DANGEROUS CONSEQUENCES

Also by Claire Booth

A Sheriff Hank Worth mystery

THE BRANSON BEAUTY
ANOTHER MAN'S GROUND
A DEADLY TURN *
FATAL DIVISIONS *

* *available from Severn House*

DANGEROUS CONSEQUENCES

Claire Booth

SEVERN HOUSE

First world edition published in Great Britain and the USA in 2022
by Severn House, an imprint of Canongate Books Ltd,
14 High Street, Edinburgh EH1 1TE.

Trade paperback edition first published in Great Britain and the USA in 2022
by Severn House, an imprint of Canongate Books Ltd.

severnhouse.com

British Library Cataloguing-in-Publication Data
A CIP catalogue record for this title is available from the British Library.

ISBN-13: 978-0-7278-2301-4 (cased)
ISBN-13: 978-1-4483-0887-3 (trade paper)
ISBN-13: 978-1-4483-0888-0 (e-book)

All Severn House titles are printed on acid-free paper.

Typeset by Palimpsest Book Production Ltd.,
Falkirk, Stirlingshire, Scotland.
Printed and bound in Great Britain by
TJ Books, Padstow, Cornwall.

For

Dot and Bob

ONE

She stood over the bed. He was the latest of them. Spaced enough apart that she hadn't noticed. She looked at his numbers and then at his missing leg. He stared up at her and mumbled incoherently about his wife. She had no idea where the woman was. She patted his hand and walked away.

She'd been working long hours lately, double shifts that left her exhausted. Maybe her recollection was wrong. Maybe she was compressing a time period or misremembering locations. She found an open workstation and started to enter parameters into the computer. Twenty minutes later she gathered a stack of notes and pulled out her phone to call the sheriff.

Sheriff Hank Worth stood on the curb outside the building. The first recruit pulled into the parking lot fifteen minutes early. The other two were five minutes behind him. It was an excellent sign. He'd given them yesterday off, even though he'd wanted them to start immediately. Hell, what he really needed was for them to have started five months ago.

All three lined up in front of him in parade position. He fought back a smile and told them that was no longer necessary. They toured the facility and then settled in the conference room. This was going to be different from the usual department orientation.

'There are a few things I need to mention before you begin your shifts,' he said as Sheila Turley slipped into the room and stood against the wall. 'When you applied for the job, I said that you'd be replacing some deputies who had been fired.'

They all nodded. That had been five months ago, before they left for the academy. A lifetime ago. He could tell at the time that none of them paid much attention – they were getting hired and didn't really care why. Now they'd need to.

'What was the reaction you got as we were walking around the jail just now?'

'It didn't seem like we were very welcome,' said Ray Gillespie, a slightly built and bespectacled thirty-two-year-old who had fortunately squeaked by on all the physical requirements. 'It seemed like we were getting glared at.'

'You were.' Hank sat back in his chair. 'And I think it's only fair to give you the lay of the land before you go in there.'

They started to look worried. Sheila, standing behind them, glared at Hank. He held up his hands reassuringly.

'Everything's just fine. We let some folks go last November because they didn't want to follow our new overtime guidelines.'

Translation: they staged a sick-out that turned into an open revolt against the sheriff's department administration.

'We can't approve overtime anymore because we don't have the budget for it. And we'd rather have every deputy keep their jobs at regular hours than lay people off so others can keep cashing in on overtime.'

All three nodded like that was the most sensible thing in the world. It was that attitude that got them hired in the first place.

'And there are still folks here who, well, sided with those deputies. So they miss their colleagues and still feel that they deserve their OT.'

Translation: they resent the hell out of you and want to see you fail.

He studied each of them. Ray had understood what he was saying from the beginning. The other man, Austin Lorentz, got it toward the end. Of the three, he was the most complete law enforcement package – mid-twenties, in good condition, and with a fantastic ability to instantly and correctly size up a person. Probably came from his years as a bartender.

Then there was Amber Boggs. She'd applied at the last minute and blown the other two away on the physical testing. She'd done the same with the entire academy class, coming in first in almost every category. Her people skills, however, were not as stellar. At all. She couldn't read a person's emotions or the unspoken currents of a conversation. And she hadn't noticed any deputies' reactions during their tour. But she was calm and attentive. Hank could work with that. Like he was doing now.

'Some of the other deputies in the jail might not like you, Boggs,' he elaborated.

That did the trick. Her face registered comprehension and then she shrugged. 'Lots of people don't like me.' And she clearly didn't care. Behind her, Sheila beamed.

'I need you all just to watch yourselves,' he continued. 'Come directly to me or Chief Deputy Turley if you have any problems or get hassled in any way. We are really, really glad that you're here and ready to work.'

He dismissed them and they filed out. Sheila shut the door behind them and turned to Hank. 'She's a woman after my own heart.'

He smiled. 'A new protégé?'

'Maybe eventually. Right now, all three are going to be under my wing, especially when they start working shifts with Bubba Berkins.' She paused. 'Are you any closer to figuring out a way to fire him?'

Hank shook his head. Berkins hadn't committed a single transgression since the sick-out. So he continued to sit there in the jail unit, a cancer slowly metastasizing into department-wide discontent and borderline insubordination. It would take surgical precision to cut him out. Hank just had to figure out how to wield the scalpel.

She was waiting in the parking lot.

'Hi, honey. What's up?' Hank started to get out of the car, but Maggie climbed in the passenger seat and closed the door. He slid back behind the wheel and turned to face her. 'What's going on?'

Maggie rarely contacted him when she was on shift. She was always too busy. One emergency after another. So not only had she called, she'd asked him to meet her. He started to get worried.

'Are the kids all right?'

'The what? Oh, yeah. They're fine. This isn't about them. This is work.'

'And you'd like my expertise in emergency medicine?'

That wisecrack at least relaxed the tense look on her face.

'No, smart ass. I'd like you to do some poking around for me – use your expertise in being nosy.'

Now *that* he could do. She pulled a sheaf of papers out of her doctor coat pocket and smoothed them out on her lap. He could see her scratchy handwriting all over the pages.

'The first one came in a week ago Monday. I didn't think anything of it.'

An elderly man, dehydrated and disoriented, had been brought in by an ambulance crew. She'd treated him and released him to his wife. Two days later, it happened again, only this time it was a woman. Even older and even more frail. Again, nothing out of the ordinary. And then it happened again today. This man wasn't leaving the hospital as easily. He was diabetic and had allowed his blood sugar to drop into dangerous levels. He'd collapsed at the scene and was brought in confused. He was still muttering things about the damn music and wanting breakfast. His wife was beside herself. She'd arrived at the hospital much later because someone mistakenly told the paramedics that the old man was there by himself. So the ambulance drove off without her, and she was forced to wait for a taxi after the tour bus driver refused to drop her off on the way back to the hotel.

'Were the first two people also tourists?' Hank asked.

She nodded.

'On buses?'

'I'm not sure. I didn't ask. I think the first one wasn't, because it didn't seem the wife had trouble getting here to the hospital on her own. But I wasn't paying much attention to all that.'

She sounded frustrated with herself. He took her hand. She took it back, gave him an *oh, please* look, and flipped to the next page in her notes.

'So I asked Chang if he'd had any similar cases.' She held up the paper. 'These were his patients, and a few more when neither one of us was on duty that I was able to find in the records. Ten total. All over age sixty-five. All tourists. All in the last month.' She frowned. 'We're kicking ourselves that we didn't get better histories from them as to where exactly they were coming from, what hotels they're staying in, that kind of thing.'

Hank was already mapping out who he would question. But he needed to be professionally skeptical first.

'It could just be that they're having such a good time in wonderful Branson that they forgot to take care of themselves. That probably happens to people on vacation a lot.'

'Yes, it does. And this could be exactly that, with just random coincidence that there are so many recently.' She shrugged. 'So yeah, I don't know for sure that something is going on. Which is why I didn't call the Branson City Police Department.'

She raised an eyebrow and held out the papers. The city police had jurisdiction over the hospital. Hank had no grounds to start an investigation there. He took the notes.

'Please just see if something's there. Then we can call BPD. And if I'm not right . . . then it doesn't cause anybody any worry.'

She kissed him goodbye and climbed out of the car as her pager buzzed. He watched her hurry back inside the ER entrance. If she thought there was more to all this, then there was. Because Maggie McCleary was almost never wrong.

They drove down the street at a slow, reassuring crawl. Two kids playing basketball in a driveway stopped to wave. Deputy Sam Karnes started to regret his choice of neighborhood.

'This is not typical,' he said. 'At all. Don't think this is how it's going to be all the time.'

Deputy Molly March finished her return wave and turned toward him. 'Oh, I know. I've seen the ones you usually deal with, remember?' Molly had been able to transfer to patrol only once the three new deputies were done with the academy. 'They'd come straight to me in the jail for booking. Drunks and wife beaters and meth heads and car thieves and a bunch of other stuff. I got quality alone time with all of 'em.'

Sam chuckled as he steered the squad car around a nicely landscaped corner. Then her words sank in. 'It would just be you? At intake?' He was horrified. That was completely against procedure. Not to mention that she was a little thing.

'Yeah. Bubba and them started making me do that after the purge.'

'Why didn't you tell Sheila?' He knew she hadn't, because Sheila would've put a stop to it immediately.

March didn't answer, instead initiating a wave with an older woman weeding her front flowerbed. Sam asked again. She stayed silent for an entire block, like the lawns were the most interesting things in the world.

'She would have fixed it,' March finally said, still looking out the passenger side window. Sam had to strain to hear her. 'And I couldn't let her do that. It would . . . it would be so bad. They already hate her. So much, those guys in the jail do. If she came in and wrote 'em all up, I don't know what they'd do.'

That hit Sam like a punch to the solar plexus. He was going to need to talk to Sheila. He turned to stare at March, who finally met his gaze. 'What about you?' He tried to keep the alarm out of his voice. 'Have they ever pulled anything else with you? Intimidated? Threatened?'

She reached down and pulled up her uniform pant leg. A holster with a Beretta semi-automatic was strapped to her ankle. She bought it about four months ago, when things really started to get bad, she said. It was with her every minute she wasn't inside the jail.

'I call her Betty. Never had to introduce her to anybody, but . . .' She trailed off sheepishly as she seemed to realize how she was talking about it and then blushed red as a hot pepper as Sam gaped at her.

'No, no,' he said. 'I'm not laughing at you. I think that's awesome. I got no issue with somebody naming their gun. And no issue with you taking precautions like that, either.'

He also had seriously misjudged March's readiness for patrol duty. That's why they were in this cushy neighborhood west of the Hollister city limits. She was more than prepared for the real thing. He swung the cruiser around. Her training was about to be taken up a notch.

TWO

He easily found the bed the patient was in, but Milt Engelman still wasn't coherent. And the nurses didn't know where the wife was. Hank tracked her down outside the emergency room entrance, gazing out over Veterans Boulevard and pulling apart a spring blossom from a nearby shedding dogwood tree. Helen Engelman looked about eighty years old and ready to topple over with fatigue.

'I couldn't find the cafeteria. I thought at least I know how to find some fresh air.'

Hank held out his hand and said he'd be happy to take her to get something to eat. They settled into a corner table with a bowl of minestrone soup for her and coffee for him. He waited until she was halfway through before he spoke. By then, there was some color back in her cheeks.

'The ER said that you and your husband were on a bus tour?'

She nodded.

'And what was going on this morning? Were you at your hotel?'

'No, no. We were at a show. *Breakfast Buckaroos*. On the Strip.'

Hank hadn't heard of that one. Which didn't mean anything. Like most locals, he avoided the Strip – that traffic-saturated four-mile stretch of Country Boulevard packed with theaters and kitsch – as much as he could.

'And how was your husband feeling when you left for the show?'

'Just fine. Everything was fine. Everybody got on the bus – we're always the first ones on, due to Milt's wheelchair and all. And I didn't take any food.'

She suddenly started to cry, tears blurring her already rheumy brown eyes. She took off her glasses and swiped at her face as Hank scrambled for a napkin. She took it with a sniffle and shaking hands. By the time she collected herself, her soup was cold. She dropped her spoon onto the tray with a moan. The poor woman had no reserves left. He'd planned to ask about her husband's diabetes and who made the decision to call the ambulance, but that now seemed unwise. Instead he concentrated on easy details: the name of the hotel, the tour company, their hometown.

They were from Wichita. Most folk on the bus were, too, not that they knew them before or anything, she said. The *Breakfast Buckaroos* show was a regular stop on the tour, as far as she could tell. So she couldn't figure out why they made such a mistake with the timing and took so long to feed them.

'Wait – so you didn't get breakfast?' That seemed a reasonable expectation to Hank. After all, the show wasn't called the *Mid-Morning Buckaroos*.

'That's why he got sick. His blood sugar . . . I should have brought his snacks . . .' She trailed off, in need of another napkin. Hank got her one, waited for her to mop up her face, and coaxed her into finishing her soup. Then he asked about family. They had a son in Harrisonville, south of Kansas City. Helen hadn't called him because she couldn't find the number. She pulled her phone out of her purse and helplessly handed it over. Hank took it and scrolled through her contact list.

'I think you just made a little typo there – "Saron" instead of "Aaron".' He pointed at the small smartphone's screen, and she started sniffling again.

He assured her that people made that kind of mistake all the time and dialed the number. Once she started talking to 'Saron', which was going to be at least a three-napkin conversation from the sound of it, he leaned back and considered things. He had meetings all afternoon but would get to the hotel and the *Breakfast Buckaroos* theater as soon as he could. First on his list, though, was the tour operator, with whom he'd be having some strong words. You don't sell a travel package to two old people this unable to manage for themselves and then abandon them at the first sign of trouble.

They always met in the park after work. Once every week or two, arriving from different access points to the Lakeside Forest Wilderness Area and rendezvousing by a rock outcrop that shielded them from views in all directions but one. The dark winter evenings had helped as well, but now it was staying light later. At least the spring foliage was coming in. That provided a little bit of cover at the one angle through which they could be seen. They never spent more than five minutes together, but it was enough.

Earl Evans Crumblit would bring along birdseed, which Sheila had to admit was brilliant. He wandered around like he'd taken it upon himself to ensure that the entire population of squirrels didn't starve. She had no such props. She was a fifty-two-year-old Black woman in Branson County, Missouri. There was nothing she could possibly carry that would make it look like she belonged.

She got to the outcropping and watched as the department's civilian jail clerk scattered stuff everywhere as he walked toward her. She suspected he was doing this less for the welfare of the department and more for the chance to act out a white-man Cold

War spy novel. That was fine with her. She'd take the information any way she could get it.

She had scheduled this evening's meeting a little bit ago, when she thought the new recruits would have a few days under their belts. But Hank, the damn softie, had given the kids those days off after their academy graduation. So now they'd been on the job less than a day – too soon for much scuttlebutt to have developed.

'Oh, Lord, that ain't the case, ma'am. All those boys had to do was get a look at them.'

Sheila pinched the bridge of her nose, but it had no effect on the ache starting to form there. 'What exactly do you mean by that?'

'They were sizing them up. Chitty-chatting about it as they were leaving work. And I just happened to be on my break out by the back door.' He grinned. Despite her creeping headache, she smiled, too. It didn't last long.

'They figure they got a bead on all three,' Earl said. 'The little guy will be easy to intimidate. Stevenson was laughing – saying that it'd take three of the small fella to equal Bubba. They should just push him around some, let him know who's the real bosses.'

Sheila sighed. Should she deliver a specific warning to poor Gillespie? It might just scare him and a scared mark was an even more inviting target.

'And I heard Bubba saying he was going to put the young lady by herself in booking, like he done with Deputy March.'

What? They'd done that to Molly? Sheila'd had no idea. Dear God. She wanted to pull Bubba Berkins's head off his obese body.

'I will not allow that.' She spat out the words.

Earl took a skittish step back. 'Um. I don't know 'bout that. You did say you wanted them not to know you were keeping an eye on things.'

She did her best not to scowl at him. He wasn't the one she was disgusted with. She managed a nod. Then she thought about Boggs, who seemed to be the opposite of tentative little Molly March. Maybe she could handle it. Sheila would damn sure be watching to see if that turned out to be true, now that she knew what was going on.

'And the other one?' she asked.

'Now that there's interesting,' Earl said. 'It was a different feeling I was getting about him. Like he wasn't a target.'

The strapping, clean-cut, sandy-haired white boy. Not a target. Not surprising.

'I didn't hear them planning to do anything to him. It was more like they figured they could bring him in, like, into the fold or something.'

Sheila considered that as she walked back to her car. Austin Lorentz had been her pick. She'd recruited him, convinced him to give up the healthy tips of a bartending job and join the force because she'd been impressed with the way his mind worked. She hoped she'd read him right. If not, she'd just created a problem instead of solving one.

The first step in what he was calling his bad breakfast inquiry was going to be the most fun. Because it involved perpetual wise-ass Larry Alcoate.

'Why exactly couldn't we do this over lunch?' the lanky head paramedic said as he met Hank outside the Hollister headquarters of Branson County Ambulance Services. 'You wanting my company I understand. You insisting that it be in this boring cinder-block office – that needs some explaining.'

'I need you to run some records for me. And your databases are here. Not at the Roark Diner.'

'Fine. But you're buying me some Flamin' Hot Cheetos out of the vending machine.'

'Fair enough.'

After Larry got his snack and a diet soda – 'gotta watch my girlish figure' – they settled in at his work station and Hank explained Maggie's concerns.

'Why didn't you tell me this was for the redoubtable Dr McCleary? I would've gotten right on it. I like her better than you.'

Hank grinned. 'Everybody does.'

Larry pecked at the keyboard with his index fingers for a minute. 'I can't give you names, dude. HIPAA privacy laws and all. But there were sixteen transports to Branson General in the past month for dehydration, dizziness, nausea – that set of symptoms.'

'How many over age sixty-five?'

'Thirteen. Two of the others were idiots in their twenties who took a leaky rowboat out onto the lake and got stuck out there for God-knows-how-long. And one was a guy in his forties who went on too long a hike.'

'Where'd you pick up the older ones? What locations?'

More hunt-and-peck typing. Two of the thirteen called 9-1-1 while shopping in stores. All of the others were transported from local theaters. Hank chuckled to himself. Maggie's estimate of ten patients had only been one off. He pulled out his notebook as Larry rattled off the addresses. By the time his friend was finished, Hank was no longer smiling. Four had come from the *Breakfast Buckaroos* show. One other breakfast theater was also a repeat offender. What was happening at these places?

Larry unrolled himself from his customary slouch and jabbed at the computer monitor. 'I'm kicking myself, man. How did we not notice this?'

'Different staff on different shifts? A pretty average call about an old person getting shaky? It makes sense,' Hank said.

But Larry was still stiff with outrage. He thought for a minute and then jackhammered at the keyboard. A whole new list came up. 'And these are calls to those same addresses that didn't result in transport. But they sure as hell did involve shaky old people.'

'And what, they got better?'

'Yeah. We treated with fluids, or glucose, that type of thing. They ended up not being in bad enough shape to have to go to the hospital.'

'I don't suppose you could print that list out for me.'

Larry made a face at him. 'Nice try. I shouldn't even be letting you see this screen. I can let you have dates and locations. Even that's skating near the edge. You're definitely not getting names.'

'Well then, I want the Cheetos back.'

'Not a chance.' He smirked and started listing the information. Then he promised to start flagging those types of calls and letting Hank know. 'You're going to go have a chat with these places, right? While wearing your jewelry?' He pointed to the badge and gun on Hank's belt. Hank's nod was slow and emphatic.

'Good.'

THREE

Wednesday was payday for a lot of folks. And some of them were the kind who went a little wild with it. Which created problems, sometimes. In some areas, especially. So a nice, slow turn through certain neighborhoods on these days was a good reminder that the sheriff's department was watching.

'Kind of like a pump on the brakes,' Sam said. 'Make folks stop and think. Just 'cause you're liquored up doesn't mean you can beat your wife. Or just 'cause you blew the grocery money doesn't mean she can beat you.'

A grim little smile flashed across March's face. 'That last one, I would love to see.'

Sam looked over at her from the driver's seat and realized he knew very little about her. She'd been a deputy for about two years and she was even younger than he was, which was a minor miracle in a department that definitely skewed middle-aged. He was starting to ask her a question when she gasped and pointed at the street in front of them.

He saw a figure leap the last several feet off the road and dive into the brush on the left shoulder. He brought the car to a stop just as a pale blur in the rear-view mirror caught his eye. Another guy was running flat across the road but was still easy to see due to the blinding white of his skin. All of it.

He pointed forward to where the first person disappeared. 'Was that one . . .?'

'Yeah. As a jaybird.'

Sam thought about the street locations in this part of the county and then hit the gas. He sped forward and then turned left as March adjusted her seatbelt and grinned. If he was fast enough, they could be on the other side of this stretch of woods when those idiots came out. They made it with time to spare. March rolled down her window and they could hear crashing through the undergrowth. He aimed the cruiser's spotlight toward the noise and waited for just the right moment. The light flashed on and they froze like deer in front of a semi's high beams.

They looked to be in their late teens – one tall and thin, the other shorter and with a little more meat on him. Sam got out of the car and told them to put their hands on their heads. They both shot looks at the approaching March and kept their hands where they were.

'Look at you both, standing there in what God gave you.' She didn't even try to hide her smirk. 'Don't be bashful on my account. Get those hands on up.'

They both looked back at Sam, who felt March tense as she came to stand next to him. He very deliberately turned toward her. 'What would you like me to do, ma'am?'

She blinked in surprise and then told him to cuff the kids, who were now paying much better attention to little Deputy March.

'Why you gotta do that?' the beanpole said, his hands slowly moving upward. 'Being naked ain't illegal.'

'It sure can be illegal. And so is not following the directions of a peace officer,' she said as she moved toward him.

Sam took the short one. He got close and started to chuckle. 'Underage drinking is, too. What'd you have, Jägermeister?'

Telltale licorice breath floated in the balmy air as the kid stuttered a denial. They loaded the pair into the back of the squad car, their butt cheeks squeaking against the plastic seats. Sam slammed the door and looked at March over the car roof. 'This is why it pays to know every street location. You never know when you'll need to cut someone off at the pass. Or return him to a home that isn't anyplace on a map.'

The teens lived near each other on a lane of widely spaced but small houses and mobile homes a distance out from Kirbyville. It was an area well known to patrol deputies. Car parts and broken furniture littered some of the yards. Others had weeds knee-high that hid who-knew-what. And a few had their occupants outside, enjoying the spring evening and newly purchased bottles of impending stupor. Sam wondered if the kids' parents were in that group.

Not at short Judah Thompson's house, it turned out. The place was deserted. Sam stood in the low-ceilinged living room and thought about what the Chief would do. Not leave the kid here alone, that was for sure. He could call Hank and ask for advice, but he didn't want to do that in front of March. He told Judah to put some clothes on and loaded him back in the cruiser. His buddy Nick Lancaster lived three doors and half a mile down the road. Sam rapped on the front door.

'Nobody's gonna answer,' Nick slurred, rubbing his wrists as March took off the cuffs.

'Why's that?'

'All sorts of reasons.' He opened the door and wobbled into a living room similar to Judah's – but much cleaner and with more firepower. A Ruger semi-automatic lay on the coffee table next to an empty bottle of Jäger. Sam slowly brought his hand to rest on his service weapon. Nick laughed.

'Don't worry. He's in no condition to do shit. See for yourself.' He pointed toward the bedrooms and then started to pick through the pile of clothes on the floor. Sam motioned for March to stay in the living room and started down the narrow hallway. The first bedroom was clearly the teen's, although a sleeping bag on the floor indicated that more than one person was staying there. The other room obviously belonged to the dad or uncle or whoever the comatose man on the floor was in relation to the poor kid.

Sam nudged away the Wild Turkey bottle and took the man's pulse. Pretty steady. He scanned the room and saw a pill bottle on the nightstand. He walked back into the living room holding it in a gloved hand.

'Who's Carmelita Ramirez?'

Nick shrugged. 'No idea.'

'So why does your dad have a prescription with her name on it? With half the pills gone?'

Nick just stared sullenly. Sam responded with a smile. This judgment call had just gotten much easier.

'You're coming with us. I can't leave you in a place where drugs are being taken illegally.'

Nick sank down onto the couch. 'Nah. My mom'll be home soon. Jude and me will wait here.'

March reached down and yanked him to his feet. 'No. You can call her from the station,' she said. 'Let's go.'

She helped his sloppy ass out to the car, where they found Judah passed out in the backseat. Sam checked that his breathing and pulse were steady, made Nick promise to warn them if he felt sick, and headed toward department headquarters.

'What do you mean nobody's claimed them?'

Sam took a step back from the gale force of Sheila's question. 'Um. We can't reach either one's parents. We picked 'em up at ten o'clock last night and we've been trying for hours.'

'We're not a coat check, for Chrissakes. We can't just hang them in a closet and ignore them until somebody shows up with the receipt.' Sheila tossed her dry erase marker onto her desk. It was more of a throw, honestly, since she was five feet away. It was that, or give in to temptation and chuck her coffee mug at something. 'Why didn't you leave at least the one kid with his dad in the first place? Then we'd only be dealing with half the problem we have now.'

'Oh, really? And what would Hank do to me if I did that? If I left a teenager unattended with the possibility he could be hurt later on? Huh?'

'Aw, hell.' She sagged down into her desk chair. Sam was right. There was no greater sin in Hank's book than the one he had committed last fall when he let that car full of teenagers go with only a warning. The county had six new gravestones as a result. Sheila let out a long, slow breath and tapped the mistreated marker on her desk blotter. She now wished she'd not come in early to work on the staff scheduling. 'If we turn them over to the child welfare people . . .'

'I know,' Sam said. 'That's what I'm trying to not do.'

'Well, let's think. Do we know for sure Children's Division would be worse than their home lives are?'

Sammy flipped open his notebook as Molly walked into the office with two coffees. She handed one to Sam and agreed with his assessment that it seemed like the Lancaster kid's mom was fairly responsible. She had been at work and the teen had expected her home soon. That's why Sam had figured it wouldn't be a big deal. She'd come pick up her son at the station, everybody would get a lecture, and that would be that. But now she wasn't answering her cell phone.

As for Thompson's parents, well, who the hell knew where they were? 'I ran their names. No record of either of them being incarcerated, and I haven't been able to find where they work. Judah's still sleeping off his Jäger, so I haven't been able to get any other details out of him.'

'That's what they were drinking? Ugh.' Sheila sighed. 'We're going to have to call the Children's Division. For all we know, they already have a record on one or both of these families.'

Sam flipped his notebook closed. Molly frowned. In a way that wasn't full of disagreement so much as consternation. She started to speak and then stopped. Sheila pointed the marker at her. 'Your opinion matters just as much as anybody else's. What're you thinking?'

Molly took a deep breath. Sheila waited. It was not her strong suit, so she spent the time feeling proud of herself. Plus, there were enough people around this place who'd earned her impatience. She didn't need to be dishing it out to ones who hadn't.

'I think . . . I'd like to give it one more try, ma'am. With the boys. See if we can find out more before we call in those people.'

Sheila eyed her. There was no harm in that. And it would be good to see how Molly approached this kind of thing. She made an *after you* gesture and followed the young deputy out the office door, with Sam clomping along behind. They walked over to the jail, where the small room set aside for non-urgent medical needs was instead occupied by hungover misery and a teenage boy stench that could fell a horse. Sheila put her hand to her nose. Deputy Gillespie looked up from the game of solitaire he was playing with an actual deck of cards and chuckled.

'Yeah, it's pretty bad to start with. Until your nose goes dead.'

This was definitely rookie duty, and she was pleased to see that Gillespie didn't seem the least bit fazed by it. He cheerfully slapped down another card and said he'd tried to get his charges into at least a round of Crazy Eights, but no-go. A skinny kid with door-knob elbows groaned agreement from the cot in the corner.

'Where's the other one?'

An explosion of retching from the tiny bathroom answered Sheila's question before Gillespie could. Molly cringed and then dragged a chair over to the teen on the cot.

'Nick,' she said as she sat down, 'I need some more information, and I need you to be real honest with me. Because I don't want to do something that . . . doesn't turn out well for you. You know?'

Nick wiped at his nose. 'Then just let me go back home. I promise, no more drinking.'

'It's more about your folks, not you,' Molly said. 'We found your dad passed out. You couldn't really tell us last night how often that happens.'

Nick shifted uncomfortably. Sheila guessed it had less to do with the hangover than with whether he was going to be truthful.

'Not very often,' he said.

Molly's expression showed what she thought of that.

'No. Seriously. It only happens when he's got money. Which ain't often. And . . . oh, dude.'

The other teen wobbled into the room and slumped onto the other cot. He at least had the decency to look embarrassed. Molly rotated her chair.

'Where your folks at, Judah?'

'They're just out. They'll be back.'

He wiped at his mouth and slouched under the weight of everyone's attention. Sheila chose to focus on the friend instead. Who'd just gotten a cue he was anxiously needing. His body relaxed and he nodded solemnly. Which meant Sheila didn't believe either one of them. Neither did Molly. She tried to coax more information out of Judah, but he had the evasive finesse of a practiced prevaricator. It would be impressive if it wasn't heartbreaking.

They were going through his denials again when Sam's phone buzzed. He looked at it and pointed to the thin Nick kid. Mom had finally arrived. A second buzz had him frowning. 'She says she's here for both of them.'

Sheila raised an eyebrow and beckoned to Nick. 'Let's go explain to her why that's not possible.'

Judah went from slouch to slump as they walked out of the room with his friend. Sheila marched Nick straight out to the lobby, where a very harried woman was waiting for them. Nick had clearly gotten his height and lack of body fat from her.

'Really? You had to go and do this now? This week? When I'm pulling double shifts?'

The kid suddenly found his sneakers fascinating. His mother shot a look heavenward and then asked where the other one was. Sheila started to explain but was stopped by a document flapping in her face.

'I got the right papers.'

Sheila plucked them out of hands that smelled like hot dogs and gasoline. It was a guardianship order. And it had been signed by both Thompson parents and a judge. Sheila would have been less surprised by a UFO landing. 'You have guardianship of Judah?'

'Wait – what? You do?' her son said.

Sheila guided the woman across the lobby and out of her son's earshot. 'What's going on here, ma'am?'

'He's basically lived with us for years. His parents weren't never around. I finally got them to sign, so I could do stuff that needs to be done. Like vaccine shots for school.' It sounded carefully rehearsed. But it also sounded like she cared about the kid. 'So I can take him?'

Sheila told her to wait, sat Nick down next to her and told him he had to listen to everything his mother was going to say to him in the next five minutes. Then she walked back and ran the whole thing by Sam and Molly, who both agreed that – based on what they'd seen – Kathy Lancaster was Judah's best option by far.

'What about Nick's passed-out dad?' Sheila said. 'Should we be wishing he signed away his rights, too?'

Sam hooted with sarcastic laughter. 'We'd be losing a lot of the parents in the Ozarks if we could use consciousness as a requirement.'

'Are we sure he isn't abusive when he's high?' Sheila pressed.

Both teens had denied it. 'And I gave 'em a look when they were wearing nature's finest,' Molly said. 'No bruises, no cuts. No healed fractures that I could see.'

Sam whistled. 'Damn . . . I didn't even think to do that while they were naked. Nice job.'

Sheila beamed. One deputy with excellent police work and another with the self-confidence and class to compliment somebody else's talents. If only the rest of the department worked this way.

FOUR

It was several days past when Hank had hoped to talk to the folks at the Buckaroo theater. His week had turned into an avalanche of paperwork and an unexpected court appearance on a burglary case. So it was Thursday afternoon when he finally made it to the boxy building off Wildwood Drive. They had softened it with landscape plantings and fancy paint, but it was still basically a warehouse. He let himself in through the unlocked front entrance and wandered through the lobby, which was nicely done up with artsy photos of the Branson area. He pushed through the doors into the theater and picked his way through the tables to a door on the right of the stage, getting there just as it swung open. A brawny man with a head shaved shiny as a pro wrestler's chest barreled through holding an iPad and a Red Bull.

'Who the hell are you?'

This was followed by a quick once-over and a stiffening as he saw the badge and gun. The man took a sip of his drink. 'What can I do for you, officer?'

Hank introduced himself with his full title. He was curious about a medical incident on Monday that involved an older gentleman in a wheelchair.

'Why do you care?'

Hank didn't respond. He was the one asking questions. He waited. It took a full minute for the guy to give in and start talking.

'He got woozy. So we called. Abundance of caution. The ambulance dudes didn't think it was too serious. They weren't in a hurry when they took him away.'

'What about his wife?'

The guy looked puzzled. 'She wasn't woozy.'

'Well, she still needed taking care of, right? Did you contact the tour company?'

The man moved to the left and started to cut through the tables toward the lobby, which meant he wasn't meeting Hank's eye when he said, 'Of course. We left her in their hands. They're the ones who had her information, who knew where she was staying, that kind of stuff.'

Hank followed, wondering why a Stone Cold Steve Austin wrestling clone with meticulously maintained muscles was working at a two-bit Ozark theater.

'And how much business do you do with Midwest Motoring Excursions?'

The big shoulders rose in a shrug. That did it.

'Sir. I'm going to ask you to stop a minute. And turn around and answer my questions.' Hank leaned against a table and folded his arms. 'First, what's your name?'

Stone Cold slowly pivoted until he was facing Hank. 'Axel Orsi.'

'And what exactly is your job here at the theater?'

'I'm the manager.'

'How long you been doing that?'

'About a year.'

'And how does the show go? It starts at, what, nine o'clock?'

Stone Cold sighed and set his Red Bull on the nearest table. Yes, they started at nine with an opening number, then a video, then a skit and more music. He waved disinterestedly at the stage and reached for his drink.

'And when do you feed them?'

'During the music. The servers come out. It's a set menu. Everybody gets the same thing. I heard they tried buffet style in the past, but with the crippledness of a lot of the folks, they figured out it's best to leave them seated.'

'And how many incidents have you had? Where you had to call an ambulance?'

Another muscled shrug. 'A few.'

Hank stared pointedly at the guy's iPad.

'We don't keep a record.'

Hank found that hard to believe. 'Do you have a guess?'

'Two or three?'

Larry's database said four.

'And Midwest Motoring Excursions?'

'We do three shows a week for them. Sundays, Mondays, and Thursdays.' Different tour companies filled the other days.

'And the tour bus drops them off and picks them up?'

'Yep. We got nothing to do with them when they're not here in our building.'

Hank straightened and stuck out his hand. 'OK. Thanks. I appreciate your time.'

Stone Cold's hand was damp with Red Bull condensation. Hank skirted a table on his way to the front and thought of something. 'Did you call the wife a taxi on Monday?'

'No. Is that how she left?'

The care for customers in this place was overwhelming. Hank thought of one more thing. 'Does the tour bus leave, do you know? During the show?'

'Maybe? I'm not sure. I'm in here the whole time. Why?'

'Just curious.' Now more than ever.

The door hissed open at Hank's knock. The driver looked down at him and gawked. 'How do I get pulled over in a parking lot?'

Hank asked to come aboard the twenty-ton road equivalent of a cruise ship. He half-expected chandeliers and white linen as he looked down the length of the thing from next to the driver, whose eyes were still wide and worried. He explained that no one was in trouble and he was just looking for some information.

'Do you usually do this route?'

Nolan, according to the silver name tag pinned to his white polo shirt, nodded. He looked about fifty based on the graying hair and the squint lines carved into his warm brown skin. He drove it pretty regularly and yes, he was here Monday with the previous batch of tourists. Took them back up north Tuesday about midday, then brought this group down yesterday. And today was indeed the *Breakfast Buckaroos* morning. 'How on earth do you know that?'

'Well,' said Hank, leaning against the dash, 'there was a gentleman in your tour group who was taken to the hospital from that theater. And his wife had a lot of trouble getting there to see him. Do you know anything about that?'

Nolan stopped making eye contact halfway through Hank's question.

'I couldn't take her, man. No personal rides, no side trips, no nothing. Not for any reason. They're real clear about that.'

'She was a distraught old lady who couldn't even work a cell phone well enough to call her son. You couldn't have asked permission to run her up to the hospital?'

'I did.'

Hank blinked in surprise. 'You did?'

'Yes, sir. I called in to base and they said they're sick of this shit and no. Can't take her.'

Now Hank felt like an ass. The guy had tried.

'I finally got her calmed down enough to get her in a cab. Took forever, though. She make it OK?'

Hank nodded. 'You said they were "sick of this shit". Does that mean it's happened before?'

'Oh yeah. Couple of times. I just took the first one. It was a gentleman whose wife fainted. He was claustrophobic and couldn't ride in the ambulance. Never occurred to me to ask first.'

Somehow the tour director found out, though, and said Nolan couldn't do anything like that without permission. So when the next one had happened at a different theater, the *Down Home Darlin'* show on Green Mountain Road, he was going to ask. But it was near the end of the show anyhow, so he just dropped the sick woman's sister at the hospital on his way back to the hotel with everyone else and forgot to mention it to his bosses.

'Then there was this one on Monday. I asked and they said no. I did not feel that they really needed to use foul language, I got to say. This is a professional environment, you know?'

'Yes, sir.'

'And I try to take good care of my passengers.'

'Yes, sir.' Hank paused. 'How would you rate their general health? How many of them are elderly?'

Nolan chuckled. 'How many of them ain't? It's a seniors-only tour. As for their health, that's a trickier question. Some are chipper as young birds. Some others, well, they don't look so good, right from the start. And then they get back on the bus after these shows, and they look even worse.'

Hank asked why Nolan thought that was the case – because Stone Cold the manager sure as hell wasn't going to say. The driver wagged a knowing finger.

'I wondered on that, too. And the thing I hear most often when folks come back on is that it takes too long to eat.' Nolan leaned forward, his shock-absorbing seat bouncing gently. 'Some of them are even sniffling and teary-eyed about it. I talked to the hotel manager about it.' He froze. 'Please don't tell them I did that.'

Hank had no intention of divulging that he'd even talked to this kind man at all. A company that essentially gave the middle finger to a frantic old lady in need of a ride wouldn't hesitate to do something much worse to a traitorous employee.

She finally got her own place. Well, she had a roommate, but it was a house, not an apartment with too many restrictions and too many neighbors. Sam fought back a yawn, adjusted the daisy bouquet and knocked on the door. He'd already been here several times – Brenna had a surprising amount of furniture – but for his first official visit, he wanted to be carrying something better than a moving box.

Brenna swung the door open with a smile that went even wider when she saw the flowers. She gave him a kiss and pulled him inside. 'I got the bookcase set up and we hung the pictures. Don't let me forget to give you back your tools.'

She waved toward the long wall of the living room. He recognized the framed movie posters from her old apartment. The rest, a few abstract art canvases and some photos, must belong to Felicia. It all looked pretty nice together.

He followed her into the kitchen. She rummaged through a box until she found a canning jar. She beamed at him and arranged the daisies just-so. Then she came over and wrapped her arms around his waist.

'Thank you.' She leaned back to look up at him. 'I couldn't have hauled all that stuff over here without you. And for being so supportive. I really appreciate it.'

She wrapped her arms tighter and rested her head against his shoulder. She came to just under his chin. In other words, she fit perfectly. He kissed her dark blonde hair and decided he could stay right here forever. Then the screen door banged. Brenna pulled away and the scent of lavender shampoo and heaven went with her. He bit back a sigh.

'Hey, guys.' Felicia flipped her stick-straight black hair out of her face and set a bag of groceries on the kitchen table. She pulled out a six-pack and several cartons of hot deli food that made her pale skin turn pink when she opened them to let the steam out. 'Dinner's on me. I figure it's the least I can do to say thank you for all your help with the move.'

She toasted Sam with a bottle and then spent five minutes finding something to open it with. Brenna took just as long rounding up enough utensils for them all. Sam didn't mind. He sank into one of the vinyl dining chairs and enjoyed the balmy breeze coming through the open kitchen window. Then he cracked open a beer and told them about last night's patrol shift. He finished the streaker story to their gales of laughter.

'This kind of stuff actually happens?' Felicia said.

'Oh, he's got lots of crazy stories,' Brenna said. 'It's a super interesting job.'

She sounded proud, maybe. Sam scolded himself. *Don't read too much into things, man.* 'Every day's always different, that's for sure,' he said.

'Well, that's pretty cool. And I'll bet the looks on those parents' faces were priceless when you hauled their naked butts home.'

Sam just nodded. He'd skipped the part about the teens' living situations. He typically did gloss over those kinds of details when he told work tales. It usually wasn't much, just small facts here and there. He hadn't had to truly censor himself with Brenna yet – nothing horrible had happened since they really started dating right after Thanksgiving. Before that, though . . .

He blinked and realized that they were starting to clear away the dishes. How long had he been staring at the tabletop with his mind wandering through past crimes? He shook his head clear and helped finish the job. Felicia grabbed another beer and gave them a cheery wave as she disappeared into her bedroom to unpack. Brenna took the last empty deli carton from him and led him over to the couch.

'You look tired. You don't have to stay.'

'No, no. I'm good. I just . . . just had a lot of thoughts floating around. That's all.'

She snuggled into him once they sat down. Like there would be any way he'd go home when this was the alternative. 'Tell me one,' she said. 'One of your thoughts.'

He tried to pick through them to find one that would work. It was like looking for fireflies and finding only mosquitoes.

'Let's see . . . oh, here's one – the Chief. I don't know what he's up to this week. He's been spending a lot of time in the city of Branson, which isn't our territory. And I saw a bunch of brochures on his desk. Like tourist stuff. I asked if he had family coming to visit from out of town. He said no, he just had a wife with a knack for diagnosing rot.'

Brenna pulled away with a puzzled look.

'I'm not sure what he meant, either,' Sam said. 'Maybe there's some problem at the hospital?'

'You're always so curious.' She laughed. 'Whatever it is probably doesn't have anything to do with a police case.'

That could be true. But Sam didn't think so. The Chief tended to get that dog-with-a-bone look only when it concerned crime. And despite his dredging up of old horrors, he found himself wanting in on it. Training Deputy March was fine and all, but it'd be nice to work an actual investigation again. He didn't say that, though. Instead he asked about Brenna's day until he started to have trouble keeping his eyes open. The last thing he remembered was a pillow slipping under his head and a kiss feathering his cheek. And the smell of lavender.

FIVE

'I'm sure I don't know what you're talking about.'

'Ma'am, six of the eleven out-of-towners who've been taken to our hospital emergency department in the past month have been on one of your tours.'

'Are you accusing us of making them sick?'

'No, ma'am,' Hank said. 'But I am accusing you of leaving their traveling companions high-and-dry.'

'The package clearly states that if a passenger wishes to go somewhere that is not on the tour, he or she must procure their own transportation and our company is absolutely not liable for anything that happens to them while they're away.'

'These folks weren't away from the tour. They were at a tour-sanctioned show. With only a tour-sanctioned bus for transportation. Can you tell me why that bus wouldn't give the sick passengers' worried spouses a ride to the hospital?' He wasn't going to divulge that Nolan the driver had already answered that question.

'I'm sure I don't know.'

'Did you forbid it?'

False outrage came through the phone line. Hank rolled his eyes and tapped his pen against his desk blotter. There hadn't been anything worth writing down so far. Just tour agency director Wendy Frederick's obfuscations. She was two minutes into her tirade and he was almost done with the morning's third cup of coffee when she finally said something useful.

'We do the bus and the hotel and we take the ticket packages from the providers. That's it.'

'What do you mean by "ticket package"?'

An exasperated sigh. 'Exactly what it sounds like. A set of music shows, bundled together at a discount,' she spat out and then realized how far she'd strayed from robotic public relations mode. 'Which, of course, we then pass on to our customers.'

'Of course,' he echoed. 'And since you're providing such good value to your guests, does your "package" include meals?'

He hoped the word would send her off again, and he wasn't disappointed.

'The package is for the shows. It's not a hard concept. If the show includes food, that's what they get for that meal. If there's no show, they can eat at the hotel. Or they can go out on their own. Which as I stated, is something that we're not liable for in any way.'

'Yes, I remember you saying that.'

He could practically hear her counting to ten. This interview was turning out to be much more fun than he'd expected. 'What's the general age range of your customers?'

'That's proprietary information.'

A laugh escaped before Hank could stop it. It sparked a round of offended spluttering on the other end of the phone line.

'You're telling me,' he said, 'that you want to keep secret the fact that your passengers are retirees?'

'Well if you already know, why did you ask?'

Police Interviewing 101, ma'am.

'How many other tour companies use these entertainment show package deals?'

'I'm sure I have no idea.'

'How many bus drivers do you employ?'

She started to protest, then sighed. 'On the Branson route? Four.'

'And they're good employees? They do what they're directed to do?'

'Yes,' she said in a tone that wearily wondered why he should care.

'So when you tell them that they have to transport travel companions who need a ride to the hospital or a doctor's office, they're going to do it?'

'Ah. I see. I don't appreciate being pushed around, Mr Worth.'

'And I don't appreciate visitors to my county being abandoned in a time of need. Especially by the folks responsible for bringing them here in the first place.'

'We are not liable for . . .' She stopped herself and stewed for a moment. 'I'll let them know. That we're being ordered to comply by the police.'

'Oh, not ordered, Ms Frederick. This is just a . . . friendly advisement. That's all.'

'My ass.'

Hank wondered if that was part of the tour package deal. He would've asked, but she hung up on him.

The man had called three times. And Sheila still wouldn't give out Hank's cell phone number.

'Sir, it is late on a Friday afternoon. You are going to need to wait until the sheriff returns on Monday, since he's the only one you say you'll talk to.'

'Well, he's the one who spoke with my mother on Monday, when she was at the hospital. Where my dad was in the ER. After being mistreated at a theater show.'

Aaron Engelman hadn't mentioned those facts in his previous messages. Sheila sighed. 'Mistreated' could mean anything from not getting cream in his coffee to slipping and falling on a wet bathroom floor. None of which would make it of interest to the sheriff's department. Unless Hank had decided to make it his business for some reason.

'I'm sorry to hear that,' she said. 'How is your father now?'

'We barely got him back to Wichita. I want to know how many other people that horrible show has sent to the emergency room. You can't hold old people hostage for hours and hours and not feed them.'

What had Hank gotten himself into? Or more accurately, what had his doctor wife gotten him involved in? She shot a dirty look into his empty office and tried to filter the exasperation out of her voice. 'I don't have any information about this at all, sir. I will certainly pass on your message, though, and—'

'Look, I've already tracked down one family. One of the ER nurses remembered they were from Lee's Summit and the hotel manager was able to narrow down who it was and gave me their name.'

That was pretty good work, Sheila had to admit. She took down the name and phone number and tried some noncommittal soothing as the guy kept launching questions. No, the sheriff's department didn't keep a list of unethical businesses – unethical didn't necessarily mean illegal. Yes, he was free to contact the local Better Business Bureau and lodge a complaint. And yes, the fact that he'd left online reviews on numerous websites was also a good way to get the word out. But no, the sheriff's department was not able to do the same thing. Posting on Yelp would not be an appropriate thing for a law enforcement agency to do.

'It does sound like you're being very proactive, Mr Engelman. I'll make sure that Sheriff Worth gets your message and calls you back. Next week.'

She hung up the phone and slapped the message slip on the top of his inbox paperwork. Whatever that man was getting himself into, he could damn well get his own self out of, too.

It was later that night before Hank told Maggie about the tour director. She had the reaction he expected. Which was why he'd waited until the kids were in bed.

'What the hell? That's bullshit.'

'Language, young lady.' Duncan smirked from his recliner over by the fireplace.

'Stuff it, Dad.' She turned away from her sarcastic father and zeroed in on her husband. 'So you mean to tell me that lady denied that she abandoned my patient's wife?'

'No. She stuck with her "not liable" line. I couldn't ask her point-blank without letting on that the bus driver basically ratted her out. I don't want him to lose his job.'

Maggie sighed. 'I figured there wouldn't be a way to make her take responsibility for it. What I really need is for it to not happen anymore.'

'After the conversation I had with her, she's not going to leave a passenger stranded again. Trust me.'

Maggie harrumphed for a few seconds then said, 'Well, what about the causes?'

'What do you mean "the causes"?'

'Why are my patients getting sick?'

'Wouldn't you be able to answer that better than a tour director could?' Hank said, then thought better of it, which turned out to be the wrong order of doing things. Maggie glared at him as Duncan cackled in his corner.

'I know what's making them ill,' she said and then paused before her voice went soft with worry. 'What I don't know is why a whole lot of people who are still capable of taking care of themselves are showing up in my emergency department with completely avoidable problems. One or two, sure. But that many? No. Something is going on.'

He looked at her, sitting there cross-legged on the couch with her long brown hair thrown over her shoulder and her blue McCleary eyes full of a devastating combination of doctorly concern and iron-willed Scottish certainty. He was no match, and he didn't even want to be.

'I think you're probably right,' he said, and he meant it. Maggie didn't overreact to suspicious circumstances. He was typically the one who did that. So if her measured, scientifically-grounded mind thought something was going on, he wasn't going to dismiss it. He told her that he'd keep asking questions, but to be prepared that they might never come up with a definitive answer.

'I'll be OK with that, as long as I don't keep getting tourists in my ER,' she said.

'That's better than the morgue.' Dunc shot Hank a grin as he hefted himself out of the recliner and started to shuffle toward the stairs and his basement bedroom. 'G'night.'

'Sorry,' Maggie said once the old dragon had descended into his subterranean lair. 'He's been even more crotchety than normal lately. I think he's worried about Aunt Fin.'

Duncan's sister was having husband problems. Hank knew the family troubles had been hard on Duncan. He smiled at Maggie. 'If it makes him feel better to get a dig in about my homicide rate, that's fine.'

She leaned forward and cupped his face in her hands. 'None of us would be getting through this without you.'

He turned his head and kissed her palm. 'At least I have one appreciative McCleary.'

She laughed. 'Better me than him.'

'Oh, God yes,' he said, kissing her long and slow. Then he took her hand and led her off to bed.

SIX

After assigning Molly that string of swing shifts, Sheila decided to move her to days for a while. The kid needed to see all aspects of patrol, and calls in the middle of the day were a whole kind of different from calls in the middle of the night. She figured Ted Pimental would be a suitable partner. He was a good cop – knew the rules and could impart the unofficial aspects, too. But mostly, he wasn't a dick. That was a difficult threshold to meet in this department right now.

She consulted her spreadsheets to double-check that the assignment wouldn't put Pimental into overtime territory. She was in the clear. Then she ran the numbers on everyone else. It was a habit she'd gotten into during the last five months, ever since the bloodletting. She came in early on Monday mornings, when she had the office to herself, and did all manner of contortions to make the duty schedule work without allowing overtime. It was painful, but it was working. They'd met their budget the last three months in a row. Of course, it helped that there were so many empty positions. But now the three newbies would bump up salary costs. That would make this month tricky – and even more important that there not be any overtime.

She tinkered with a few things and closed the computer file, finally as satisfied as she could be. Then she thought about the instructions she would give Pimental. Molly reported right on time ten minutes later. Sheila put down her almost empty coffee cup and waved her into the chair in front of her desk.

'Deputy Pimental comes on duty in an hour. I'm going to have you shadow him this week. I thought that in the meantime, we could go over a few things. How do you think last week went?'

The child's face lit up. 'I loved it, ma'am. So much. There was so much to do, and everyone was so nice.'

Sheila looked down at the reports on her desk. There'd been a drunken brawl out at the Red Bone Hound Dog bar, a couple of fender-benders with drivers yelling at each other, several homeless person transports, and of course, the streaking teenagers.

'Everyone was *nice*?'

'Yeah. Some of the drivers we stopped called me "ma'am". Me – can you believe that? One of the homeless gentlemen did, too. We were able to get him fixed up with a meal and a place to sleep.' She beamed. 'And Deputy Karnes explained everything real good. He never even yelled at me.'

Sweet Jesus, those asshole jail deputies must've done that all the time. Sheila pretended to write something on a notepad in order to collect herself. When she could speak again without her voice shaking, she started on an overview of evidence procedures. She was barely past 'remember to always carry gloves' when her cell rang. She looked at the caller ID and her eyebrows shot up. Molly leaned forward curiously.

'Dale? What's up?'

'Good morning, my friend.' A voice that sounded like Michael Jackson came through the phone. 'I thought you'd like an early head's up since it came in to our dispatch. It'll take forever for it to officially reach you. There's been a hit-and-run out on Fall Creek Road. That stretch that belongs to you guys.'

'What kind of injuries?'

'Don't know yet,' Dale Raker said. 'I just heard it come over the scanner. I know they've sent an ambulance, but I don't think it's there yet. I'm sure we'll respond and secure the scene for you.'

The Branson city detective said a few more things before hanging up. By then Sheila had made up her mind. Molly's patrol training would start before Pimental got in.

'Let's go.'

The doorbell rang as they were feeding the kids breakfast. Maggie groaned. 'Please let the dog not have dug up Mrs Crawford's geraniums again.'

Since she was still in her bathrobe, Hank went to the door and looked through the peephole. It was not their neighbor. He had a feeling that fact was going to turn out to be a good news-bad news thing as he opened the door to a squirrely-looking guy in a wrinkled blazer. 'Can I help you?'

'You're Henry Alejandro Worth?'

Hank backed up a step but the packet of papers was already coming at him.

'You've been served.' The guy stepped away, leaving the papers to either fall or be caught by unwilling hands. Hank let them fall. They smacked on the foyer tile. Squirrely spread his arms and shrugged. 'Still counts, pal.'

Hank watched him get into his old Nissan Maxima and drive away before he bent and picked up the packet. He unfolded it and saw what he figured he would. He walked back into the kitchen as Maribel and Benny ran out, racing to get to their toothbrushes first. He dropped it on the table and sat back down.

'Well, it wasn't Mrs Crawford holding dead plants and cursing the dog at least.'

Maggie picked up the papers.

'It's a lawsuit. The department's getting sued,' he said. 'By Gerald Tucker and those other couple guys we fired for not showing up for their work shifts after we took away their overtime last November.' He sipped at his coffee as Maggie flipped through the pages. 'We knew it was coming. I'll say, though – I am not happy they came here to the house. That was uncalled for.'

Maggie frowned. He thought it was in agreement but then she leaned forward. 'Honey, you're named.'

'Of course . . . I . . . am.' He slowed down as he realized what she was saying. He took back the papers.

'I think they're suing you personally. And Sheila.' She pointed at the first page. He felt all the blood leave his head. He carefully reread it. She was right. Him and Sheila in both their professional and personal capacities. He glared down at the words until Maggie patted his hand.

'It'll be OK. The county lawyers said when you did it that you had legal cause, right? So it will all be just fine.' They stared at each other, neither one knowing if what she said was even remotely true.

Sheila had always thought it looked like someone sneezed on a map and they'd drawn the city limits around what hit the paper. There were tiny carve-outs and slightly larger carve-outs where property owners had clearly fought against being annexed, so the city just went around them. Then there were bigger chunks with few tax-generating possibilities that the city didn't care about and so passed by as well. This particular section was a half-mile stretch of Fall Creek Road as it ran east to west just north of Lake Taneycomo. On either side, the road continued within the city limits, but here it was county jurisdiction – two-lane and shoulderless and currently decorated with flashing emergency lights.

She and Molly, all the way from the county seat of Forsyth, pulled up at the same time as the second city police cruiser. She'd have to remember to kid Dale about his agency's response time. They parked down from the ambulance district vehicles and walked closer, Sheila taking advantage of the teaching opportunity to point out the flare placement on the pavement. They got nearer the rig and Sheila saw Larry Alcoate wading through the tall spring weeds on the side of the road. He turned and saw her and quickened his pace. Sheila waited for him at the edge of the asphalt.

'I'm sorry.'

'What for?'

'We probably ruined your scene.' He took his baseball cap off and ran his hand through his hair. 'We thought it was urgent.'

'What, no injuries?'

He stepped to the side so she could see the path he'd trampled through the weeds, and just at the end of it, the crumpled, contorted body of a woman. 'No injuries that were survivable.'

Molly sucked in so much air that she started to cough. Sheila looked upward, as if the sky would deliver her from yet another mess. It stared back, full of clouds but no help. She took a second to breathe and then leveled her gaze at Larry as she briskly took out a pair of nitrile gloves.

'That path through the weeds – that was you? Or was that already there?'

'The call came through as a live victim. So we went rushing in with our equipment. Plus, it wasn't completely light out yet.'

He waved at the strip of weeds and tall grass that stretched maybe ten yards away from the road. She snapped her gloves impatiently. He wasn't answering the question. He cringed.

'I don't know. The path is definitely me and Patrick, going back and forth to the rig. I'm sure we put other footprints around everywhere, too. While we were trying to find her. But I don't know what was already flattened before we got here.'

She sighed and took the same path they had, since any evidence on it was already trampled. She told Molly to stay put and walked the length of it, coming to a stop at a body with more bones broken than not. The blond white woman was mostly on her right side, with her arms flung up around her head. She wore workout clothes – trendy leggings and a fitted Nike running jacket. A Fitbit and a gold bracelet circled her left wrist.

Sheila knelt, balancing on the balls of her feet. She couldn't touch the body until the coroner got here, and she was afraid to move around the woman because she might compromise evidence even more than Larry already had. She sighed and walked out of the weeds, calling out for the Branson police guys to shut the road down completely. Then she turned to Molly, who was still frozen to the spot.

'Deputy? You all right?'

Molly disguised a sniffle as a cough and said she was fine. Sheila told her to get the evidence markers out of the car and then turned to Larry.

'This one's going to be a shitshow no matter what,' she said.

'You didn't necessarily make anything worse. Just be sure Alice gets a look at your shoeprints, though, for elimination.'

Larry nodded and quickly got while the getting was good. They both knew her magnanimity was unlikely to last long. She watched him climb into the ambulance and pull it farther down the road, then she pulled out her cell. Her first call was to forensic technician Alice Randall, who would have quite a time collecting evidence from this crime scene. Then she dialed the next number.

'You need to get out here. We've got a fatality.'

SEVEN

He came at it from the opposite direction Sheila had. He could see her cruiser on the other side of the roadblock, but she was nowhere in sight. He tossed his coat over the papers on the front seat and got out of the car, striding along the blacktop and nodding at the two city officers manning the perimeter. Nice of them to respond to the scene. He ducked under the crime scene tape and waved at Larry, who was sitting behind the wheel of his rig filling out paperwork. He got around the ambulance before he saw Sheila, who was standing in the middle of a patch of wildflowers and staring at the sky. A compact woman with bristly, short, gray hair was methodically moving in a circle, taking photos of something on the ground. Jesus – the victim had been thrown that far from the road? He quickly pulled paper booties on over his work boots and started down a well-trod path through the vegetation.

'We did that?' he pointed at the flattened weeds when he got where the women were standing. Alice stopped taking pictures and pointed at the ambulance.

'They thought she was still alive. Came galloping through like a herd of buffalo.' She shifted her point toward him. 'You get one more foot forward. No closer. I haven't done around the body yet.'

Hank took his allotted distance, which was enough to see the poor woman crumpled on her side, her limbs contorted and jogging clothes askew. He stretched to see around a tuft of long grass and then looked back at the road.

'This was called in as a hit-and-run?'

'Yep.' Sheila was now staring at the ground around the body. She looked up at Hank, raised a skeptical eyebrow, and pointed at the woman's feet.

'Exactly,' he said. 'Why the hell does she still have her shoes?'

They both turned and looked toward the road, which was – in this particular situation – very far away. March was standing at the edge of the blacktop with a measuring wheel. Sheila gestured and the kid started carefully down, the wheel spinning along the flattened path. She stopped when she got to Hank. Seventeen feet, two inches. And they were still at least four feet away from the victim.

Once she had the measurement, March drew back slightly and started fiddling with the wheel. Her nose was pink and raw, like she'd rubbed it quite a few times. This might be her first body. He was about to ask when Alice, single-mindedly looking only through her camera and scouring the weeds for evidence, reached a point in her circuit of the area where her lens fell on the woman's lower half.

'What the . . . she's still wearing her shoes.' The camera came down and Alice straightened with a frown.

'Yep,' Sheila said again. 'Seventeen-plus feet sailing through the air and she stayed in her shoes.'

Hank was still eyeing March, whose puzzlement had overcome her aversion. She stared at the victim's Nikes in confusion.

'When someone's hit by a car going fast enough, a lot of times they're knocked out of their shoes,' Hank said. 'And for her to be hit hard enough to land this far away from the pavement, she should've been pulled right out of them.'

It was a crime scene detail that had always struck him more than any other in these investigations. Shoes blithely stepped into by owners who thought they were just starting an ordinary day. Shoes that ended the day violently abandoned.

Sheila looked over at March. 'So what does her still having her shoes tell us?'

March's cheeks blushed the same pink as her nose. 'Yes, ma'am.

It tells us that maybe – probably – this wasn't a hit-and-run.' She looked back at the road and then around at the grass and flowers swaying in the breeze. 'But then how did she get here?'

That was a very good question.

It was taking more than an hour for the damn bodysnatchers to get there. Those people drove Sheila crazy. Couldn't touch the victim, definitely couldn't move the victim. Not until they got there and gave the OK. Which always took forever. In the meantime, Alice's partner Kurt had taken casts of every dirt impression they could find and some of wildflowers, which Sheila thought were artsy and unnecessary. The delay did give her a chance to catch up with Dale Raker, who showed up because 'it was this or do paperwork'. Blunt honesty was one of the many things she loved about the Branson city detective.

'Plus,' Dale said as he shook Hank's hand, 'it's so much more fun to gloat in person.' He looked down Fall Creek Road to the east. 'Only a couple hundred feet in this direction and this would've been my problem, not yours.'

'Yeah, I'd wish it were yours, except . . .' Hank trailed off with a glint in his eye that Sheila knew meant trouble. 'We don't think it's a hit-and-run. There's something else going on. Could be interesting.'

Dale blinked slowly, reminding Sheila more than ever of a bullfrog – something his squat shape and naturally downturned mouth evoked even without that movement. Hank explained the shoes and the lack of skid marks on the pavement, his eyes doing that glint thing the whole time.

'We won't know anything else until we can get a better look at the scene,' she said, trying to slow down whatever theories were starting to form in that head of his. 'We haven't even been able to see if she's got ID on her.'

Dale stared contemplatively at the swath of weeds. 'Could be anything at this point. Jealous husband, business partner argument, drug deal gone bad.' He winked at Sheila.

'You stop egging him on,' she said. Fortunately, Hank's attention was on the coroner's van just pulling up. About damn time. Soon they were all standing in a circle around the woman as the body-mover knelt and carefully moved her arm away from her head and down to her side. As he started to roll her onto her back, a gold necklace caught the sunlight. Something about it tugged at the edges of Sheila's brain. She started to point when Hank sank to his knees and brushed carefully highlighted blonde hair off the woman's face.

'Oh, my God.'

He wasn't sure whether he'd said it or if Sheila had. Vivian Gillam. Lying dead at his feet. He flashed to the last time he'd seen her – hostile and haughty and ferociously protective of her clients' interests. And their anonymity. He looked up at Sheila and saw the same shock on her face.

'There's no ID,' the coroner deputy said.

'We don't need one.' The words came out scratchy and weak. He cleared his throat and rose to his feet. 'Any initial observations?'

The guy shrugged. 'Dead at least eight to ten hours.'

Sheila held up her hand, like she was trying to stop what was coming. 'We need—'

'Yeah. Right now,' he said, moving back along the trampled path. She followed and they stopped when they got to Dale, who had walked halfway down from the road. They told him who the woman was. He let out a low whistle. He also had the dubious pleasure of making her acquaintance during a joint investigation last fall. Before that, none of them had ever heard of the businesswoman, she kept such a low profile.

So low a profile that whatever scant records she kept could already have disappeared. Hank pulled out his phone. They had to get someone over to her office immediately.

'Pimental just came on duty,' Sheila said.

He shook his head. 'It's got to be Sam. He knows where the office is. It's just an unmarked door. He's the one who tracked it down in the first place during that investigation.'

He made the call and then thought about how carefully Gillam had guarded the details of those who hired her. People with pockets deep enough to afford exclusive luxury accommodations in the area. And pockets deep enough to get very litigiously annoyed at someone going through supposedly private files.

'Pimental can still help. Have him get a search warrant,' he told Sheila. 'I think we need to tread very carefully on this one.'

He felt bad that he didn't feel bad. Sam was sorry she was dead, sure. But to get access to her drawers full of files? That was a flat-out jackpot. He raced across Branson to the office plaza where Concierge Travel Consulting was tucked away behind a blank door. It was a swanky one-room setup that he'd been in only once before, while investigating that old country music star who rented a house from one of Gillam's clients. Euford Gunner had a washed-up singing career and a murdered friend. And Gillam hadn't cared. She refused to give them any information until they came back with a warrant. Even then, they'd only been able to access stuff related to Mr Gunner, not the lady's full range of who-knew-what kind of juiciness about area landowners. But now . . .

He had to wait for Ted, who should be asking a judge for a new warrant right now. He pondered the locked – and very solid – door. The building manager must have a key. He couldn't find a phone number on the website, so he took a deep breath, braced himself, and walked into a doctor's office halfway down the open-air corridor. He finally escaped ten minutes later with the needed contact information, a questionable-looking homemade cookie from the new receptionist, and thankfully only one hug from the medical practice administrator, who happened to be his mother.

He paced around the parking lot, antsy as anything, until the building maintenance manager showed up. The guy had an average build but stooped shoulders that took several inches off his height. It made him seem grandfatherly even though he couldn't be any older than Sam's dad.

'You want into which office? That one? Son,' the guy said, 'that would not be a good idea.'

Sam knew why, but he wanted to hear the guy's take on Gillam, so he asked.

'The lady who leases that is . . . particular.' He stared at the unadorned door from a safe six feet away. 'Under no circumstances is anyone allowed in there without her authorization. And that includes me.'

'What if a pipe bursts or something?'

'I wait for her to get here. I don't go in without her. That's what her rules are.'

Sam's phone was quiet, no call yet from Ted. So he decided to keep with the conversation. 'It's not her building. She can't forbid you access if property damage is occurring.'

'You obviously ain't been lucky enough to make her acquaintance. She's the kind of personality makes a honey badger look warm and cuddly.'

Sam coughed to cover a snort of laughter. 'How many run-ins have you had with her?'

'One. That was enough. Tried to get the carpets cleaned in there. Gave prior notice and everything. She never responded, so that's supposed to mean everything's OK. I opened the door to let in the little lady who does the rug shampooing, and she was sitting there in those tiny dollhouse chairs with some big meaty guy in a suit. Rose up like my pastor says the devil's going to. Came at us real deliberate and quiet. Which was scarier than getting yelled at, I tell you. Made the little rug lady cry. Said if she ever laid eyes on me again, she'd have my job and my credit rating and all sorts of things. She even knew where my wife works.

'So you look like a nice kid, but I ain't opening that door.'

'I understand where you're coming from,' Sam said as his phone buzzed. 'I have met her, so I get it. But I have a search warrant, as of just now. A judge is giving me permission to go in there and look through everything.'

The guy just shook his head and didn't budge from his safe spot in the corridor.

'The other thing I can tell you is that she's dead.'

'What's that now?' He stared at Sam. 'You're kidding me, right?'

'No, sir. Not at all. That's why I'm here. She was found deceased this morning. So we need to . . . do a little investigating.'

'You sure? You take her pulse?'

Sam didn't know whether to laugh or put his arm around the guy. He split the difference and gave him a pat on the shoulder. 'I am absolutely certain that she has passed away, sir.'

It might have been his imagination, but he thought the man's stoop lessened just a little. He held up his phone and the picture Ted had sent with Judge Sedstone's flourish of a signature on the warrant. The guy squinted at it, then pulled out his key ring.

'I guess between that and you promising me she ain't going to rise from the dead, I'll open it up.'

Sam hoped he was joking.

EIGHT

So Hank was sending an off-duty deputy to search this woman's office. Sheila paced the pavement in frustration. It wasn't that Sam would do a bad job of it. It was that he wouldn't do a time-and-a-half better job of it. There would be his overtime, and possibly some for Pimental, too. And Alice and Kurt, of course. She sighed. Such huge overtime costs. It was why she hated homicides. Well, that and the loss of human life, she supposed.

She stopped as the coroner's people finally finished and started through the weeds with an occupied gurney. They were a glorified transport service and it drove her crazy that they could dictate things at her crime scenes. The coroner wasn't even a doctor. He was some corn-fed, white-boy insurance agent who won the office in the last county election. He never even bothered to show up on site if a death was already confirmed. He just sent his flunkies to take the body to the real doctor – a forensic pathologist – up in Springfield.

She managed a weak smile at them as they scooted past her to the van, Vivian Gillam body-bagged and balanced between them. What had that woman been up to? Cosseting more music stars in town for limited engagements? Leaving dozens of pissed-off peons in her wake?

'I think we could end up with one hell of a long suspect list,' Hank said, walking up behind her as the van pulled away.

'Because of her sparkling personality? Yep.' She turned. 'What was Larry able to tell you?'

'Not much,' Hank said. 'They were dispatched to a possible

hit-and-run with injuries. Came racing out here and were only able to find her fairly quickly because their lights caught the reflective strip on the windbreaker otherwise obscured by the weeds and grasses.' Hank looked around. 'Where's Raker? I wanted to ask if he could get us tape of that phone call.'

'He had to leave, but I did ask him for it.' She paused as Kurt hustled his sizable frame through the weeds toward them.

'She wasn't killed here. Very little blood. Some of those wounds would've bled some, at least.'

'Any idea how she got so far off the road?' Sheila asked.

'Not yet. I'm not even done with all the footprints.' He mopped at his face with the honest-to-God actual handkerchief he always carried. ''Course, I got a feeling they'll all turn out to be the EMT guys.'

He headed for his truck, stopping to introduce himself to Molly with a handshake and a smile. She looked stunned as she finished the last little distance to Sheila and Hank. 'I can't get over how nice it is on this side of things.'

In some ways, yes – and in some ways, no, she thought as she looked at the sad little clearing where Gillam had come to rest. She took a breath and refocused. 'Did you find the address?'

'Yes, ma'am. She lives right around the corner.' Molly pointed in a vaguely southeastern direction.

Hank smiled. 'Ted's search warrant covers it, too. Do you want to do it, or should I?'

'Oh, I'll go,' she said, already heading for her car. 'If I see Kurt pick any more wildflowers, I'm gonna lose my mind.'

It looked just as it had the last time he was here. If someone had searched it, they'd done a very good job. Nothing was out of place. Sam stepped inside with paper booties on and walked carefully into the center of the small office. The Chief had said to treat it as a crime scene, since they didn't know where she'd been attacked. He quickly checked the closet-like space in the back that had been outfitted with a microwave and refrigerator. It was just as immaculate. They'd do Luminol when Kurt and Alice arrived, but from first appearances, it sure didn't look like anybody had been killed here.

He decided to start with the room's centerpiece. The desk was spotless – further proof of her insane meticulousness, he thought. Two pens, a clean pad of paper and a cork drink coaster on polished wood held up by spindly carved legs. That was it. The computer sat on a small table behind the desk and chair up against the wall. The plants on top of the filing cabinets were lush and healthy, despite the low lamp lighting that was the room's only source of illumination. No overhead fluorescents for the elegant Ms Gillam.

He started dusting for fingerprints and once Ted got there, the job went quickly. Toward the end, he couldn't resist tugging on one of the filing cabinet drawers. Locked. Of course. He was dying to get inside. When he and Hank were here last October asking about Euford Gunner, they'd realized she had information on not only companies and wealthy landowners who rented out their properties, but also the rich and famous who insisted on that kind of luxury. Both he and Hank practically swooned over it, but they had no right to look. Then.

Now he eyed the heavy wood filing cabinets and the single drawer on the desk. All locked. Sam was quite sure Gillam kept the keys in a safe, separate location. Ted flipped open his knife and knelt at the desk.

'Wait.' Even though the woman had been frustrating as a Missouri mule, he couldn't bring himself to deface property that clearly had been important to her. 'Let me get in some practice.'

He pulled out his lock-pick set and went to work. It took him only two minutes and he didn't scratch a single thing. Better treatment than she'd ever given him. He chuckled as Ted looked at him like he was crazy. 'You had to have met her, dude.'

'Oh, I wouldn't have wished that on anybody.'

They looked up to see Hank standing in the doorway, the building manager hovering worriedly behind him.

'This guy just came walking up like he owns the place.'

Now Ted chuckled. He explained who Hank was as Sam started on the filing cabinet lock. The Chief shook the manager's hand and began asking questions. Sam stopped paying attention to the conversation as soon as he opened the top drawer. There were no neatly hanging file folders. Just a spare hard drive. There was a manila envelope tucked underneath. He pulled it out and felt a set of familiar rectangular dimensions.

'Uh, sir?' He laid it on the desk in full view of everyone and pulled out several stacks of cash. All hundred-dollar bills, it had to be at least ten grand. Ted let out a whistle. Hank sighed.

'That complicates things. Let's get to the files and see who those clients are. Who was she manipulating and pulling strings for?' The Chief raked his hand through his hair. 'Unless Sheila finds something at the house, that's the only avenue we've got.'

Sam pulled open the second drawer of the tall cabinet and Ted started photographing the neatly hung files. Hank headed to the desk, and as he knelt down in front of it, a jolt of déjà vu seemed to smack Sam in the head.

'Sir, the last time we were here . . . didn't you take a picture when you were looking in that drawer? Trying to find the Gunner file?'

Hank bolted upright, swore at himself, and yanked out his cell phone. Two minutes of furious scrolling later, while Sam picked that lock, and he found it. If anything was different from the photo, that would be a good place to start. They all peered at his phone screen and then the drawer. The Gunner file was gone. Nothing suspicious there – it had been subpoenaed as part of that ongoing court case. Otherwise, there were three new files. Could be new business over the ensuing months. It was as good a place to start as any.

There had been no set of keys on the body, so Sheila decided to show Molly how to break into a house. Only it was sealed tighter than her mother-in-law's pocketbook. Gillam had put deadbolts and interior chains on all the doors and wedged wood dowels in all the window frames. It might be the only home in Branson so thoroughly secured. Some people didn't lock up at all, and most only used whatever doorknob lock came with the house.

She wasn't surprised Gillam thought differently. The woman came from Chicago, where Sheila guessed every door got locked every time. Plus, she struck Sheila as someone who thought very highly of herself and wouldn't hesitate to protect that most valuable asset.

They chose a window in the back where they could reach the inside door bolt. Molly did a good job with her baton and they were finally inside. The interior was pale gray with splashes of color and inexplicable flooring. 'White carpet. Honest-to-God white carpet. Who does that?' she muttered as they put on fresh paper booties. The woman had to have walked around in a pair herself in order to keep this all so damn pristine. Not a single thing appeared disturbed or even out of place. Until they unlocked the deadbolt and stepped into the garage.

'Something doesn't feel right,' Molly said, sidling nervously to the left of the door.

Sunlight came through the one side window and lit the back wall. The rest of the space lay in shadow. Sheila walked around the back of the car, her flashlight playing over the Lexus. She stopped at the rear driver side door and felt her stomach twist into a perfect knot.

'Hit the light,' she ordered, and Molly's gloved hand obeyed.

A smear of blood ran across the bottom of the window. The back of the driver's seat cover was ripped clean through and a crowbar lay on the floorboard. Sheila moved forward a foot and looked in the front seat, but nothing there was out of place. There weren't even scuff marks on the floor mats. She stepped back again and pulled open the rear door. The bloodstain extended from the glass all the way down the door. There was more on the seat, but the black leather upholstery made it hard to tell exactly how much of Vivian Gillam had been left behind in her car. Because Sheila was damn sure the blood was hers.

'Killed *in* a car, not killed *by* a car,' she said to Molly as she straightened up and looked at where the girl had been standing by the door into the house. She wasn't there.

'Around front, ma'am. Watch where you step.'

Sheila found Molly kneeling in front of the shiny Lexus grill. It was spotless. But the concrete wasn't.

'I figure she got out and came around here to get to the door.' Molly pointed at the door to the house and then at the blood on the floor. 'And somehow the guy sneaks up on her and gets her right here. Hits her a bunch and forces her back in the car.'

Sheila's stomach knot convulsed and she tried not to vomit. Pulling into the garage and having an intruder slip inside just as the automatic garage door was closing. It was every woman's worst nightmare.

NINE

Hank found the Hickory Sticks Motor Lodge owner trimming hedges along the front of the drive. The motel had been the only readily identifiable entity out of the three new folders in Gillam's desk drawer.

'Concierge Travel? Never heard of it.' Warren Swink put down his clippers and shook Hank's hand. 'Why?'

'How about Vivian Gillam? Ever heard that name?'

'Now that, sir – yes, I have. Called me up a few months ago.'

'What about?'

'She wanted to see if I was interested in selling.'

'Were you?'

'Oh, hell no. Where would I go? We live in the back, so I'd be selling my business *and* my home. Told her I wasn't interested.'

'Do you have any idea why she approached you in the first place?'

Warren shook his head. 'Nope. Not a clue. Came out of the clear blue sky.' He squinted at Hank in the noonday sun. 'Why you asking? She do something?'

It would be in the newspaper soon anyway. 'She was found dead this morning. We're just trying to track down what business she might've been working on recently. To see if it helps us figure out what happened to her.'

'I'll be damned. That's nuts. I mean, it's too bad, but I didn't even know the lady.'

'Was the phone call the only contact you had with her?'

Warren had thought it would be. He was not hesitant in his rejection of Gillam's offer. But she showed up in person anyway, about a week later. Very nice lady, quite gracious if a bit overdressed for a chat in the lobby of a sixty-year-old motor lodge. She made the offer again. He said no again.

'Did you happen to ask why she wanted to buy?'

'I did. I thought I had a right to be curious. But all she'd say was that she was interested in my property. Which is a good way to say something without saying anything, don't you think?'

Hank was thinking exactly that. It was the same deflecting and obfuscation that Gillam excelled at when he dealt with her last fall. Only now he couldn't confront her about it. And her file was no help. All it had was Warren's contact details. He looked around the guy's business. It was trim and tidy and well past its heyday.

'How much land you got here?'

'An acre and a half.'

'How much did she offer you?'

'Eight hundred-and-fifty thousand.'

'I got to be honest – I have no idea if that's a good price or not.'

Warren chuckled. 'I wasn't real sure, either. But I talked to a real estate agent I know, and she said this property is worth way more than that.' He picked up his clippers. 'One more reason I'm glad I said no.'

Sam had been super excited about getting the important job of searching Ms Gillam's office, but now he was realizing it came with a hefty price – as in how much God-awful paperwork it had. He and Ted finally decided to truck everything, including the filing cabinets, over to department headquarters. They had a secure room there, where they could spread out and examine all the files properly and someone could get to work on that hard drive and her desktop. Only now he'd never get to leave, there was so much to go through.

There appeared to be two types of clients. One set was like Euford Gunner, ritzy out-of-towners who needed special high-end places to stay. The other set was made up of companies where Ms Gillam acted as their local representative. Some of those looked like they owned the places where celebrities stayed, and others looked like . . . well, they looked like they didn't want anybody knowing what they did.

'Where the hell do we even start?' Ted said as they stared at the drawers.

'It'd be great to get a look at her emails. See what she was actively working on.' Sam frowned at the computer, smugly sitting there protected by, like, five different passwords. He scratched at his ear. 'Maybe the highway patrol has somebody they could lend us to break into that thing?'

'No need, young man,' a high-pitched voice said from behind him. Both he and Ted turned toward the door to find Mr Raker standing there with a laptop, portable printer, and tangle of cables. Sam hadn't seen him since they'd finished the Gunner case. He still looked like a bullfrog and sounded like Michael Jackson.

'Sheila said I could help,' he puffed as he laid it all down on the conference table. 'She said you guys didn't really have anybody. And I just took a continuing education class on this computer stuff. I didn't think I'd get to try it out this quickly.'

Sam was delighted to see him for more than just that reason. To have a detective with years and years of experience sitting here as he and Ted tried to decipher all this would be a big help. He'd been starting to get a little nervous about them muddling through it on their own.

While Mr Raker pounded away at both his keyboard and Ms Gillam's, they decided to Google the VIP visitors. That made Sam feel a lot less overloaded. This paperwork might be manageable after all. Many of the folks seemed to be just passing through. Music stars with limited engagements mostly. They moved on and were never connected to the area again, according to both Ms Gillam's documents and their own tour schedules and promotion materials. Except one guy. Sam put that folder aside and kept going. A few names he didn't recognize turned out to be rich businessmen. They tended to come to town during times of the year when the fishing was good.

'They strike me as being more potentially suspicious than the entertainers,' Ted said, holding up the file for a big-time Kansas land owner who rented the same house out on Table Rock Lake every spring during paddlefish season. 'They come back annually. They could've had repeated contact with the victim.'

Sam agreed and started a separate pile. They had five files and were looking at a stack of loan application paperwork when Mr Raker suddenly smacked the table.

'I'm in. That wasn't as hard as I— oh, crap.'

Her email had a separate password. So did her word processing program. Mr Raker said a few unrepeatable words and started pounding away again. Ted mouthed, 'I like this guy,' and went back to work. They had piles and sub-piles and off-shoot piles by the time Mr Raker finally cracked into her email account.

'Cameron Cooper.' The detective hit print, and paper started spewing out of the printer sitting on the floor. 'Her last email was from accounting@godismusic.com, regarding somebody named Cameron Cooper.'

Sam snapped his fingers and reached for the one file he'd set aside. It was twice as thick as most of the others. Cameron Cooper. Recording artist. Pretty big in the world of Christian music. He and Hank had noticed the singer's name the first time they were in Ms Gillam's office – he'd been staying at the luxury hotel out by Table Rock Lake. He'd left there, but he hadn't left Branson.

'It looks like the hotel kicked him out in February. Now he's at the Whistler Hollow Cabin Resort,' Sam said. Curious, he pulled out his phone and Googled the guy. A handsome oval face popped up. Sleepy green eyes, light brown hair that was tousled just right. One successful album, then one much less so.

'And these folks are saying that they're cutting off his gravy train.' Mr Raker continued, squinting at the computer through the little reading glasses perched on the end of his wide nose. 'This email says the bills that this guy is running up are too high, and they're pulling their sponsorship. Are they the same ones who were paying for him at the hotel?'

Sam started going back through the neatly chronological paperwork and shook his head. A church had paid for his hotel stay – half of the two-inch-thick file seemed to be room service bills – and then finally had enough and dumped him. At the behest of his record company, Gillam went searching for another sponsor, eventually coming up with God Is Music, Inc.

'Damn. I wish someone would "sponsor" me,' Ted said. 'I could do with a few all-expenses-paid months at a resort.'

Mr Raker was in the middle of agreeing when he stopped scrolling through emails and let out a low whistle. 'Hold on – it looks like Cooper knew he was getting cut off. He sent this on Friday. And not to the company. To Gillam.'

> You better find me someone new. I'm not leaving town and I'm not paying. Get off your ass and find me a gig or find me a sponsor. Or I'll be showing up at your door and you don't want that.

That was certainly not the most Christian of responses, Sam thought. 'Did she reply?'

'No,' Mr Raker said. 'She sent God Is Music an email on Saturday asking them to reconsider, and that last email she got was their very polite version of a "hell, no" – on the Lord's Day, no less.'

'And now it's Monday, and she's dead.' Sam tugged on his ear and glanced at Mr Raker, who was looking at him a little too much like a parent.

'This ain't my rodeo, son.' He sounded like he was encouraging Sam to take a first jump off a swimming pool diving board. 'You think you ought to do something, then you two go and do it. I'll keep at the emails on this end.'

Sam and Ted were out the door before he finished the sentence.

Alice crossed herself, and even then had trouble stepping over the threshold into the garage. Kurt, typical oblivious man, hustled right in and started to work up by the front of the Lexus.

'I think about this exact thing, when I pull into my garage,' she said. 'Not every time. But a lot.'

Sheila nodded. 'Yeah. Me, too.'

Alice frowned. 'But my car's so old, it doesn't have a back-up camera.'

'Yeah. This car's only two years old and has all the bells and whistles. The camera would've caught someone sneaking in down low after the car pulled in. Except . . .'

She walked around to the front and pointed at the blood. 'I figure maybe she turned the car off, so the camera was off, then the person slipped in, then the garage door closed.' Alice nodded at the order of her theory, then whipped out her camera and started snapping ferociously. Sheila quickly stepped out of her way and ended up standing on the front lawn as she pondered things.

She decided to make two assumptions. One, that Gillam's

clothing wasn't just for show, that she had indeed been working out. And two, that she had come home from the gym immediately afterward. If only her purse had been in the car. It would have a gym membership card and a phone and all manner of God-sent evidence. But no. The SUV held nothing but the awful crowbar, and a yoga mat in the trunk.

She sent Molly back to comb the roadside between the house and the body dump site and texted Sam to have him start contacting gyms in the area. Then she put on her friendly face and walked across the street. The Gen X resident came out on the porch before she even got to the door.

'What's happened? Where's Viv?'

It was hard to imagine the suffocatingly proper Gillam as 'Viv'. Sheila said as much, more politely.

'Oh, no. We never call her that to her face. It's always "Vivian". And I'm pretty sure she thinks even that's too informal. But there's no way I'm calling someone barely ten years older than me Ms Gillam.'

'How often do you see her?' Sheila said.

The neighbor, white with dark hair in a messy bun and wearing rolled jeans and a green tee, was having none of it. 'What happened?' she asked again. 'Did her house get burglarized? Is she OK?'

No and no, Sheila thought. She told the woman that Gillam had been found dead out on Fall Creek Road, but not that they suspected the actual killing took place a hundred feet from where they were currently standing. 'Did you see her at all yesterday or last night?'

'Yeah. In the morning. She loaded one of those gift baskets in her trunk and drove off.' Viv was always coming out with things like that. Not tacky things with bows and balloons, but heavy, woven baskets full of what looked like wine and cheese. 'I always thought it had to do with her business. She was happy to tell you she owned her own company, but we could never get out of her exactly what it was. What the company did. I figured, with all the gift baskets and her dressing so nice, she must be in real estate. She has a license, but no listings, no website, and no advertising. So we never have figured out exactly what she does.' The woman blushed. 'Oh. That sounds really nosy, doesn't it?'

Sheila assured her it was perfectly natural and then encouraged more of it. 'What other habits did she have? Regular trips anywhere? People coming over?'

She never had people over, but did seem to have a social life. She'd leave in the evening, clearly dressed to go out. Otherwise, her schedule seemed haphazard. Weeks of nothing and then weeks of numerous comings and goings.

'She ever jog or walk around the neighborhood?'

That got a laugh. Viv seemed more the type to have a treadmill in her spare bedroom than someone who would stoop to sweating in public.

'Could she have belonged to a gym?' Sheila pressed.

'I guess so. She came and went often enough, and she wasn't dressed up every time. She could've been going somewhere to work out.' It was at this point that the woman explained she wasn't a stalker, just a graphic designer who worked from home and so was familiar with her neighbors' movements.

'Did she have any friendships with anybody else on the street? Or on the flip side – any disagreements with anyone?'

The graphic designer pointed across the street to the house next door to Gillam's. 'He's got two dogs. If she was going to have a disagreement with anybody, I'd bet it would be with him.'

TEN

'I count four.'

'Four what?' Sam asked.

'Commandments. That this dude has been breaking.' Ted stood in the middle of the room with his hands on his hips. 'If he tried a little harder, he could hit an even half.'

Sam snorted a laugh and stepped gingerly over a puddle that smelled like a Bourbon Street gutter. There was an overturned table and several empty bottles of premium tequila on the floor. A video game console sat on the couch half-covered with dirty designer clothing.

'High-class taste, low-class living,' Sam said.

'Last night was insane.' The Whistler Hollow Cabin Resort manager stood in the doorway. 'He honestly wasn't that much of a partier – not a homebody, sure, but not this nuts. He was mostly just demanding. Always wanting something or other from room service. Having delivery people in and out at all hours. That kind of thing.'

Not exactly what God Is Music, Inc. signed up for, Sam thought. Ted muttered the same thing as he picked his way through the mess toward the bedroom. The cabin consisted of the small kitchen and living room where they were standing, the bedroom, and a bathroom with access from both rooms.

'Do you know where he is?' Sam eyed through the foodstuffs on the kitchen counter as the manager wisely stayed on the threshold.

'Nope. I thought I'd see him today in here packing up, to be honest. We sent a bill on Friday which that lady was not happy with.'

They both snapped to attention and stared at the guy, who started to fidget. 'Look, we keep her up-to-date. She knows what kind of spender Cooper is. This bill was higher, sure, but not hugely different. This time, though, she actually called.'

Yeah, her name was Vivian and she worked for something-or-other travel services. She was the one Whistler Hollow dealt with about anything concerning Mr Cooper. The manager only actually spoke with her when she set everything up in February, and then last Friday. She'd seemed a little stressed and more than a little annoyed.

'At you?' Sam said. 'Or at Cooper?'

'Definitely more at him. She said she'd be speaking to him right away to get a handle on these expenses.'

'Do you know if she did?' Ted asked.

'No, sir. I got off that phone as quick as I could. Even her being only a little annoyed with me was too much. She was some kind of fearsome. I got no idea if she talked to Cooper after.'

'When did the party start?' Sam said, resuming his kitchen rummaging.

'Sunday afternoon. About four or five o'clock. Music and noise and door slamming.'

'And nobody complained?'

'That's our usual turnover time. If guests are here for a week, it's always Sunday evening to the following Sunday morning. So that afternoon is always the gap where we do the cleaning. But he wasn't going anywhere, so he partied on through it. Plus, we're not real full this time of year, so this week I put the folks we do have in units as far away from him as possible. 'Cause of the ruckus.'

They kept poking through the remnants of the ruckus – taking care to not dig through Cooper's personal belongings because they didn't have a specific search warrant. Ted made it into the bedroom and yelled out that there was no wallet or cell phone in there, either. Sam looked at the half-full kitchen trash can and rubbed at his ear.

'Did you see how many people were here?' he asked.

'Lots. All the lights were on, and the music going. Voices.'

'But how many people did you actually see? Coming? Going? Sitting on the front step drinking margaritas?'

The dude stared at him and the light bulb slowly came on. 'Oh. I see what you mean. I guess . . . I mean, I guess I saw none. Nobody. By the time I heard the music and the laughing, everybody was already inside here. Or weren't they?'

Sam didn't answer. Instead, he scooted past the man as he stood in the doorway and circled the cinematically rustic cabin. People around here hadn't lived in something that looked like this in decades, if ever. It was what the movies thought the Ozarks should be. But it wasn't just the façade that was unrealistic. He looped around the little building again and was standing by the spotless porch when Ted came out.

'What're you smiling for?' Ted said.

'There's no trash. No bottles, no cigarette butts, no red Solo cups. No footprints in the dirt right here, either. No signs that anybody came outside to get some air or take a piss or cut through the grass to the parking lot. There's nothing.'

Ted cocked an eyebrow and turned to look at the manager, who was busy turning fire-engine red and studying the artistically weathered porch boards.

'With a party as intense as this one looks, you'd expect at least some of those things, wouldn't you?' Ted asked the manager.

There was a little more fidgeting before the manager finally spoke. 'I never actually came down here. I saw from a distance, and I heard the noise. But I didn't walk down here.' He pulled at his knuckles. 'I just didn't want to deal with the guy. I'd had it up to here and I figured that the Vivian lady could take care of it. It's her job to babysit that idiot, not mine. But she wouldn't answer her phone.'

'You called her? When?'

Sam's tone had the man yanking his phone out of his pocket. 'Twice. Once at five twenty-five p.m. and then at eight forty-five. The first time it rang and the second time it went straight to voicemail. I left messages both times.'

Ted came down the porch steps and faced away from the manager as he leaned toward Sam. 'If it looked like there were people inside, it could look like Cooper was inside, too.'

'Yeah. Even if he wasn't.'

Hank expected to see Sam and Ted hard at work, ideally ready to hand him a list full of potential suspects. Instead, he found a solitary city detective battering a laptop and yelling at his cell's speaker phone.

'Raker?'

'Gotta go – there you are, Worth. They said you were on your way. The scene's all wrapped up?'

'For the most part. Forensics just went to her house on Country Bluff Drive.'

Raker's keyboard pounding stopped. 'What now? Country Bluff Drive? Within-the-city-limits Country Bluff Drive?' He leaned back in his chair and folded his arms. And scowled. 'That woman puts Machiavelli to shame.'

Hank knew he must be talking about Sheila, but he had no idea what she'd done. Or where she'd sent Sam and Ted.

'She makes these crumbs' – Raker gestured at the computers and stacks of files – 'look like the main dish. Makes me happy to lend a hand. And the whole time, the real meal is in a location that's mine to begin with.'

That's what was going on? Sheila had steered the senior police detective away from a site in his own city that might turn out to be where the killing occurred? If it did happen at Gillam's house, that would make it Raker's homicide and not theirs. Unless he'd been diverted elsewhere. By someone who knew her boss's predilection for holding onto interesting cases. Hank fought to keep from smiling.

'I'd think you were in on it, but she said you ran off to interview someone Gillam had a file on,' Raker said.

Hank nodded and was about to say something about the remaining paperwork when he realized how many years of local expertise was sitting in front of him. He pulled over a chair and sat down. Raker scowled some more.

'Why would Gillam have been interested in the Hickory Sticks Motor Lodge?'

'Warren's place? No idea. It's a good salt-of-the-earth facility, but everything's grown up around it. You got the highway real close by, and then the fire department and its sirens just down the road, so it's not like it's optimal real estate. On the other hand, great visibility.' His thick fingers drummed the table. 'There wasn't anything else in the file?'

Hank shook his head. It looked like there could be papers missing, he said, but there was no way of knowing for certain. And the other two new files in her desk had even less information. One had the name 'Charolais, K.' and involved the purchase of a house. The other was labeled 'Property 162' and had nothing in it. Was there anything about them on Gillam's computer? And what about this loan paperwork?

'I'm working on it,' Raker said. 'Too many damn passwords. I haven't gotten into her word processor yet.' He nudged the computer in frustration. 'Any documents at the house?'

'I don't know.'

'You should call Machiavelli and ask her. Since she's there anyway.'

Hank shook his head. 'No way. She doesn't like taking phone calls at a scene. Texting is safer.'

He pulled out his phone as Raker scoffed knowingly. When he was done, the detective turned the computer monitor so Hank could see the screen full of emails.

'Gillam was emailing pretty hot and heavy last week on only two topics. That churchy singer that your boys just went to talk to, and this. It looks like she was making deals and more than one, if I'm parsing these messages right. Toss me that cord. I'm gonna redo the printer connection.'

As Raker fiddled with the hardware, Hank stared at Gillam's email inbox. More than half involved the same domain name, something called TWS. He clicked on the most recent. It was just a string of letters and numbers and one phrase at the very end.

Time Well Spent.

'Everyone loves Puffin.'

Sheila looked down at the yappy little furball and doubted that statement very much.

'So you never had any disagreements with Ms Gillam?'

'Not since we put the fence up. That was about three years ago. Because, I admit, the girls did like to use her lawn. Such nice, soft grass. But the fence solved that issue. And now, poor Marshmallow is so old, I have to carry her outside anyway. No worries about her running over to the neighbor's.'

Puffin yipped her agreement. Sheila said she'd be happy to wait while Mr Murchison put the little dog inside. When he returned to the front step, she asked whether he'd seen anything unusual lately.

'Nope. She was real quiet, never really had visitors. She was always coming and going, though. In and out, always dressed real nice. What did she do for a living? I always wondered.'

Sheila ignored him. 'And last night? Did you see or hear anything? Anywhere on the street?'

Mr Murchison shook his head. 'Not a thing. And I would've noticed something at her house. She's got those security lights that pop on if something moves. Very bright. Too bright, if you ask me. They glare through every window of my house. But they didn't come on last night.'

She turned and stared over at the lights tucked under the eaves of Gillam's garage, then thanked Murchison and quickly cut across his yellow-spotted lawn. She stared up at the partially obscured light fixture and wished she had a few more inches of height on her five-foot-four. Well, there were ways around that. She walked over and yanked open the rear door to the evidence van, pulling out the stepladder she knew was inside. She needed to climb all the way up to see over some wire mesh that had been placed on top of the metal bolts attaching the light fixture to the wall. Once she did, the weird contraption made sense. A ramshackle bird's nest sat precariously along the edge. The mesh had clearly been added later to help prop up the egg-laden twigs, some of which were coming loose anyway. Vivian Gillam, friend to the birds. Who would've thought it? She leaned back a little to get a better view of the whole thing and suddenly understood why Mr Murchison hadn't seen anything. She carefully reached in and moved several bits of stick and leaves to the side, away from where they'd fallen directly onto the motion sensor. Not even an invading army would have triggered the lights with that in the way.

She climbed down and slumped against the ladder. Vivian Gillam, the queen of the perfectly neat, being kind to some messy birds. And look what it got her.

ELEVEN

Mr Beckham,

I am pleased to inform you of a new and unique opportunity for your enterprise/business/organization. I represent Time Well Spent, an exclusive collection of properties specifically created for your customer demographic. A presentation during your performances would benefit your audiences as well as add to your bottom line. For more information or to see an example of our entertaining and persuasive presentation materials, please contact me at your earliest convenience.

Sincerely,
Vivian Gillam
Time Well Spent, Inc.

Ms Gillam,

We have established timeshare partnerships in place. We would only be interested in changing our arrangement if your offer is substantially more beneficial to us. Please send financials and a list of your properties to this email address.

Travis Beckham
CEO, Darlin' Entertainment

Mr Beckham,

Thank you for your response. I'm attaching full information on our financial package. You'll see that it is fifty percent more lucrative for you than any other arrangements currently available in this area. We have also, in recognition of the key role your company will play in our joint success, incorporated a bonus structure if certain benchmarks are met. Those figures are in the second document attached to this email.

I do apologize regarding your other request. Our list of properties is proprietary information and unavailable for release until contracts have been signed. Please let me know if you have any other questions. I am happy to meet in person to discuss.

Best,
Vivian

Dear Travis,

It was wonderful to see your facility yesterday. The care you put into your business is quite evident and will be a great match with Time Well Spent. I and the Time Well Spent team look forward to a long, successful and prosperous partnership.

Talk soon,
Vivian

Dear Viv,

The signed contracts are in the mail. We'll start using your presentation this coming week, when we'll have five audiences full of our key demos. I'll have sign-up numbers for you next Monday.

Travis

'This guy is calling her Viv?' Raker said. 'I can't imagine that woman letting anybody call her that.'

'I guess familiarity breeds a good business deal,' Hank said, flipping through more of the documents. There were back-and-forths like that with multiple companies, most of which had shows playing somewhere in the Branson area. He got to the bottom of the stack of correspondence and smacked his hand on the papers in frustration. They'd been at this for hours. And not a single email or computer file had more than a passing mention to the 'presentation'. There were no details about how Gillam expected these shows to convince people to buy timeshare vacations at her properties. Which – since this was a woman who obviously had no problem putting other things in writing – was highly suspicious. She had to have slipped up somewhere, he thought. He shuffled everything into random order to force a fresh look. That earned him a smug grin from Raker.

'Do you regret yet that my boss agreed to let you keep this case even though it's my jurisdiction?' the Branson detective said.

Hank looked at the piles of paper. 'I'm starting to.'

That earned him a chuckle from Raker and more frustration from the paperwork until he got about two-thirds of the way through the stack. Tucked at the bottom of an email was a random comment about blood sugar levels. *You're right, the research on blood sugar levels and decision-making is fascinating. We will definitely incorporate it into our procedures.*

He pondered that for a minute. If it meant what he suspected it did, it was certainly interesting. Possibly even criminal. Definitely unethical. He waved the paper at Raker, who ignored him and jotted something on a notepad.

'All right, I finally traced back one of these corporate names,' the detective said. 'Axelrod, Inc. Doing business as something called The *Breakfast Buckaroos*. Must be new – I've never heard of that one.'

'Oh, I have.'

Cameron Cooper hadn't come back to his luxury cabin overnight. Aside from updated charges added to his bill by the irate manager, there was nothing new to be learned there. So Sam started his morning with the previous irate manager.

'That guy ran up such a bill. I've never seen one so high. And we've had major rock bands stay here.' Dave Yates offered Sam a seat in his nicely furnished but small office at the Kamarra Hotel. 'I don't think I can show you the invoices, though, without permission.'

Sam assured him that was fine, not telling him they had all that in Ms Gillam's files anyway. What they needed was information about Cooper's friends, his activities, his personality. And Sam was hoping that this hotel, with its closer quarters and more numerous staff, would have a better idea of all that than the more isolated cabin resort did.

'I think,' the manager said, 'that the best folks to talk to would be housekeeping. Oh, and room service. They would've had the most contact with him.'

Sam agreed and then declined the offer to interview them here in the office. Having a boss hovering in the background never made for a productive conversation. 'I'll just go to where they are. Less disruptive that way. And then you can get back to work.'

'Oh. Well, all right.' Mr Yates dejectedly reached for a walkie-talkie on his desk and radioed for someone named Joan. 'It might take a minute.'

Sam rose to his feet and then paused. 'Say, there is one thing that I think only you could help me with.'

Mr Yates perked up immediately. Soften them up first, with either flattery or disappointment. Then ask the important question. They'll be a lot more likely to help – that's what the Chief said about interviewing.

'About Ms Gillam. Did you ever get a sense of how she felt about Mr Cooper? You know, when you talked to her about the bills and everything.'

Mr Yates thought on that one for a minute.

'She was always real businesslike. Very professional. But very friendly and always remembering details – like if we had a big event here, she would ask how it went. That kind of thing. But towards the end, right before she said she was moving him to a different accommodation, she got a little . . . well, I could tell she was annoyed.'

'Just annoyed?'

'Yeah, OK. Pissed off. She was definitely pissed off. The folks who were paying Cooper's bills had just quit. She was flustered about it, which I definitely never saw before. We talked about where would be a good place for her to move him and came up with Whistler Hollow.' He paused. 'I was puzzled about why she didn't just drop him, honestly. I hadn't asked up to then, but she seemed so frustrated and needing to talk at that point, I felt like I could ask. And she said, "Dave, if you know a way to dump family, please tell me, because I'd do it in a heartbeat".'

Sam sat back down with a thump. A relative? 'Did she happen to say how Mr Cooper is related?'

'She muttered something about her sister, then switched back to talking about the bills. I wanted to ask more, but it was like she iced over. That probably doesn't make sense. Sorry.'

It made perfect sense to Sam, having met the woman. In fact, a lot more than just her cold demeanor was starting to make sense. A troublesome relative explained why she would take on such a client, and it could be the answer to the other – and far more pressing – question.

There was no admiring the lobby this time as Hank strode through it. He grabbed the interior door that led to the showroom and had it halfway open before he saw the sign. *No Outside Food Allowed* on a flimsy computer printout held up with Scotch tape. He pulled it loose and stomped inside.

'You change your policy since I was here last?'

'What the hell? None of your business, asshole. Gimme that.' Stone Cold ripped the paper out of Hank's hand. 'You can't come in here and start accusing me of stuff.'

'I haven't accused you of anything.' He examined the part of the sign he'd hung onto, which now read *owed*. 'I'm merely asking if you've had a change in your business policy.'

The bald man crumpled his half of the sign into a ball and started to walk away.

'It wouldn't be because you've recently studied the research on blood sugar levels and decision-making, would it?'

The sudden falter in his step was answer enough.

'When was the last time you talked with Vivian Gillam?'

'Who?'

He hadn't turned around. Hank moved through the tables in order to get a better look at his face.

'Dude, you need to leave. We're closed on Tuesdays. If you got questions, you go through company headquarters.'

He was pretty sure Stone Cold was the company. The man had used his home address when he registered with the state.

'You're the one who signed the contract. You're the one who presents the shows. I'm going to ask you one more time: when did you last communicate, in any way, with Vivian?'

The man crossed his massive arms over his chest and stayed silent.

Hank shrugged. 'Fine. I'll get a search warrant for your phone records, and your business records.'

The little color there was in Orsi's pale face drained out. 'You got no grounds to do all that.'

Hank took a step forward, glad he had three inches on this guy since Stone Cold so significantly surpassed him in the muscle-mass department. 'I have simple questions about Vivian. I will get that information any way I can. Whether you make it easy or hard is up to you.'

If the crumpled sign in Orsi's fist were coal, it would be a diamond by now. Hank knew he could make this whole thing much easier by just saying Gillam was dead. But he wanted to see just how long the man was willing to fight. It was always a useful measure of how much a person had to hide.

Stone Cold turned and walked toward the stage, which was more of a waist-high platform set in an alcove on the back wall. He leapt lightly onto it and started moving boxes stacked along the edge. Hank leaned against a table and waited. Ten silent minutes later, he slammed down a carton of dishwashing detergent and spun around.

'You're not going to leave, are you?'

'Nope.'

He hopped off the stage and muscle-walked over to Hank, who made sure to stay in his nonchalant slouch against the table. And then tried not to laugh. Stone Cold clearly wasn't used to his flexed biceps failing to intimidate. They stared at each other until Stone Cold caved.

'We talked on Sunday. I don't know why you're so interested.'

'What was so urgent that you needed to talk to her on a Sunday?'

He hesitated. Hank straightened back to his full height and pulled out his phone. He dialed a number and told the other end to go ahead with the search warrant applications.

'Whoa. Hold on. Fine – we talked about the ambulances.'

Hank hung up. 'Go on.'

Vivian had just found out Hank was asking questions about audience members having to go to the hospital, he said. She hadn't been pleased. 'She turned on a dime, man. Always been real accommodating, friendly-like. But she got frosty. Was not happy to hear that we'd called 9-1-1 so many times.'

'So which one of you advocated withholding food to make people more susceptible to the time-share pitch?'

'That was her, man. All her.'

'Really? You already forced people to sit through long presentations – even before you went into business with her. Now you're trying to blame her?'

'It's different. The order of this is dictated by the contract. She was set on that. It was non-negotiable.'

'And that was OK with you?'

'Our percentage of the sales was going to go up. And . . . and I didn't know that it would cause all those kind of emergency health problems.'

That last statement was bullshit, and they both knew it. Hank decided to keep the focus on Gillam.

'So you weren't happy with her?'

'I wasn't happy with you, man. You are not something I need. And I told her that.'

'And you two argued?'

'No. Yeah. I don't know. We disagreed.' He waved his hands around, trying to gather all Hank's accusations so he could dump them in Gillam's lap. 'She has hardcore requirements, man. Nobody who hasn't already signed a contract gets food for any reason until after the presentation. And the presentation has to come after at least a half-hour worth of show.'

'And how long is the presentation?'

'An hour minimum. And that's if you hit your target right off. If you need more sign-ups, you go longer.'

So elderly people who hadn't eaten since the night before showed up expecting breakfast shortly after sitting down, and instead had to wait at least ninety minutes, and likely more. All while getting bombarded with a high-pressure sales pitch. And that was after a lengthy process to get everyone on and off the bus from the hotel. It was a wonder Larry's ambulances hadn't been called even more often.

'Did you ever talk to anyone else at Time Well Spent?'

'No. Just Vivian.'

'And they're the ones who have these properties? The time-shares that you're trying to sell?'

'Yeah.'

'I'm going to need a copy of the presentation and the list of the properties.'

'No way, man. I signed a nondisclosure agreement.'

'Then I'll get a warrant.'

'Why are you coming at me? I'm one dude. One show. You want all this shit, why don't you search-warrant Vivian? She's a one-stop shop for you. Has all the info on all of it. Go hassle her.'

'I would. Except that she's dead.'

Stone Cold stared at him, first in surprise and then in calculation. For such a fearsome face, it was remarkably easy to read. Hank watched as he took only seconds to decide who would bring greater dividends – the sheriff or Time Well Spent.

'I still can't help you.'

Hank nodded and made a show of turning to leave. 'Oh, one last thing – where were you Sunday? From five p.m. until Monday morning at six?'

'At home. And yeah, I live alone.'

Hank gave a slow nod and left through the lobby, ripping down another No Food sign on his way out. He crumpled it into his own diamond-hard ball as he walked to his cruiser. Stone Cold hadn't batted an eye when asked for an alibi. And that was not, in Hank's experience, the sign of an innocent man.

TWELVE

There were way too many skinny white women. Sheila hadn't thought there were this many physically fit people in the whole county. They trotted out with stainless steel water bottles and dewy glows. She kept her distance until the yoga studio was empty, then cautiously went inside. One wall was exposed brick and the opposite had a row of ferns in a planter under high windows. It smelled like incense and potting soil. The one woman left was in the corner making notes on a clipboard. She wore black leggings and a light peach tank top that was just a shade darker than her skin.

'Well, hi. Are you here for the next— oh.' She stopped and took in Sheila's uniform. 'It doesn't look like you're here for the next class.'

Sheila chuckled and showed the woman a photo of Gillam.

'Oh, yes. Viv. She's a regular.'

That answer was worth the lungfuls of incense. 'When was the last time you saw her?'

'Oh, a day or two.'

'No. I need you to be as specific as you can, ma'am. Do you have sign-in sheets, or some kind of record of who comes?'

She looked a little taken aback. 'Uh, OK. I do. Have a sign-in.' She walked to the door, where there was a spindly little carved table and a frou-frou binder that said, *Be Where You Are, Not Where You Think You Should Be*. Sheila tried not to roll her eyes.

'It's kind of haphazard.' The yoga teacher flipped through it. 'Not everybody signs it.'

'How do you know to charge them?'

She held up a hole punch. 'I stand here and punch their card. They buy ten classes at a time, and I punch each one when they come through the door. When they hit ten, they need to buy a new punch card.' She shook her head. 'I got to tell you, Viv isn't much for the sign-in. She sails in, gets her card punched, of course – she doesn't mind that. But she can't really be bothered to stop and sign the book, you know?' Her peach complexion reddened. 'I don't mean that she's rude. More like you can tell that she's busy. Like every minute is plotted out.'

'When was the last time she came?'

'Oh, yeah, you asked that.' She looked again at the uniform and Sheila could see the pulse start to hammer in her throat. 'Did something happen to her? Is she OK? Why are you wanting to know exactly when?'

'Ms Gillam was found dead yesterday morning. We're still trying to figure out what happened, and part of that is tracing her movements over the weekend.'

She sagged against the little table, almost toppling it. Sheila steadied her and led her to the front of the room and her water bottle. She sank onto the rubber mat on the floor and sipped until she was able to stop shaking. Sheila loomed over her and looked around. There were no chairs. She sighed and pulled another mat out of a bin. Several popped joints later, she was sitting on the ground, her service weapon digging into her side and her knees promising revenge.

It must have been Sunday night that she last saw Viv, the teacher named Trish said as she clutched the water bottle to her chest like a teddy bear. It wasn't a class the older woman usually came to, but she hadn't acted any differently than normal. She took her typical spot at the end of the front row, did the nod-and-smile thing with the ladies around her and left as soon as it was over. All that was normal.

'But it didn't seem like it helped.'

'What do you mean?'

'Usually, my students leave more relaxed. You know – more at peace, more centered. And Viv always does. This is her de-stressor.'

Trish looked proud at that, justifiably so. Sheila wouldn't have imagined it possible to de-stress the high-strung Gillam. The teacher must have read the thought on her face.

'I know. She comes across as real high-powered. But most times, she just floats out of here after a class. She told me once that I was the best part of her day. And now . . .' She blinked hard and then burst into tears.

Sheila gave her a tissue and pressed on. 'And she didn't give any indication what was making her so tense on Sunday?'

Trish shook her head.

'What time did the class end?'

'Nine p.m. No one stayed to chit-chat.'

'Do you have cameras in your parking lot?'

That got a laugh through the tears. 'In this strip mall? You got to be kidding.'

Sheila asked for a list of everyone Trish remembered attending Sunday night's class. The woman unfurled from the floor in one impossible movement and went to get a notepad. Thankfully it was a long list, which gave Sheila time to leverage herself off the mat without her gun digging into her side even more. It took both hands, a few hip contortions and one muffled grunt. She was on her feet just in time to take the paper.

'You didn't say anything about what happened to her,' Trish said. 'Was she . . .'

Sheila didn't make her finish the question. 'No. She wasn't sexually assaulted. Beyond that, we don't know much. We don't even know if it's more likely to have been someone who knew her or a stranger.'

'I didn't know her real well,' she said, using the past tense for the first time. 'And I know that some of the ladies felt that she thought too highly of herself, and they'll probably tell you that. But please don't go into this with that kind of bad image. She would stop and have kind words for people. And she donated anonymously to a raffle we had to raise money when someone in the morning class got cancer. I just think she was trying to run her own business and she was used to doing it someplace other than a small town. She was more of a big-city personality. She wasn't mean – I just think she didn't feel real at home here.'

Not at home here. Sheila thought about that all the way back to the office.

Sam found Joan in Room 207, scrubbing God-knew-what out of the bathroom sink.

'Make-up,' she said. 'Expensive stuff is always the worst. More thick and gooey. Not good for the drains.' She straightened and dumped the glop in her hand into the trash can. 'Mr Yates said you had questions about Room 210?'

'Yes, Cameron Cooper. I'm interested in anything you can tell me about him.'

She eyed Sam carefully. 'You're a policeman. You care that he didn't hang up his towels? That isn't why you're here.'

Sam looked at the short, stocky woman with tired eyes and other people's dirt on her hands. And now he was lengthening her day. The least he could do was level with her.

'He's missing. From the resort he went to, after he left here. And we really need to talk to him. Because the lady who co-ordinated all of his accommodations and funding has been murdered.'

She mulled that over for a moment. 'Now that is a reason for a policeman. You have her picture?'

Sam pulled out Ms Gillam's driver's license photo. She shook her head. 'She is not the one who visited.'

'There was a woman who came to see him?' Sam asked.

She was much younger than Ms Gillam, maybe a year or two younger than Cooper, Joan said. She didn't see the woman come often, but she was definitely Cooper's most regular visitor. And the baby was adorable.

'Baby?'

'A *niño. Ocho meses*, maybe?'

A woman with an eight-month-old boy? Sam asked more, but Joan hadn't anything about how the woman knew Cooper or where she was from. Otherwise, the only visitors were silly men like Cooper. Different ones every time, but always loud and full of drink. She would see them occasionally, leaving in the mornings as she came onto the floor to clean. And she could always tell, of course, when she got to his room.

'Bottles and smoke – and not just from cigarettes. Trash from the take-out food. Nothing too horrible, but . . .' She shrugged. 'It was not the kind of thing that Mr Yates likes. The mess left behind, he doesn't care how big that is. But it needs to be done quietly. Not loud and rude.'

'Did you hear anything about when Mr Yates made him leave? Did he just go quietly?'

She laughed. 'No. That was loud and rude, too. I was working down the hall when Mr Yates came up. I didn't know he was up here on this floor until I heard them both yelling.'

The first thing she remembered was Cooper yelling that he had a sponsor who'd already paid, so the hotel couldn't kick him out. Then there were some lower volume murmurings from Mr Yates that she couldn't hear clearly. He started out sounding professional, then irritated. After a sudden crash of glass he shot right up to furious – and very loud.

'"That's right, they cut you off. And it doesn't matter anyway, because I'd be kicking you out no matter what." That's what he yelled. Then he said Cooper had twenty minutes to pack up and get out,' she said. By that point, Wilton the daytime security guard was there and Mr Yates told him to escort Cooper from the premises. The ridiculous man started stomping around and throwing things from the sound of it. And he kept shouting for Yates to call someone named Lillian.'

Sam rubbed his ear. 'The woman with the baby, was her name Lillian, do you know?'

'I don't think so. I heard him a few times, and he called her Cheeks.'

'Cheeks? Like . . .' Sam patted his face.

'Yes. Exactly. Cheeks. Like, "Hey, Cheeks, the maid is here. Get out of the way so she can clean up".'

Sam got a full description of the woman – pretty with pale skin, dark hair and a curvy build – as the name rolled around in his brain. 'Do you think he could've been saying, "Call Vivian," maybe?'

Cooper's voice had been muffled behind the closed hotel room door, so it was possible she heard the name wrong, Joan said. 'Is that the woman who's dead?'

Sam nodded.

'And you think he did it?'

'We don't know. We definitely want to talk to him, though,' Sam said. 'Were you still close by when he left?'

'You bet I was. I was *not* going to miss that.' Twenty minutes exactly and Wilton was marching him to the elevator. It was hard not to cheer. She and the other two housekeeping staff on the floor rushed to a room with a front-facing window and watched him try to stuff all his luggage in the Uber car he'd ordered. There was more arm waving and yelling and he was gone. They did cheer at that point. Then they saw the room. It could have been worse, but not by much.

'Lots of things broken?'

'Oh, yes. Everywhere. Toothpaste all over the bathroom walls. Spilled tequila soaked into the mattress. Curtains stained and smelling like barbecue sauce.'

Sam looked around the comparatively pristine bathroom they were standing in and asked, not because it was important, but just because he wanted to know. 'And what about the towels?'

'Oh, he took those.'

THIRTEEN

Four different shows – one breakfast, two lunch, and an afternoon matinee – had all come up empty. The folks at the matinee didn't have a clue what he was talking about. He figured Gillam hadn't bothered with them because they didn't serve food.

The man running one of the lunch performances said Gillam approached him, but he declined to switch from the timeshare company he currently worked with. The other lunch show guy refused to divulge anything Gillam told him, even though he hadn't actually seen a contract yet, let alone signed one. The lady at the breakfast show was much more cooperative, but it didn't matter – she didn't know anything. Gillam tried to set up a meeting, but the woman said she hadn't even had a chance to respond to the email. Hank must have looked as dejected as he felt, because she sent him on his way with not only an apology but also a blueberry muffin left over from that morning's show.

He sat in his cruiser and finished off the food while staring at a list of these theaters. They were all home-grown, not ones that could be dictated to by some corporate entity out of a big city. That made sense – those types didn't like the potential for litigation and bad publicity. And they had deep enough pockets to not need the infusion of cash he was sure Gillam was bringing to these shoestring-budget local shows.

There was one last production in that category. And *Down Home Darlin'* had also been one of the starring players on Larry's list of ambulance calls. He found the showrunner walking across the almost empty theater parking lot to his car. Hank pulled up directly in his path, got out and introduced himself to Travis Beckham, he of the cozy 'Viv' emails. He was a tall, blond thirty-something with a strong jaw and direct gaze, even after Hank told him what he wanted.

'I'm sorry – I can't divulge any of that. Unless you can override the nondisclosure agreement. In which case I'm all yours.' He smiled. Big and toothy.

Hank could see now why Gillam let this guy get away with calling her 'Viv'. He'd probably been student body president in high school and then transitioned into a nice sales job somewhere before taking on this show. Excellent people skills and an easy charm. He'd bet the guy was Viv's top performer.

'You deal with the timeshare company directly, then?'

'Yeah . . . with Viv. She is Time Well Spent. And I checked it all out,' he said. 'No worries there. It's a fully incorporated company. And she's the registered agent.'

That was what Raker was finding as well. Fully legitimate, with no names attached. Which did their investigation no good. Hank would happily sacrifice a sheriff's department laptop to the detective's ferocious pounding if he could come up with any other people connected to the company.

'Do they have certain guidelines you need to follow? Maybe regarding when breakfast gets served?'

Toothsome took a moment to smooth the front of his shirt. 'They do recommend that we have their undivided attention during the presentation, so we don't serve the food at the same time.'

'Do you ever serve it before the presentation?'

'No. The rhythm of the show isn't laid out that way. The presentation needs to come before the meal.'

'Anybody ever have issues with that? Get mad, get sick, anything of that sort?'

The guy looked puzzled for a split second before switching to panicked. 'We have the highest kitchen standards. We're fully licensed and inspected. We've never made anybody sick.'

'How come the ambulance had to be called five times in the past month?'

'Those had nothing to do with the food. Breakfast hadn't even been served in any of those incidents.'

Hank smiled. Gotcha. 'I know. In fact, that was the point, wasn't it? Keep the old folks from eating so their blood sugar gets low and they're less able to resist your persuasive presentation, right?'

Beckham looked like a bird who'd flown full tilt into a window – disoriented and wondering when he'd be able to pick himself up again. He even let out a few chirping stutters before finding his balance. 'I don't . . . know what you mean. We choose the order of things based on entertainment value.'

'Oh. I thought it was based on science. You know, like those studies that talk about how hypoglycemia makes people confused and more susceptible to high-pressure sales tactics?'

He could see that the guy was dying to ask how Hank knew all this. But instead, he smiled and slid his hands into the pockets of his slacks, forcibly relaxed and ready to take flight. 'I don't know how else I can be of help, sheriff.' *I'd like you to leave my parking lot now* remained unspoken.

'When was the last time you talked with Ms Gillam?'

Toothsome blinked in surprise at the change in subject, but answered readily enough. 'Friday. We were supposed to meet for coffee, but she had to postpone. We're going to do it tomorrow.'

'Did she say why she needed to reschedule?'

That was too far. He frowned. 'I think I need to know why you're asking all these things.' He walked the few steps to his Honda Accord and pushed at his key fob. 'Why do you need to know about Viv from me? You should go and ask her.'

This was the first person today where Hank felt like he was breaking the news to a friend of the deceased. He spoke softly. Beckham staggered back a step and turned white.

'Oh, God. Of course you'd want to know then. What did she tell me?' He put a hand to his head. 'She said something came up. She did sound flustered, which wasn't like her.'

That was sure true, Hank thought. He stayed put as Toothsome started pacing slowly in front of him, recalling the conversation as he went.

'I had some ideas to promote both of our brands even further. We were going to meet at the coffee shop downtown and talk about it. She called that morning and said she couldn't make it . . . another client had an emergency.' He paused. 'No, not an emergency. "Urgent matter" is what she said.'

'Any idea who this other client is?'

She hadn't named anyone, but her tone when she said it was different. He'd just lumped it together with her general flusterment, but now that he replayed everything in his head, the way she said those particular words was almost sarcastic. Which made plenty of sense to Hank if the 'client' was in fact the troublesome, freeloading relative Sammy was looking for right now.

'You said you were going to meet to talk to her about promoting your brands?'

Still choked up, Toothsome nodded.

'What does that mean?' Hank said.

'Bringing in some of her individual clients to perform here. She said she could swing bigger stars, increasing crowds and therefore increasing timeshare sales. That sort of thing,' he said distractedly. 'I can't believe . . . you're sure? That she was murdered? Really? How did it happen?'

Hank ignored the questions. 'Where were you Sunday night?'

'At home. Why . . . good heavens. You don't think I . . .?'

'We're just checking with everyone who knew her. Do you live alone?'

Toothsome nodded. 'I, uh, I did get take-out. Near my house. I'm sure I still have the receipt. Would that help?'

Not really. 'Sure. Could you email me a copy of it?'

The guy's tensed shoulders relaxed a little bit. Hank thanked him and started to move toward his car. 'Oh, in any of your conversations, did Vivian ever mention having problems with anyone?'

'She never talked about other people. She was very discreet.'

That was an understatement. She kept everything under wraps and for the most important information, apparently didn't even keep records. And if no one she worked with was going to help him get what he needed, he'd have to help himself. And for that, he thought as he drove away from the theater, he had a plan.

Vivian Nesbit Gillam kept her husband's last name after he died, but her maiden name came up easily enough on a records search. That left Sam with the wonderfully uncommon combination of Nesbit Cooper, of whom there was only one. She lived in Joliet, outside of Chicago. The local PD agreed to do an in-person death notification. He asked them not to leave Mrs Cooper until she called Sam. When he told the duty officer it was because the woman's son was a murder suspect, she offered to have her guys stick around for the whole conversation, maybe see if it looked like Cameron had been home to see his mother lately.

His cell phone rang two hours later. Harriet N Cooper sounded very tired.

'These officers here said that my sister was murdered but they don't know anything else.'

Sam outlined what had happened and that they were looking at several possible perpetrators. He would get to one particular suspect in a minute. He needed background before he got to the questions that would almost certainly tick her off. 'Can you tell me why she moved to Branson from Chicago?'

'Oh, when Jim died, she needed a fresh start. She couldn't stand to be in the area any more, I think. Being in the same places where the two of them used to do things. Certainly in their house. She sold that within three or four months, and boom, she was gone.'

Sam wasn't sure how to ask his next question without it seeming like he was dogging on his hometown. 'Any idea why she chose Branson specifically?'

'Oh, I know. Why on earth would anyone set up shop there? But she told me that she did her research and the need for high-end service, the "quiet market" she called it, was basically untapped. Nobody was doing it. So she could build from the ground up. Now, that doesn't mean I know anything about her business – like a hotel concierge for people too rich to slum it in hotels? I never understood it. I just told people she was a real estate agent.'

'How was business going for her, do you know?'

'Mmm, not really. I mean, I guess it wasn't going bad. I would've known that. But ah, we hadn't talked much about her work lately.'

'Why's that?' He tried to keep his tone neutral.

There was no answer. The silence stretched until finally he heard faint sniffling and someone in the background offering a tissue. He was curious how genuine the emotion seemed to the officer witnessing it in person.

'Because I asked a favor of her,' she finally said, sounding even more tired than before. 'And it was going . . . badly.'

'How so?'

More silence, this time without sniffling. Sam bit his lip to keep from talking. Let them fill the silence, the Chief always said. Let it stretch until they can't stand it. It took Harriet Cooper more than a minute to get to that point.

'I needed her help with something that, ah, turned out to be more difficult than either one of us anticipated.'

'What was that, ma'am?'

'Oh, it isn't important. Now, definitely.'

Sam frowned at his phone. He would get her to talk about Cameron's arrangements. But maybe a new tack first. 'Are there other family members?'

'I'm it. Her only relative. Our parents have passed on. And we're the only siblings – we *were* the only siblings,' she corrected with a sob. 'She never had children. I have a son, so yes, there's him, too. I raised him by myself. Viv was always supportive.'

More crying. Sam spent the time trying to picture Vivian Gillam as a doting aunt. He couldn't do it. He took so long trying that Ms Cooper filled the silence again, talking more to herself than to him.

'Viv was very . . . transactional. Everything was about what came next. Not in a monetary way necessarily. More like in a results way. She would help him out, like with his homework or the cost of sports equipment. But then she expected him to get good grades and attend every practice. That was the deal.'

'Where is your son now, Ms Cooper?'

A pause. 'I don't know. He's a musician, so he travels a lot.'

'And was Vivian helping find him lodging?'

Now the silence felt like a smack. Sam bit his lip again.

'I really have to go now . . .'

'Ms Cooper, no. You and your sister talked about Cameron's behavior, didn't you?'

They had, she finally admitted. And Lord, Vivian was furious about it. She said Cameron was ruining her reputation, with both the Branson hotels and the sponsor companies she also used for other clients. Harriet said family should come before reputation. Vivian said that was bullshit and family should be expected to behave in a civilized fashion just like everybody else. Harriet said that Cameron wasn't like everybody else and Vivian said he was worse and hung up. That was three weeks ago, and it was the last time they spoke.

'Did Cameron ever mention a baby to you, ma'am?' Sam said.

There was confused silence. 'What do you mean a baby?' she finally said. 'Like, we talked about babies in general? Or are you saying *his* baby? I don't even know what you're talking about. He doesn't have a baby.'

She started to full-on cry. Sam hated it when interview subjects did that. He took a deep breath.

'Where is your son now, Ms Cooper?' he repeated.

'I honestly don't know.' Her voice was very small. 'He called on Sunday and left me a voicemail. He said he was sick of Branson and was leaving. He didn't say where.'

Sheila had lost count of how many rushed meals she'd eaten in this conference room. This particular McDonald's drive-thru would not go down as one of the better ones. She pushed away her hamburger and got up to stand in front of her whiteboard. Dale continued to eat.

'You gonna finish your fries?'

She told him to go ahead and started drawing a timeline. At only the second dot on the line, she turned around. Dale didn't even look up from his food as he plucked a paper from a pile and handed it to her.

'Our call log. Times and transcript.'

She looked at the Branson Police Department shield on the top then at the six fifty-eight a.m. time stamp. *Something's happened on Fall Creek. I think somebody got hit. By a car. A jogger maybe? It looks bad.*

'And this is verbatim? Where's the rest of it?'

'He hung up.'

'What? No one called back?'

Dale shook his head and took a napkin to the ketchup spot on his shirt sleeve. Sheila cleared her throat.

'Another call came in. We're down to only one operator for the 9-1-1 line. The other one's out on maternity leave.'

'You got to be kidding me,' she said. 'Did your guys run down who the phone number belongs to? Or were we supposed to be doing that?' These dual-jurisdiction things were always one step away from chaos.

'No, no, it's us. And we did,' Dale said. 'Guy named Cliff Watkins. Who apparently likes to harvest roadkill.'

The image of Gillam's body flashed through her head and Sheila felt her burger start to come back up.

'He saw some flattened grass on the side of the road,' Dale said. 'He pulled over, then saw some tire marks on the dirt shoulder. Thought he might have found himself a deer. Seems he's well known at the Department of Conservation. They've issued him several of their free wildlife dispensation permits.'

'Dale.' She loved him but Lord, he sure could sidetrack himself. 'Focus, please.'

He pushed his food away. 'Mr Watkins walked on over and saw that it was . . . not wildlife. Ran away as fast as he could.'

Sheila sighed. 'And don't we wish we could do the same.'

FOURTEEN

The knock came as they were eating breakfast. Sheila hadn't managed to haul herself out of bed as early as she'd intended to, but at least the consequence was getting to share an omelette with her husband. Tyrone paused with a bite halfway to his mouth as the sharp rap faded away. It happened again as she pushed back from the table, heading for the bedroom and her service weapon. He went for the laptop and the video feed from the camera mounted on the porch.

'It's some white guy in a suit.'

'At six thirty in the morning?' She came out strapping on her duty belt. There had never been anything good from an unexpected knock on their door. The number of times she'd had to hose off bags of shit . . .

'I don't see anything else on the street except what's probably his car,' Tyrone said.

Sheila took a look for herself and then they both sat back down and resumed eating, the laptop on the edge of the table between them. Four knocks later, the man finally gave up and drove away. Sheila set down her glass of orange juice and stood up.

'We're going to leave at the same time, baby. I don't want you pulling out on your own later.'

Tyrone rolled his eyes. 'Just because I don't have a gun don't mean I'm little-old-lady vulnerable. I'll be fine backing my car out of the garage.'

An image – unbidden and unwelcome – flashed through Sheila's mind. Her fingers tightened around the dishes in her hands. 'Even rich white women aren't safe in their own garages.'

He gaped at her.

'Just . . . please, baby. Leave with me. You can read the paper at work before your shift starts.'

He gently took the plates away from her. 'OK. Let me get dressed and we'll go. Together.'

'This is an interesting theory, man.' Ted put down his copy of the list. 'That we're going to find "Cheeks" in a crowd of women who all had babies at Branson Valley General eight months ago?'

'Seven to nine months ago. The housekeeper said she was guessing about his age,' Sam said. 'And it's all we got. We just have to hope she had the kid here in town. I don't want to do this with other hospitals. It was enough of a pain in the butt with just ours. I spent half the night matching addresses with names.'

'I guess we can count ourselves lucky that the maid noted that it was a boy.'

'How possibly could that be a detail someone would miss?' Sam said.

'Oh, you young, carefree ignoramus,' said the father of two. 'You go to enough Gymboree infant classes and you realize that the only way to tell with a lot of babies is the color of their clothes. I remember one mom who put her bald girl in blue denim overalls and then got mad at me when I complimented "him" on rolling over. That's not fair play, man.'

Sam laughed at the thought of Ted on some floor mat with a bunch of infants. He'd probably see just as many babies today if all these mothers were home when they showed up. If they were lucky, Cheeks was one of them and she knew where Cooper was. They divvied up the list. Since this was his bright idea, he got stuck with the far-flung addresses. Ted took the convenient in-town locations.

Seven hours later, Sam had ruled out a third of his list and called the state Children's Division twice. Once because the mom was on meth, and once because there was no mom at all – only the baby and a five-year-old sister in an apartment with no food. He was pretty pissed off with the whole world, to be honest, when he pulled up at what he promised himself would be his last stop of the day.

It was a street off Spring Creek Road in Branson with little houses in semi-decent shape although few seemed to consider front landscaping to be necessary. An older woman opened the door with a baby on her hip and a disinterested expression on her face that changed to hostile in a nanosecond. 'You got a warrant?'

Sam swallowed a groan. 'No, ma'am, I'm just looking—'

'Then get off my land.'

'Ma'am, I only have a couple of questions, and then I'm out of here. Really.'

'No.'

He could feel a flush crawling up the back of his neck. He took a deep breath. 'Ma'am, I'm working on a murder investigation, and I need your cooperation. It can be some quick answers to questions right now, or it can be me coming back with a warrant.'

'Natalie, come get the baby. I got to show this boy off our property.'

A much younger woman materialized behind the unfriendly grandma. The baby started squirming to get to her and the grandma handed him over without breaking eye contact with Sam. He planted his feet more firmly and moved his right hand to rest on his belt near his Glock. He wasn't going anywhere. Because the young woman had long, dark hair and some significant curves.

'Cheeks?'

She froze and turned white as her baby's bottom. The older woman, who was clearly her mother – same oval face and slashing eyebrows, just marinated in years of hard work and nicotine – demanded to know what the hell he was talking about. The young one, standing a foot behind, stepped back even farther and shook her head.

He was so tempted to simply flat out ask where Cameron Cooper was. Get all this over with. Whatever this woman was keeping from her mother wasn't his problem. But then he took in the pajama bottoms she wore and the changing table in the corner of the living room. It didn't look like she and the baby were just visiting. Did she depend on her mother for housing? He sighed and focused again on the older woman as she started advancing on him.

'Hold on now, ma'am.' He did not want to have to take a step back. She kept coming and he held out his hand in a stop motion. He'd made a decision. 'I obviously have the wrong house. So I'm going to leave. But I need to ask that you give me the space to do that. OK?'

He made himself as tall as possible, which was a good six inches more than her, and looked stern as he walked backward for several paces before turning sideways toward his cruiser. She came out onto the bare wood porch and watched him. That put her out of reach of whatever guns she might have perched inside the front door, which put him enough at ease to walk normally to his car. He drove away with two new tasks on his plate – canceling his date with Brenna tonight and setting up surveillance for when Cheeks inevitably left Grandma's house.

'Oh, yeah. I call him "The Politician".' She smiled and handed Hank back his phone. Hank looked down at his screen and the photo of Toothsome, the breakfast show manager. The guy did look a little bit like one, he had to agree.

'And this is the man who would come in with Ms Gillam?'

'Yep. A bunch there for a while,' Brenna said. 'Then it tapered off. I think the last time I saw him was about two weeks ago. Her I saw only a couple of days before she died. It was a weekday, so maybe Friday?'

If only every interview was this easy. Sam's girlfriend was answering questions he hadn't even gotten around to asking. And she apparently had a habit of nicknaming people. He liked her more and more each time he saw her.

'Did she meet with anybody else?' Hank asked. He laid the Gillam photo, enlarged from a snapshot they found in her house, back on the coffee table. Brenna sat back on her couch and thought about it. She seemed to be replaying things in her head, which meant she probably had excellent recall. He didn't want to put pressure on her by staring, so he surveyed the room instead.

He was sitting in a nicely broken-in brown corduroy easy chair. She was cross-legged on a green microfiber couch that drooped on one end. There was an IKEA bookshelf in the corner and a mish-mash of modern art prints and framed landscape photography on the walls. Through the kitchen door, he could see a bouquet of flowers on the table that he suspected came from Sam. The whole thing was clearly a collision both of tastes and of hand-me-downs from two different households. Tied together with a triumphant, out-on-your-own vibe that made it work perfectly.

He relaxed into the recliner's sizable butt divot and waited as Brenna pondered the photo.

'She didn't really. Meet people. I remember her a lot, but I think it was mostly her coming in and getting something to go. She didn't usually sit. You know, at a table with people. That's why I remember her with the Politician.'

'Did she ever come in with anybody else? Even if it was just to-go?'

'She was always by herself. And always in a hurry.' She paused. 'I don't know if that's it. She was just very . . . brisk. Always very polite, but no chit-chat. Just order a large soy milk half-caff latte with minimal foam, pay, move down the line, take it, drop change in the jar, and go.'

He wasn't surprised at all that Gillam would have such a nit-picky order. At least she tipped.

'Exactly a dollar. Every time. Not our most generous, but definitely not bad. Half the people don't leave anything.' She suddenly snapped her fingers and leaned forward. 'There was once, after she got her order and left. I could see through the front window that she was talking to somebody, but I couldn't see who. It seemed like it was an argument, actually.' She bit her lip. 'I guess that's actually not super helpful, is it?'

That was fine, Hank said. He started to ask a follow up when a petite young woman came out of the hallway, waved and disappeared into the kitchen.

'That's Felicia. My roommate.'

The other half of the home-decorating collision. They heard the clunk of cabinet doors and she popped out holding a slapdash sandwich and a Red Bull.

'I'm late for work. Sorry. Hi. Nice to meet you.' And then she was gone, the screen door banging closed behind her.

They both laughed through Hank's follow-up questions. He didn't have many and rose to his feet soon after Felicia's breezy exit. On his way to the door, he thought of one more.

'I'm just curious. What name did you give Vivian Gillam?'

She turned a little pink.

'"The Perfectionist".'

Earl was sprinkling birdseed like he bought it by the individual grain.

'Since when did you turn all miserly with that stuff?'

'Since I almost used it up waiting for you. The bag ain't bottomless, you know.'

'Sorry,' Sheila said. 'I lost track of time. That murder we're working on . . .'

He nodded. 'Heard about that. Imagine you all been busy.'

She stuffed her hands in the pockets of the green sweatshirt she'd put on to cover her uniform shirt. The temperature hadn't dropped as it got dark, and she was starting to get hot. Which was making her cranky. Which would not do, because Earl was a sweetheart and out here as a favor to her and the department.

'How my newbies doing?'

'Pretty good. The young one is fitting right in.'

Austin. 'Fitting in with his duties, or fitting in with the other staff?'

'Both, I'd say.'

That wasn't good news, actually. She wondered what to do about it.

'And the other guy is fine,' Earl continued. 'He's not a back-slapper, so he just kind of comes in and does his thing. You can tell he's soaking things in, though. Lots going on up there.' He tapped his temple.

'And Boggs?'

'The girl?' He backed away at the look on Sheila's face. 'Sorry. Woman. Female. The female deputy?'

'Yes. Her.'

He doled out a few more seeds.

'Are they treating her like they treated Molly March?' she asked.

'Yep. Only she ain't taking it.'

'What do you mean?'

'She ain't taking their crap. They'll say rude things and she just walks on by. Or she looks at them all bored, like they're reading out a grocery list and she's just waiting for them to finish. They don't know what to make of her, I think. Like, the other day somebody got released and Stevenson was bringing him out. He musta been teaching Boggs the procedure, 'cause she was with him, taking it slow 'cause the guy had a gimpy leg.'

Earl had swung into action behind the lobby counter, offering bus fare if the inmate didn't have a ride waiting. It was one of Hank's policies that drove the penny-pinching county commissioners nuts. Stevenson made some crack about the department being a welfare state paid for by the folks who actually worked for a living. 'And what does your rookie do? She quotes chapter and verse from some university study about how little expenditures mean bigger savings later in incarceration and social service costs. Statistics and everything.'

Then she turned around and walked back into the locked down portion of the building, leaving a flabbergasted Stevenson standing next to the counter. 'Took him about a minute to come around. Then he got real red and called her – well, I won't repeat it. Sidetracked me so as I didn't notice the releasee was almost out the door. I yelled after him about the bus voucher, but he just kept going. Can't say I blame him, with that look on Stevenson's face.'

'Did Stevenson say anything else?'

'Nah. But I saw him and Bubba later. Heads together. I couldn't hear what they were saying, though. Coulda had nothing to do with Boggs, I guess.'

Sheila laughed. If it wasn't about Boggs, it was about her. Either way, it was nothing good.

FIFTEEN

Cheeks hadn't budged. Molly watched the place all night and now Sam was back, parked behind a patch of trees that allowed him a view of the house. Thankfully, the street was a dead end, so if the young mother wanted to leave, there was only one way to go. Right past him. And really, Sam thought, that was the least she could do. He hadn't given her up to the grandma, which he totally could have. Now she should return the favor and lead him straight to her baby daddy. Because Sam was positive that's what Cameron Cooper was.

Cooper seemed just the type to leave a knocked-up girlfriend to live with her mother instead of taking care of her. So maybe the grandma wasn't real fond of the guy. Understandable. And Cheeks hadn't wanted to start an argument by having Sam ask about him. Also understandable. But since she'd visited him at the fancy hotel, she was obviously choosing to stay in contact. So why the hell wasn't she contacting him now? She could be calling him, sure. That was a lot more practical than sneaking out to see him, Sam knew that. So did the Chief and Mr Raker, who were trying to get a search warrant for her cell phone records right now. But he'd so gotten the feeling yesterday that she was making him a deal – his silence in exchange for her help with the man who called her Cheeks.

He slouched down in the driver's seat and questioned his judgment until Ted interrupted him with a text.

Any luck?
Nope.
Me either. He hasn't checked into any other local hotel.
That Yates manager guy probably put out the word. Don't let him check in.
Lol.
Damn. Activity. Gtg.

Natalie Lambert walked across the weedy yard and got into the old Chevy hatchback in the gravel driveway. She'd switched the pajama pants for sweats, but still had on yesterday's T-shirt. Sam waited for her to putter down the street and turn onto Summit Drive before he started his car. He followed her and she wound her way through Branson and onto Highway 65. She sped over Lake Taneycomo and took the Hollister exit. She puttered through the residential streets, the old car burping exhaust the entire way.

Sam's hands tightened on the wheel. He was getting close. He hoped. If he could find Cooper – apprehend him, really – and the dude ended up being the killer, then he'd end up solving a homicide. Well, him and Ted. But what a thing that would be. The Tag-Along Kid solves a murder.

He knew what a lot of the deputies thought of him. Even before the bloodletting, but especially after. The department splitting in two. And him deciding to back the Chief and Sheila instead of the fired Tucker and his friends. At the beginning, back in November, he'd felt forced into a corner about having to choose a side. But he'd never regretted his decision, not even when the other guys put that stink bomb in his locker or egged his beloved Bronco. Thank goodness he'd gotten to that one before the gross yolks dried onto his paint job. He'd never uttered a word about either to Sheila or Hank. He didn't want to put them in a position where they felt they had to take some kind of disciplinary action against the guys who did it – or worse, not be able to figure out who did and then look impotent when they didn't punish somebody. Either outcome would make things even uglier.

So he laid low and kept his mouth shut and hoped it would all eventually blow over. Although as the whole thing dragged on, even he was starting to admit to himself that the likelihood of mending fences was, well, unlikely.

'Damn nigh impossible,' Ted had said the last time they talked about it. 'Don't fool yourself, kid. It ain't gonna happen. Somebody's going to go down in flames. And to be honest, I'd say the odds are even as to which side. Hank's got the brains and the authority, but Tucker and Bubba got the means. They're just nasty operators.'

They wanted their influence back, and their plum work

assignments, and their way of treating folks. Traditionalists, the Chief called them. It was not a compliment.

So if Sam could make an arrest in this case, it would help their side a lot. And it would be awesome. He tapped the brakes as Natalie turned left onto yet another residential street. He wasn't familiar with this area – Hollister had its own police department, so he never had to patrol these neighborhoods. He could see her slowing down and thought about driving on by and not tipping his hand. But what was the point in that? She knew that he knew who she was and—

'Oh, forget it,' he muttered and swung the wheel left. He coasted to a stop on the side of the road as the Chevy continued to crawl along past the small one-story houses. She finally came to a stop in front of a yellow one with crisp white trim about a hundred yards away. She got out and walked up the driveway and then around the far side of the house. Sam swore. He couldn't see a thing. He didn't need Cooper's baby mama having enough time to warn him so he could slip away out the back.

He thought about knocking on the door and decided that the pursuit of a murder suspect was sufficient grounds to put off that little nicety. He'd ask permission of the owner once the guy was in handcuffs. He walked along the side yard and turned the corner to find a scuffed camper trailer parked in the backyard, a row of just-bought petunias planted along the front and the little attached awning propped up with weathered two-by-fours. He ducked under its absurdly low height and banged on the door.

It swung outward slowly, Cheeks's slender arm pushing it wide. She stared at him with a mix of resignation and contempt, then wearily shifted her stance so that he could see the tall figure behind her.

'Who the hell are you?'

The words came out before Sam could stop them. The guy was tall and thin and angularly good looking, but he was not Cameron Cooper. He swung back to Natalie. 'Who the hell is this?'

She blinked in confusion and opened her mouth, but the guy spoke first.

'Who am I? Who the hell are you, asshole? And what are you doing here?' He advanced more quickly than Sam would've thought possible, forcing him to step back from the door and whack his head on the awning. The immediate identification of a uniform would come in handy right about now, he thought as he fumbled with his civilian windbreaker. He yanked it back and showed his badge. And his gun.

The guy stopped with one foot out the door in mid-air. Cheeks slipped into the trailer's interior shadows and started crying.

'I'm going to ask again. Who are you?'

'Jason Nilquist.' He slowly lowered his foot and turned back. 'You led him here? Really?'

'He came yesterday,' she said. 'To Mom's. I can't get kicked out, Jason. And she'll do it, if she knows I'm over here. And he' – she jabbed a finger at Sam – 'was going to say something. Right in front of her. And then Brody and me would be out on our asses. So I had to get him to not say anything then. I had to let him follow me here.'

Jesus. It made him sound like the worst arm-twisting low life. And it wasn't even true. About this guy, anyway.

'I haven't done anything wrong.' The Jason guy was still facing Natalie. 'Why would you—'

'Where is Cameron Cooper?' Sam knew he was beet-red, but he didn't care.

They both stared at him. It was clear that the Jason guy had no idea what he was talking about. That left Cheeks. Sam stepped out of the way and invited her to join him outside. He walked her to the end of the row of flowers, using the time to take several deep breaths.

'Your nickname is Cheeks?'

She nodded.

'So when I called you that, you thought . . .'

'I thought you were going to ask about Jason. Mom doesn't like Jason.'

'Is Jason the only one who calls you that?'

She dug a flip-flopped toe into the freshly turned dirt. 'No.'

'Who else calls you that?'

'Cameron.'

She didn't know where the singer was now. She didn't know why he vanished. She hadn't seen him since late January, which was right before he got kicked out of the hotel.

'Yeah, I knew that was coming,' she said. 'He trashed that place.'

'Why'd you visit him there in the first place?'

The other foot started in on the dirt. Sam rubbed at his ear and then considered Jason, who was leaning against his camper door and glowering at them.

'You know what? We're going to continue this somewhere else,' Sam said. 'Somewhere we have time for you to tell me all about everything. So let's walk back to our cars.'

He pointed to the side yard. Her tears started up again, now the angry kind that had him worried she might kick him in the shins. They stared at each other for a minute and then she trudged slowly around the side of the house. She didn't look at Jason again. Sam did.

'How long you been living here?'

'Three months.'

'How often do you see Natalie?'

'Too often.' He stepped inside and slammed the door, shaking a two-by-four loose. It toppled forward and Sam instinctively grabbed for it. He caught the end and wedged it back under the awning, then hurried after Cheeks, yanking splinters out of his fingers as he went.

He came at Sheila from the side, right there in the employee parking lot. She had the trunk of her Forerunner open and he approached from the left, tickling her peripheral vision. She spun around and a full view brought instant recognition. The little ferret in a wrinkled suit.

'You are not authorized to be here.'

He peeled his lips back in a smile. 'It's public property, Ms Turley. And I wouldn't need to be here if you just answered your door at home.'

She was aching to put her hand on her Glock. Or punch him in the face. But either one would just make that smile wider. So she stood completely still. And waited. He pulled a tri-folded sheaf of papers out of his coat's inside breast pocket and held it out. She didn't move. So he weaseled his face a little more and reached forward, like he was thinking about laying the thing in her trunk. She allowed herself a raised eyebrow. Not the 'that's interesting' eyebrow. No, this was the one Tyrone called the 'slow and painful death' eyebrow. The one her brother said meant his little sister was about to cold-cock you, then stick around and make you thank her for it when you woke up.

The ferret froze. Then he shifted cautiously away and laid it on the ground about eighteen inches from her boots. Genuflecting almost. She would've smiled at that thought, except now she knew what he was. And what that was, the white slab of documents on the dark asphalt. She watched him get in a shitty sedan and drive away, then she turned back to her SUV. She looked at the bird seed bag in the trunk that had pleased her so when she bought it an hour ago. She slowly closed the door hatch and walked toward the building, the papers trembling in her uncertain hands.

SIXTEEN

Hank was in the conference room contemplating Sheila's whiteboard timeline when she walked in. She quietly closed the door and laid a letter on the table. He looked more closely. It was not a letter. Shit. He'd completely forgotten to tell her about getting served on Monday. His copy was still on the front seat of his cruiser, under a pile of case paperwork.

She waited, hands resting on the back of one of the conference room chairs. Which was a bad sign. She should be telling him she was irritated, or pissed off, or ready to fight, or some other Sheila-ish reaction. He fumbled for something to say.

'I'm sorry. I totally forgot to tell—'

'They're naming us personally. Not just in our capacity as officials.' Her knuckles were pale against the chair.

Hank held up his hands, patting the air like he was trying to calm a child. He realized it a split second later and dropped them to the back of his own chair. Placating was not a good idea with a grown woman. Especially this particular woman.

'I know. That surprised me, too. But I don't think it matters.'

Her eyebrows shot up and then came down in the start of a scowl.

'No, no.' Now his hands were up in surrender. 'What I mean is that the lawyers said we were on solid legal ground to fire Tucker and the others. So if we were solid there, we should be solid on a personal level, too.'

He wasn't sure about any of that, but she looked so uncharacteristically anxious that it was starting to worry him.

'If that's true – and it's probably not,' she said, 'that doesn't mean we won't have to hire our own lawyers. Spend our own money and time.'

'Maybe. I don't know.' He swiveled the chair around and sank into it.

'You know they're going to go after our assets. All Tyrone and me got is our house and our retirement, Hank.'

'I know. Us, too.' He raked his hands through his hair. 'We're not going to lose those. They're not even going to get close. We'll talk to the government attorneys first. See what they say. And then . . . well, do you know any private lawyers?'

'I've never gotten divorced and I've never had call to sue anybody. And since my country club membership lapsed, I don't have any in my social circle, either.'

The sarcasm felt like sunshine on a winter day. It meant her disturbing disquiet was fading. He smiled at her. She glared at him. All was right with the world. She shook her head and pointed to the murder timeline. Except where it wasn't.

He walked up to the board and tapped at the point two months ago when Gillam had started emailing about Time Well Spent. 'So . . . I have an idea,' he said. 'We can have officers pose as tourists and attend the shows. Watch the presentations, hopefully experience some high-pressure sales tactics. Maybe even be treated so badly we could file charges against the showrunners.'

She stared at him, something clearly dawning on her. 'You haven't checked your inbox, have you?'

'My email?'

'No, the actual physical inbox on your desk. Where I left a message Friday night from some guy whose father was mistreated at a show and rushed to the ER.'

'Milt Engelman?'

'If he's the one with a very pushy son, then yes. Demanded to talk to you, demanded you talk to the other folks, demanded—'

'Other folks?'

'Yeah, he said he tracked down another victim. It's all on the message slip. Which you would know if you bothered to look.'

'This is great. The more of them, the better we can show a pattern.'

Her hands went to her hips. 'We're looking for a murderer, not somebody who was late serving breakfast. I know Maggie brought this to you, which makes it important. But you need to stay focused.'

She had so little faith in him.

'I am focused. The point I'm trying to make,' he paused to shoot her a look, 'is that if we're able to get them on elder abuse or something similar, it would be some good leverage to get them to give up Time Well Spent and what properties Gillam had, who she might have made angry.'

She thought about that for a minute and then gave him a begrudging harrumph.

'Some of them have to know something. I don't buy that somebody like the smooth guy in charge of *Down Home Darlin'* couldn't wheedle more information out of ol' Viv,' Hank said. 'If divulging a little bit meant the difference between closing a deal and not closing it, I think Viv would side with closing it, don't you?'

He could tell she was warming up to the idea. 'That's true. She would close the deal above all else,' Sheila said. 'And she was the type of person who would think she remained in control of everything at all times. Even if she wasn't.'

They both took a minute to enjoy the other's self-satisfied expression. Hank's disappeared when Sheila shook her marker at him again. 'So who are you planning to send into these places that matches the demographic? We don't exactly have seventy-year-old deputies walking around.'

'Yeah, the oldest woman in the department is—'

'Don't. You. Even.' She glared at him.

'I didn't mean you should do it.' He waved his hands defensively. 'All I'm saying is that it seems like it'd be better to have a couple go in, be interested in a timeshare to use for vacations with the grandkids. That kind of thing.'

'Well, it needs to be white folks. Nobody's going to believe Black people want to come down here year after year.'

She had a point.

'I think we're going to have to ask for volunteers from outside our agency,' he said.

'Why? 'Cause Bubba Berkins is the only old deputy in the department?' She spat out the name, then got that pinched look on her face that appeared every time the jailer came up in conversation. 'He can't write a basic report, let alone handle a sensitive undercover job.'

Hank scoffed. 'I'd rather put Sam and Molly March in gray wigs than send him in.' Maybe the State Highway Patrol would loan them some people. Or Springfield PD. They were a big department and could probably spare two officers for a few days. He'd call both places today.

Wanted: elderly looking, preferably still mentally sharp law enforcement officers able to withstand high-pressure sales tactics and mediocre country music theater.

Natalie Lambert had a nice ass. At least she used to, until she got knocked up. The pregnancy made things sag that hadn't sagged before. 'Nobody would nickname me Cheeks now,' she said, sipping at the coffee Sam bought her when he decided that taking her back to an interview room might not be the most productive of plans. Instead, they were strolling along the little Hollister business strip. Which meant, thank God, that he wasn't having to look her in the eye when she told him stuff like that. He could feel the blush crawling up his neck.

'And they both call you that?'

She scoffed into her to-go cup. Jason called her that because he was the one who came up with it when they were dating in high school. Cameron called her that because she was stupid enough to tell him the truth when he'd asked if she had a nickname. She'd met him at the St Louis Landing about a year and a half ago. Sam decided not to ask how she managed to frequent a famous strip of bars that long ago when she wasn't even legal age right now.

They'd totally hit it off. She didn't even know he was a rock star. Sam had heard Cameron's music, and that wasn't how he'd label the guy. More like a lite Christian FM star. They spent a month together while she was in St Louis visiting friends, then went their separate ways. She didn't find out about his career until she got back to Branson. That did not, however, turn out to be the biggest shock from her whirlwind romance.

'My mom was so pissed off. She wanted me to go to college. Not get pregnant and have to keep living with her.'

'When did you hook back up with Cameron?'

She stopped dead. 'I didn't. No way. I was letting him see Brody, but that was it. We were *not* together.'

She started walking again, faster now, with Sam trying to keep up in every sense. Her story bounced around, but several things finally became clear. Cameron had tracked her down. After the baby was born. He said he just happened to be in Branson to do some recording, but then he stayed. And stayed. So her mom started to get on her to go after child support. He kept brushing her off. He liked playing with Brody for a few hours here and there and he liked the hotel, but he wasn't interested in a permanent place and he definitely wasn't interested in paying his fair share.

She started to be sick of the whole thing, and then he got kicked out of the hotel. She grabbed that opportunity and pretended she didn't know where he'd gone. It felt good to not answer his phone calls, which only came a few times before he stopped trying.

'And now he's not at the Whistler Hollow Cabin Resort anymore?' she asked. 'Did he skip out on his bill? Is that why you're after him?'

'As a matter of fact, he did skip out,' Sam said. 'Did he ever say anything about how he was paying for stuff? Like the hotel?'

She swished the remnants of her coffee around in her cup. 'Just that he had sponsors. I figured it was some kind of Christian group, once I figured out that was his music type.' She cocked an eyebrow at Sam. 'They obviously weren't checking in on him real close, were they?'

He couldn't help laughing, but shut up quickly as she started talking again.

'He was super mad when he thought they might stop paying for the hotel. Like, furious mad. I heard him on the phone once, yelling that they needed to find more money. It was nuts. Like, wouldn't it be smarter to kiss the ass of the people paying the bills? Instead of being a dick?'

That certainly made sense to Sam. It wasn't sounding like Cameron Cooper was a very logical thinker, though. He asked if she'd ever overheard the singer talking to anyone else. Family perhaps?

'Does he have relatives here?' Her eyes widened in fear. 'Am I gonna have to worry about somebody else showing up and wanting to see Brody?'

'I don't know about that. But we are trying to figure out whether he knows a lady who was killed over the weekend. That's why it would really help if we could find him.'

'Damn. He's mixed up with a dead person?' She stopped short again. 'I picked the wrong hot guy in a bar, that's for sure.'

The proper spin could help him out where there was not a natural inclination to cooperate, Sam thought. 'So call me. If he shows up. I can stop him bothering you. Maybe make it so he doesn't come around anymore at all.'

She took his card eagerly. 'My mom will like that. If we can't get child support from him, at least we can get him out of here.'

Sam came to a halt. They were back at their cars. 'If Cameron is the one who's not doing right by you, then why is your mom mad at the other guy? Jason? You said at his trailer that she didn't want you seeing him?'

She rolled her eyes. Even though Jason was actually a ten times better guy than Cameron, her mom was worried that hanging out with him would decrease the chances of getting support from the singer. 'I keep trying to tell her that's not how it works, but she won't listen. She's gone a little nuts about everything, basically. But she's letting me stay at the house, so . . .'

She trailed off and opened her car door. Sam held up a hand. He had one more thing.

'When I came by yesterday, why did you think that I was after Jason? If he's a good guy and Cameron isn't?'

She shrugged. Not in an I-don't-know way, but in a that's-the-way-it-is way.

'Because you guys don't go after rich people. They can do plenty of mistakes. It's the poor guys you're always after.'

Aaron Engelman was still livid about the way his father had been treated at the hands of the *Breakfast Buckaroos*. And that was nothing compared with how Lisa Fettic-Posky of Lee's Summit felt.

'My mother still isn't well. She went down on a package tour deal to see some nice shows – not to be trapped in a room with no food or water and pressured into signing an egregious contract for a goddamn timeshare.'

The date and time of the elderly Mrs Fettic's ambulance trip to Branson Valley General matched up with one on the list Larry gave him last week. She'd needed to be monitored overnight, which meant the daughter had to drive down and get her.

'She was in no condition to take a long bus ride home,' Lisa Fettic-Posky said. 'I honestly thought she should've spent more time in the hospital, but they said she wasn't dehydrated anymore and her glucose levels were fine. So I brought her home, and she's been shaky and upset ever since.'

'And she did sign a contract?' Hank asked.

'Yes. Those bastards. I nullified that quicker than you can say "sleazeball tactics". Missouri law gives you five days to back out of something like that, did you know?'

Hank didn't know that. He should have. The murder had completely pulled his attention away from following up with mistreated showgoers. He pictured Maggie's face and pushed aside the guilt.

'I barely got the Barkers out of theirs in time.' Lisa was still heated. 'Mom's neighbors. They went on the tour, too. Resisted the first day. But the second day, it was a different show and they gave in. Just to be able to get back to the hotel. Plus, they'd been freaked out by Mom getting taken off in an ambulance.'

'That second show – it was selling the same timeshare place?' Please let her still have the contracts.

'Of course I've still got the contracts. And I'm going to be getting a lawyer. But let's talk about you. Can't you charge them with, like, elder abuse or something?'

He was going to damn well try. He gave Lisa Fettic-Posky his email address and asked her to send all the paperwork she had. And then he called the Barkers.

They seemed to be in better shape, health-wise, than Mother Fettic. Neither one had needed medical attention.

'But my goodness, I'm glad I've got a strong ticker, because the stress of those sales pitches would've given me heart palpitations otherwise,' Mr Barker said.

'Sir, did you know you'd have to sit through all that when you signed up for the tour package?'

He sighed. No, he hadn't realized that. It wasn't one of those packages where you got a hotel getaway only if you sat through a special presentation. So it hadn't entered his head to check whether they'd have to endure the same thing just for some discounted show tickets. He felt very silly.

'Oh, we feel worse than that,' a feminine voice came through the line. 'We're just mortified that we talked Martha Fettic into going. I mean, we felt shaky and disoriented by the time that second day was over, but poor Martha actually collapsed. "I'll never forgive myself" I said as that ambulance took her away.'

'Did you think about leaving the tour at that point?' Hank asked.

'We had no way to get home,' Mrs Barker said. 'We called Lisa, so we knew she was coming down to be with Martha, but we didn't know how long she'd have to stay in Branson. So Ray and I decided to stick the whole thing out and just come back on the bus.' She paused and Hank thought he heard sniffles. 'But it was even worse the second day. That man was right up in our faces. He started out so friendly, and then kept moving closer and closer. And putting papers in front of us. And fancy drawings of buildings. And talking about our grandkids. Did we really love them? Didn't we want to see them?' More sniffling. 'And it just went on and on.'

Her husband interrupted. 'When we got back to the hotel room that second day, I was close to calling a taxi to take us to the emergency room.'

'You were not.'

'I was so. You were woozy.'

'I was cranky. There's a difference.'

'And you don't think I can tell, after forty-six years of—'

'Mr Barker. If I could ask you about the contract?'

Yes, they signed one. And yes, the sheriff could certainly see it. They'd given it to Lisa Fettic when she offered to extricate them from it. They would ask her to send Hank a copy.

'She's such a dear,' Mrs Barker said. 'She went racing down there to Branson again once she found out what we'd gone through. She's a busy lady, and to give up her weekend like that, just to try to talk some sense into those awful people – well, we just think the world of her.'

Hank looked at the dates in his notes. 'That would have been just this last weekend? Your tour was last week so you mean Ms Fettic came back down just a few days ago? How did she say her trip went?'

She hadn't been in touch after she returned, they said. They assumed she hadn't been able to find anyone at the shows to complain to.

Hank wasn't so sure about that.

SEVENTEEN

It had not been a pleasant conversation with Tyrone. *Hi, honey, I'm getting sued and our whole financial future is at risk. How's your day going?* Now she was glaring at her whiteboard timeline and trying to focus. The conference room door opened and she heard the clump of a laptop hitting the table.

'That isn't doing you any good.' Dale came around the table and stood next to her. He uncapped her marker and ignored the redirection of her glare toward him. A minute later he'd taken over the left edge with a list of names. 'We got no new time elements. We need to talk to more people.'

She turned slowly, barely able to get the words out. 'So you think I need Investigations 101? That I need help figuring out what to do next?'

He leaned against the table and loosely crossed his arms. Deliberately non-threatening. Which she knew because she was an experienced investigator and interrogator. She was also about to become a murderer. And her victim just stood there smiling at her.

'Look, Sheila – Hank told me about the lawsuit. I'd be furious, too. It's bullshit you don't need. Especially in the middle of a homicide investigation. Which I know that you know how to run. I'm not stupid. Or suicidal.'

He grinned at her. Lord, he was the definition of exasperating. And he was still talking.

'. . . interview somebody. Who's left on this list? I don't know who that lanky guy has talked to.'

Ted Pimental. He'd finished the neighbors and a bunch of the yoga ladies and come up empty. Sheila plucked the marker from his hand and crossed off more than half the names. Dale grunted in disappointment. She considered the rest of the list and jabbed at the crossed-off Warren Swink.

'The motor lodge has been eliminated, but what about the other two new files Gillam had?' She pivoted to the table and plucked out the folders. 'Preliminary paperwork for what looks like a house purchase for the elusive Mr Charolais and Property 162, which is apparently just a bunch of dirt.'

She tossed a soil report onto the table. Dale picked it up, but his mind was clearly a million miles away. Sheila gave him a minute and then softly cleared her throat.

'We should talk to Reggie.'

'Who?' she said.

'Reggie Silver. She's a real estate agent. Helped us buy our house, actually. Knows everything about local property. You've probably seen her signs.'

Sheila already had a house, so why would she pay attention to neighborhood For Sale signs? She was about to tell him so, when he got up and walked out the door.

'I'll drive,' he hollered from the hallway.

'You can't just pick up the phone?' she called after him.

He poked his head back in. 'Nope. You gotta get out of here. Otherwise you're just going to stare at that board until your eyes melt.'

She hustled to catch up and thirty minutes later they were parking his car and walking past the two 'Strike Gold with Silver' lawn signs leaning against Reggie's building in Branson. Dale held open the door and then followed her in. She had to lunge out of the way to avoid the air kisses that followed.

'Dale Raker, my dear. How are you? How's Ellen? And Logan? Hannah?'

Even Sheila didn't remember the names of his kids. And this white woman with the helmet of chrome-colored hair was rattling them off like she'd found them a house a year ago instead of when the now-teenagers were in diapers. She sidled even farther away as they started in on Ellen's job teaching at the elementary school. She was perusing the framed listings for ranch-style homes when she noticed the talking had stopped. She turned. Reggie Silver was looking at her with an expression somewhere between a puppy that wants breakfast and a wolf that wants dinner.

'To answer your question, Reg – no. My friend's not in the market for a house.' Dale grinned at her. 'This is Sheila Turley. She's chief deputy sheriff and we need your expertise.'

Reggie shrugged and smiled as she shook Sheila's hand. 'Never hurts to ask.' She waved them toward comfortable seats around a table in the middle of her office. Her desk was tucked against the back wall. It looked, Sheila realized with a jolt, a lot like Gillam's set-up.

Reggie sat, propped her elbows on the shiny surface, and folded her hands under her chin. The two-inch stack of silver bangles on her wrist jingled. She waggled her fingers. 'So this is exciting. Fire away.'

'We need to ask if you've heard anything about a property sale involving someone named Charolais.' She spelled it out. 'First name starts with "K". Probably something very high-end.'

'Well, I don't have any clients with that name. Or anybody on the other end of a sale, either.'

Sheila handed over a copy of the paperwork in the Charolais file. It was definitely for a residence, Reggie agreed. But that was it. Nothing was filled in – no address, no legal property description. It was as if the process had been started, or the agent was getting things prepped. But for what property? She pursed her lips. 'High-end, you say? There aren't too many of those. Let me see.'

She got up and walked over to her desk. As she tapped away at her computer, Sheila took a better look around. While the office set-up was the same as Gillam's, the vibe was completely different. Framed family photos lined the bookshelves and a bulletin board next to the back door was tacked with hundreds of holiday cards from what Sheila guessed were satisfied clients. Reggie's desk held so many neat stacks of papers that the wood was barely visible. The desktop computer had a film of dust across the top, just as any normal person's would. Gillam's, of course, had not.

Sheila felt herself relaxing at the differences. Where Gillam was tightly-wound sleek chic from the big city of Chicago, Reggie Silver was native Branson blowsy. Jewelry from Kohl's instead of Nordstrom. Sensible flats (silver) probably purchased at the outlet mall down the street because she was too busy for the nonsense of high heels. Hair just a smidge too high and wide and lacquered into place. And blouse not quite tucked into an expanding waistline due to her expansive gesturing. Which she did again on her way back to the table, after printing a few pages. A lakefront house in Hollister and another one near Table Rock Lake, and a mountaintop home out by the Arkansas border. All three had buyer and seller names that were not Charolais.

'There hasn't been much on the market lately in that kind of price range. People are hanging on to them, not putting them up for sale,' Reggie said. 'The big deals now are mostly with commercial properties or vacant land.'

Dale plucked a mint chocolate out of the crystal bowl in the middle of the table and unwrapped it slowly. 'Would those possibly involve something like a soil analysis?'

Good question, Sheila thought. She slid the Property 162 paperwork across the table. Reggie flipped through it with a practiced eye.

'I'm not going to pretend I'm an expert,' she finally said. 'But I think I can safely tell you this is mostly a typical report. Not great, but not awful. Too bad there's no company letterhead on it. Then we could just ask them who commissioned it.'

That was already on Sheila's list of irritations regarding Gillam's paperwork. She moved on to the dead woman's third new file.

'The Hickory Sticks Motor Lodge. Anything going on there that you might have heard about?'

Reggie snapped her fingers. 'Now that's funny. Just a week or so ago, Warren Swink called me out of the blue and asked what I thought his property was worth.'

Both Sheila and Dale knew the details of Hank's interview the day of the murder.

'What did you tell him?'

'That it was worth more than eight hundred and fifty thousand dollars. Not by much, mind you. I didn't tell him that, though. I've known the dear since our kids were in elementary school. I'd never want to hurt his feelings. But I also didn't want him to get dazzled by some random offer and do something he'd end up regretting.'

'Did he tell you anything else about the offer? Who made it?' Dale said.

Reggie shook her head and took a candy out of the dish. Sheila leaned forward and put her elbows on the polished tabletop.

'Did the name Vivian Gillam come up?'

Reggie's arm dropped to the table with a metallic clink. 'Her? She made the offer? Oh, Lordy, that's why you're here. I read in the paper that she was killed, but . . .'

Sheila and Dale looked at each other. 'You knew her?' Dale asked.

Back when Gillam came to town four years ago, she swooped in with cash offers to snatch multiple high-end properties away from Reggie's buyers. Then she turned around and rented them out short-term to wealthy outsiders. But there was only a small amount of expensive housing available, so she and Vivian didn't cross paths often. She hadn't seen her in more than a year. The snooty woman certainly wasn't one to show up at things like the Chamber of Commerce luncheons. 'She didn't need the local riff-raff. Just the high-profile out-of-towners. She's put off a lot of folks in the business community by not having any care for locals.'

'And if the expensive houses aren't as hot a market, she's fishing around for commercial properties?' Dale asked.

'Warren's call is the first I've heard of that happening,' Reggie said.

'What about timeshares?' Sheila said.

Reggie drew back from the table with a look of revulsion.

'That is not a term we utter at Silver Real Estate. Those things are horrible. A chain around your neck as far as I'm concerned.'

Sheila leaned forward, elbows on the table. Reggie did know everybody in town. 'And if Gillam did branch out into something like that, what would the effect be on the local market?'

Reggie smoothed out her empty candy wrapper as she thought. 'She'd either have to start new theater shows or find some other way to corner people into listening to the sales pitch. And that's coming close to having a hand in entertainment, not real estate.'

Sheila hadn't looked at it in those terms before. 'And what would that mean?' she said slowly.

'Well, that market has pretty much already been cornered.'

Sheila raised her eyebrows. *Go on.*

'There are the couple of old local families who've had shows forever, of course,' she said. 'They're untouchable, and should be. The soul of Branson, they are. But otherwise, right now, there's one who's built up a pretty interconnected entertainment operation. I can see him not wanting it unbalanced by some random woman with a stable of out-of-town country stars.'

Dale stopped, his hand halfway to the candy dish. Sheila didn't move.

'And who,' she said, 'would that be?'

'Henry Gallagher, of course.'

EIGHTEEN

Everyone said no. Well, what they'd all said was, 'Sorry, don't have the people to spare.' Which meant Hank still had no suitably aged officers to send to a seniors-only theater show so they could endure a timeshare sales pitch. A presentation Vivian Gillam had concocted so her marks would be completely vulnerable to manipulation. He thought of those elderly tourists in Maggie's ER and the show presentation that could hold clues to Gillam's business, and thereby her death. He could feel his teeth grinding in frustration again.

If he couldn't come up with something, he'd be forced into

The Nightmare Scenario. And that contained a whole bucketload of problems, including the questionable legality of using a civilian and the questionable judgment of having it be his father-in-law. So he needed to keep looking. He spread the list of non-deputy staff across his desk and stared at it until his head hurt. Most of them were too young. They did have sixty-year-old Wanda, the records clerk who shared her life story with anyone unfortunate enough to get within ten feet. If it was gossip about somebody else, the tell-all radius was even wider. She was old enough, but she'd give away the operation before *Down Home Darlin'* even raised the curtain.

He shuffled the pages around and landed on one with the jail support staff. Of course. Earl Evans Crumblit. Very decent guy who manned the visitor entrance to the jail. Sixty-seven years old. He'd been a big help last fall during the bloodletting, which meant he was capable of deputy-level duties. And most importantly, Sheila thought he was great. That was as gold-plated a recommendation as you could get. He picked up the phone but paused before he finished dialing the jail extension. He should wait until after work. He didn't need those asshole jail deputies overhearing anything about this investigation. God knew what they would do.

He grabbed some chips and a Diet Coke from the vending machine and decided to spend some quality time with criminal databases while he waited for Earl's shift to end. Stone Cold, the muscled *Breakfast Buckaroos* manager, despite looking like he should be decorating a Post Office bulletin board, was clean. But the guy from *Down Home Darlin'* – that was a different story. Toothsome stared back at him from a mugshot on the computer monitor. Two counts of breaking and entering. Too bad his probation was over. The threat of revoking it would've been a good stick to use.

'Look up Natalie Lambert.'

Hank almost tipped over his Coke can. He looked up at Sam, who was hovering over his shoulder. 'Where the hell did you come from?'

'I've been standing here. Said "hi" twice.'

Hank moved his drink out of the way and closed the screen with Toothsome's mugshot. 'What name did you say?'

Sam explained. It took ten minutes and ended with Hank's compliments. When neither she nor maybe-boyfriend Jason Nilquist had records, Hank waved for Sam to sit down. 'What do you think?'

Sam flipped through a few pages of his notebook without really looking at them. Hank leaned back in his desk chair and watched. A year and a half ago, that question would have flustered his Pup into bright red embarrassment. Today it just prompted a calm assessment and an unconscious tug on the ear. He'd come a long way.

'There's definitely some family issues going on. My guess is that when Ms Gillam's sister asked for help coordinating Cameron's upkeep, neither one of them had any idea it was going to turn into what it did.'

'Really? Neither of them knew he was a self-entitled little jerk?'

Sam shook his head. None of his hometown friends knew, either. He'd called around and found out that Cameron apparently did the typical partying in high school, but afterward just quietly focused on his music. Then he got a recording contract, left town, and nobody saw him again.

'I think he's got a drinking problem,' Sam said. 'That he was able to hide from his Christian fan base. And if he was capable of that, it wouldn't have taken much more effort to also hide it from Aunt Viv. At least until she started getting the extra bills for it.'

That was when the sisters started arguing. And then stopped speaking altogether. Which would certainly make Harriet a suspect, but he'd checked. Her alibi was rock-solid – she'd been in Chicago at some kind of continuing education seminar all weekend. Sam flipped his notebook closed and leaned back in the spare chair.

'Cameron's mom thinks it's possible he did it. She was trying to hide it, but . . .' He shrugged. 'I've told her to call me if she hears from him. I think that whether she does will come down to who she decides deserves her loyalty. Given the circumstances, I hope it's her sister.'

Hank looked at the childless young man sitting across from him. He was charming in his naiveté. On the karmic balancing scale, yes, that was how Harriet's decision should play out. But the parental scale didn't balance things the same way. He smiled. 'Get a search warrant for her cell phone records. Just in case.'

They needed to look into this without telling Hank. He'd turn into a dog with a bone the minute he heard about it. Then Sheila would have to smack him on the nose to get him to behave, and she had too much on her mind to do that right now.

'Henry Gallagher? The guy who bought the old *Branson Beauty* showboat?'

'And the outlet mall off Gretna Road that's getting redeveloped and two different hotels on the Strip,' Sheila said, buckling into the passenger seat of Dale's car. 'And he's the one who backed Gerald Tucker in the sheriff election last year.'

'Ooooh. So that's why you don't want to tell Hank.'

'Oh, not at all. The election is the least of it. I don't want to tell Hank, because Hank's positive that Gallagher ordered his own boat blown up so he could collect the insurance money. He's never been able to prove it, though. He's also never been able to prove that Gallagher has at least one of the county commissioners in his pocket.'

Dale gaped at her. 'That's insane.'

'Oh, no. It's true. Some of it anyway. I didn't believe the *Beauty* thing until Gallagher backed Tucker – who just happened to be the deputy on guard duty at the boat right before it went boom. Why the hell else would a suave business developer choose a good ol' boy sheriff candidate with no business sense, no establishment contacts and no campaign platform?'

Dale ruminated on that. 'And the county commission? I admit, I don't pay much attention to them. It's the city council that controls our police department budget, so they're the ones I concentrate on.' He paused. 'It's the little guy with the spiky hair, isn't it? Very pro-business with his commission votes.'

She nodded. 'Which in itself is fine. But he's also very anti-sheriff-funding with his commission votes. It's that combo that's got Hank thinking the way he does. Me? I think that might be a stretch too far.'

Dale looked out the window, muttering what sounded like city councilman names to himself. Great. Now she had him seeing his own Gallagher conspiracies where there probably weren't any. Time to shift focus.

'So we'll just look into whether Gallagher ever bumped up against Gillam's business before we brief Hank,' she said quickly. That way, if there was no link, she wouldn't have to deal with Hank becoming obsessed with the guy all over again. She glanced over at Dale. 'Please. As a favor.'

They both knew how unusual that kind of request was for her. Dale sighed. 'OK. It's your call.'

She nodded a thanks and turned to look out the window. They were nearing department headquarters. The fields were an explosion of foliage – tree leaves, low brush, wildflowers. A crumpled body flashed through her mind. Her hands tightened into fists and she spent the rest of the ride in silence.

He was pretty sure he could do it. He'd read over the law and unless there was something lurking in the state statutes that he hadn't seen, he was well within his rights to temporarily deputize a sixty-seven-year-old clerk with bad knees and the beginnings of a comb-over. The law wasn't that specific, obviously. It placed no limits on him at all, actually, except the requirement that the person live within the county limits and serve for no more than thirty days. Earl was a lifelong Branson County resident and Hank prayed the investigation would take no longer than a week.

'What do you think?'

Earl slowly set his coffee cup down on Hank's dining room table, his face alight like a kid's on Christmas morning. Home had seemed the safest place to have this conversation – no chance of anyone connected with the department overhearing.

'Really? You think I can do it? I know I can do it. You bet I can do it. Wait, I ain't going to have to run, am I?'

Hank shook his head. 'The only thing you might have to do is get on and off one of those big tour buses.'

Otherwise, it would just be sitting still and paying very close attention. From the way Earl was hanging on his every word, it seemed safe to say the guy was going to excel at that part of it.

'How many shows do you want me to go to?'

He looked ready to take on the entire Strip. Hank made a stop motion with one hand while he put down his own coffee mug with the other. He reached for the manila folder sitting on the edge of the table. There were two shows in particular they were going to focus on, he explained.

'You're going to need to keep careful track of what they're saying and the time that they're saying it. How far into the show they do the presentation, and when they finally feed you. That kind of thing.'

He slid a more detailed list across the table. Earl plucked his reading glasses out of his shirt pocket and perched them on the end of his nose before bending forward to go over the sheet. Central casting couldn't have delivered Hank a more perfect infiltrator. He fought to keep from grinning and waited for Earl to finish.

Finally, his visitor sat back and took off his glasses. 'Can I pretend that I'm interested in a timeshare for my grandkids? I can say they live far away and I think this'll get them to come spend time with me, if I give 'em a vacation every year. How's that?'

'That sounds perfect.'

This would get them specifics on the presentation – exactly how the sales pitch went, particulars on the time-share property locations – that previous audience members hadn't been able to remember in enough detail when interviewed. They needed every scrap of evidence they could get in order to convince Judge Marv Sedstone to issue search warrants for the theaters' business records. Hank couldn't think of any other way to peel away the Time Well Spent layers Gillam had laid, and figure out who she'd made angry enough to kill.

And, to be honest, he was also hoping this operation would lead to enough proof about deliberate health dangers to satisfy a certain emergency room doctor who would not stop asking about it. And there she was now, walking past the doorway after putting the kids to bed. He and Earl kept talking, but he heard her footsteps stop halfway through the living room and then she was back, standing on the threshold. He started to introduce her.

'Shush,' she told him, pulling up a dining chair and sitting down next to Earl. She took his hand. 'Sir, you're the one Hank's sending in to these shows?'

Earl clearly didn't know whether to be charmed by her focused attention or alarmed by her worried expression. He chose charmed. Hank couldn't blame him.

'I am, ma'am, thank you for asking. I'm getting deputized and sent in to investigate.' He sat up a little straighter as he spoke. Maggie noticed and gave him one of her gorgeous smiles. Thank you, honey, he thought.

'He's lucky to have you,' she said. 'I do want to go over a few things with you, just about eating beforehand. And ask you a few questions about your health, if I could?'

Earl cheerfully gave up his entire medical history. Hank would've been fine without hearing about the hernia surgery or the broken toe, but Maggie listened attentively to it all and gave him a list of instructions, including what to eat before attending a show. Then they both walked him to the door. As it swung closed, Hank turned to his wife.

'I was going to say thanks for not minding when I told you I was inviting him here to the house,' he said. 'But now I see that you had your own agenda.'

'Of course.' She leaned up and kissed him. 'I always do.'

NINETEEN

It had been almost two weeks on the job, and the golden white boy seemed to be settling in fine. She took him for Friday morning coffee after his graveyard shift, just to make sure.

'Yes, ma'am. I think everything's going pretty good. I mean, it's tough doing the overnights, I won't lie.' Austin Lorentz grinned. 'I thought working until the bar closed was bad, but this is a whole different kind of middle of the night.' He slurped at his coffee, which he'd ordered without cream or sugar. One more point in the column for why she liked him.

'I got to tell you, ma'am, I never imagined when you came into the bar to ask if I'd seen an old country singer, that someday I'd end up sitting here with a full-on career and benefits and retirement.' His eyes saucered at the wonder of it all.

Sheila laughed in spite of herself. Welcome to an increasingly rare kind of adulthood, kid. 'Well, there are a few good aspects to the job.'

'Oh, no. Sorry, I didn't mean those were the only good things. It's really interesting. So many different types of folks. I love it. Like, I released a guy today, but I just got a feeling he'll be back. Pretty quick. I think he's too into the drugs. But then, I also think that he probably wouldn't hurt a fly. So that made me feel better. That he's not a threat. Like, to society.'

Sheila leaned forward and wrapped her hands around the mug of her own black coffee. This was why she'd recruited him. He drew a bead on people right away, and he always seemed to be right. She figured it was natural talent, but years of tending bar certainly hadn't hurt. She was curious if his hunch was right.

'You remember the inmate's name?'

'Guernsey, maybe? Like the cow?'

Gursey. A spindly limbed addict who stole from every convenience store in the county. But he was so good-natured about it, nobody ever ended up pressing charges. They just had him hauled off to jail so he could dry out for a few days. Everybody and their uncle had tried to get him into rehab, but it never worked. She told Austin all this and then pinned him with a look.

'You're good at this. You can read people real well. I want you to keep sizing up everybody you meet. Everybody. Trust your gut. And if you come across ones that are the opposite of ol' Gursey, tell me. They might not be doing something too bad now, where I'd know it and track it. But if you can sense they're capable, you let me know, OK? I trust your instincts.'

He left the diner with a spring in his step and a promise to hone his skills on everyone who came through. She watched him go and sipped thoughtfully. She'd got as close as she dared to flat-out asking him to report on his fellow deputies. She might trust his instincts, but she didn't know him well enough to trust his allegiances. So this would have to do.

Earl was on his way to Kansas City to catch the Midwest Motoring Excursions bus, which would bring him right back here to town. It was three-and-a-half hours there and three-and-a-half back, when he lived only fifteen minutes from the theaters – but it was the only way to make him a legitimate part of the tour. He couldn't very well show up for the first time right before a show. He'd be outed in a hot minute by crabby seniors complaining he'd cut in front of them in line.

The old guy hadn't minded at all. Showed up at the crack of dawn with a suitcase and a grin and got in an unmarked department car with Deputy March, who'd been tasked with driving him up there.

Sheila pulled into the parking lot as they were pulling out. Hank waited for her. They stood next to each other and watched the departing car. And then they stood some more. He shoved his hands into the pockets of his jeans. She checked that her name plate was level on her uniform shirt. He thought about just going inside and starting his day. But not bringing it up wasn't going to make it go away.

'About the lawsuit . . .'

A slight change in posture was her only response.

'I talked to the lawyer at the association of counties—'

Now she finally turned, the raised eyebrow showing what she thought of that.

'Hey, it's not my fault this damn county doesn't have a county counsel office,' he said. 'And he's the one I talked to before we went through with the firings in the first place.'

'And that's why you're getting this look,' she said, her eyebrow climbing even higher. 'He's the one who told you we'd be in the clear, and look where we are now.'

Not in the clear, that was for sure.

'The case law is on our side.'

'That doesn't mean they can't drain us dry in legal fees.' She was now facing him full-on, balled fists thankfully still down by her sides.

'I know,' he said. 'That's why – since we were acting in our capacity as employees of a county entity – we get the county to pay for the legal work. Then, in our personal capacity, we just piggy-back on that.'

Her fists moved to her hips. 'You are a fresh-up idiot if you think the county is going to look out for our interests.'

'I know the county doesn't give a rat's ass about us,' he said. 'But—'

'No. No way. That isn't it. That implies they don't care one way or the other. They very much care – a passionate hate kind of care.' She stuck a hand in his face to stop him responding. 'They hate me out of reflex. They hate you because you go pokin' the bear all the time. You think they're going to put anything but the bare minimum into defending how you run your department? That's what we're supposed to piggy-back on?'

She should be the one to argue for them in court. They'd win in a heartbeat, if only because the judge would desperately want to escape her fusillade. 'Look, maybe we can get it thrown out before it even gets to that. That's happened before. I've got a friend up in KC who—'

'Do not give me some bullshit comparison,' she said. 'We're in the Ozarks, with Ozark politicians and Ozark judges. They do whatever they goddamn well please.'

Which was what Hank was hoping for. That the folks who operated this way would decide they were fine with him doing the same thing – running his fiefdom as he damn well pleased. He allowed himself a rueful smile. So much for the equitable, collaborative philosophy of leadership he came into office with.

'You're going to play the same game?' Sheila said, interpreting his expression correctly. Or maybe she was to the point where she could straight-up read his mind. He nodded. She searched his face for a moment, not seeming to find what she was looking for. She stepped back.

'I hate this place.' She spun on her heel and strode into the building, leaving him standing in the parking lot alone.

Sam waved the marker with a flourish. 'I have news.' He pointed at Sheila's timeline on the conference room wall, where he had chicken-scratched a date in late March. 'This is when Cameron Cooper's record label dumped him.'

Mr Raker tossed his bag on the table. 'Really? That is quite interesting, young man. They just told you that?'

'Yeah, I finally got through to the CEO.' And now he finally had an audience. The Chief had been locked in his office all morning, and Sheila was nowhere to be found. Even Ted wasn't around – it was his day off. He'd been itching to tell somebody. Mr Raker peered at the timeline and then turned toward Sam, who had spent enough time with him by now to know what the city detective expected of him.

'So . . . I think this was huge for Cooper,' Sam said. 'Now he doesn't have any hope of another album or a tour or anything. The fame he was trading on is going away. He's just some dude with a guitar, not a recording star.'

Mr Raker nodded. 'He's well and truly up shit creek. No record deal, no charitable Christians paying his living expenses, and a furious Aunt Viv who wouldn't bail him out anymore.' He tapped the record label spot on the timeline and then the larger bullet point further down that marked when Gillam was killed. 'Do you think she knew?'

'I can't see how she didn't,' Sam said. 'The record label has no paperwork saying they notified her, but that's not proof they didn't. Somebody could've just called her up and told her. Or maybe one of his sponsor groups heard about it. If that happened, then you can darn well bet they immediately called her.'

'But there's nothing in Gillam's files about it?'

Sam shook his head.

'Those damn things,' Mr Raker said. 'A whole forest worth of trees sacrificed for all that paper, and none of it worth anything.'

They both turned to look at the antique oak filing cabinets, which sat against the far wall. Careful as he and Ted had tried to be when they transported it, they still managed to twist the metal tracks of one so that the drawers didn't fit back in correctly. It sat all askew and made Sam feel guilty every time he saw it. He looked away and watched Mr Raker pull out his laptop. There was a new crack along the outer edge. The detective ignored it and fired the thing up. Sam picked up a stack of files and flipped through them.

'Have we ever figured out this loan?'

Mr Raker looked up and shook his head. A bank out of Chicago had confirmed they approved a $500,000 business loan, but no monies had yet been paid out. Before Sam could respond to that, Mr Raker cleared his throat.

'Do you know what's going on with the two of them?'

Sam kept his eyes on the whiteboard. He knew exactly who the detective meant, and exactly nothing about why Hank and Sheila had been so skittish all week and made themselves scarce today. Sure, he could mention the overtime rebellion. Or the low morale. Or the destabilization plots constantly being hatched by jail staff. But he didn't want to be telling tales out of school.

'I don't know,' he finally said.

Out of the corner of his eye, he saw Mr Raker slowly nod. 'OK,' the older man said. 'You pass on for me, though, that there's folks in my department who have their backs. Not everybody, but some of us. So if something new's come up, we're ready to help if we can.'

Now it was Sam who cleared his throat of the lump that suddenly formed there. He nodded without taking his eyes off the board. Raker muttered something about the vending machine and headed for the door, giving Sam a pat on the shoulder as he went.

TWENTY

He felt like he was in a bunker, under assault from every direction. It would probably help if he bothered to open the window blinds. The only light was the God-awful fluorescent over his desk. The cheap aluminum clacked as he wrenched them up and then stood there pondering the parking lot. He'd acted sure of everything with Sheila, but . . . He wasn't going to get anything other than mocking laughter when he went to the county commission, and he knew it. Edrick Fizzel's nasally voice echoed through his head. The little porcupine was going to have a field day with this. In as public a fashion as possible. Thank God he still had three years before he needed to run for re-election as sheriff. Maybe folks would forget about it by then. He scoffed. Even if the lawsuit was resolved, the bad feelings in his department wouldn't be. On both sides.

He turned back to his desk, where Gillam case paperwork was stacked everywhere. He was frowning at it when his email alert chimed. It was a response from the Greene County Associate Court with several attachments. Excellent. He opened the first one to see a younger Travis Beckham staring back at him.

Disheveled and angry. Which Hank supposed he would be too, if he'd just been caught breaking into a house. After the mugshot came the charges and conviction papers, with the date and location. He opened the second attachment and found Toothsome's other burglary. For the same address. Interesting.

No victim information was included in either file. He mapped the location and then tried to use a reverse directory to find a phone number. No luck. He settled in and dug deeper. A half-hour later, he had a name off property records and a phone number off a cosmetology license. He dialed the salon.

'Yeah, Tina's here. Hang on.'

There was a low hum of background conversation and the sound of running water, then Tina came on the line. Hank declined an appointment and explained who he was. He was met with silence. He tried adding more information.

'I'd like to know more about what happened. Mr Beckham has come up in an investigation down here in Branson, and I'm just trying to find out more about him.'

More silence. Now he stayed quiet, too. Finally she spoke. 'Gimme your phone number.' Hank did. And then she hung up. He groaned. Now he still had no information, but had added an intense curiosity as to what the hell happened four years ago. It was not a good combination. He drummed his fingers on the desk and contemplated driving up to the hair salon. But if she wouldn't talk to him on the phone, the chances that she would talk as he loomed over her in front of customers were next to nil. Then his phone rang.

'Why the hell did you call me? I don't want to talk about him.'

The tightness in her voice confirmed what Hank had started to suspect when he saw that the burglarized house belonged to a young woman.

'Ma'am, I apologize. But there was no explanation in the court file about what happened. What Travis was after. I need to find out more about what kind of person he is.'

Tina snorted. 'The court file. Please. They gave him a plea deal. Say yes to trespassing and they wouldn't charge him with stalking. Or attempted assault. It was a pretty good deal. Unless you were me.'

Just as he thought. 'What happened, Tina?'

'No. I'm not reliving this.' But she stayed on the line.

'Look,' he said, 'I understand. And I'm really sorry.' He stayed on the line, too.

Finally, she cleared her throat. 'What'd he do? Is he harassing someone else?'

'Not exactly. A local businesswoman was murdered several days ago, and he was one of the last ones to speak with her.'

He could hear her suck in a breath and hold it. Then it came out in a rush, along with enough anger and bitterness at Beckham that Hank needed to hold the phone away from his ear. They met at work, both of them waiting tables at an Applebee's in Springfield. She was in beauty school and needed the extra income. He was trying to get into sales and busy applying for different corporate jobs. She personally thought he was over-reaching – he kept trying for good ones where you needed experience, which he didn't have. But he was like that. Wanted to be at the top, but didn't want to do the work it took to get there. Otherwise, he was an OK guy. To start with.

A bunch of the wait staff would sometimes hang out after a shift, so she socialized with him like that. But never one-on-one. Especially once she started getting the vibe that he liked her. She wasn't interested, so she just ignored it. Then it got uncomfortable. He was like a laser. Super focused in on her – what she wore, how she spent her time off, where she went after work. She'd shrugged it off. Some guys were like that. Couldn't take a hint, right? She'd had it happen before. What woman hadn't? So it was a relief when she finished beauty school, got her license, and was able to quit the restaurant.

'Yeah, I thought that would be a natural end to any contact with him, you know?' She paused. 'And man, was I wrong.'

He started pestering her. Found out where she worked at her new hairdressing job. Followed her home, so he knew she lived in a neighborhood west of the Bass Pro flagship store in a little house she inherited from her parents.

'And that fucker broke the windows. The two by the back door. Then he let himself in. That was after all the phone calls and the knocks on the door and all that for months. And me telling him over and over to *get lost*.' She stopped and took a moment to compose herself. 'I came home that night and found glass all over the floor and a dozen roses on the kitchen table.'

Hank winced. The fear in her voice was still there, even after four years. She reported it to the police, changed the locks and put plywood over the broken windows. She made sure friends knew where she was at all times, which was an extraordinary pain in the ass.

'The cops talked to him. He admitted it. He said the broken windows were an accident. He was just trying to surprise his girlfriend with flowers. But I had already told the cops what was really going on. That I was most definitely not his girlfriend. I don't know what the officer said to Travis, but after that, it all stopped.'

But it must not have worked for long. Hank looked down at the second criminal court document on his desk.

'That's for damn sure,' Tina said. 'About a month and a half. Then he broke in again. This time he picked the lock. He must've spent the downtime learning how to do it. I woke up to the sound of him trying to bust through the door chain. But he couldn't move the chair I jammed under the doorknob. I called 9-1-1. He was breaking a window on the side of the house when they showed up.'

That would explain the belligerent, scruffy mugshot. An out-of-control man with anger and boundary issues. And lock-picking skills.

'So what happened in court?' Hank asked.

He'd flashed that smile and his lawyer was able to talk his way into a plea deal. Something that could be written off as a youthful mistake, not an aggressive obsession. Part of their bargaining was that Toothsome would move from the area. Head down to Branson for a job.

'And how is forty-five miles away not in my area?' She scoffed. 'He would still drive by every once in a while. That lasted for about two years.'

'And he hasn't been back since?'

'Not that I know of,' she said, 'But I still wedge a chair under my doorknob. So there's that.'

The fancy wood beams-and-windows building sat nestled on meticulously groomed grounds of strategically placed hillocks and bursts of flowers. Some landscape designer had gotten one hell of a commission in a city where most businesses went with Home Depot boxwoods for their street frontage. Sheila cruised past twice, pondering it from behind the wheel of her Forerunner. She'd been inside, once. That was in the dead of winter, though, with icy snow everywhere. At that point, they hadn't even been able to see the Gallagher Enterprises sign – which was rustic carved wood and objectively, quite lovely. Subjectively, it was a pain in her ass, as anything to do with Henry Gallagher always was.

She pointed her Toyota away from the building and toward the main location of On Ramp Racing, which was the actual reason for her trip into Branson. There were rumors, according to Dale, that the owner of the little chain of go-kart tracks was thinking of selling to Gallagher Enterprises. It had always struck her as a pretty vibrant business, full of long lines of tourist families on the weekends, so she wasn't sure why they'd want to sell.

'The wife wants to retire.' Tom Powell ushered her into the company office, which was a large shed-like structure at the back of the main location. The inside was comfortable, with carpeting and a small reception area. He bypassed that and offered her the chair in front of his desk, then poured her a cup of coffee. She didn't want any but took it with a smile – the best way to show this wasn't a hostile visit.

'Actually, she wants to move to Arizona to be closer to the grandkids,' he said with a sigh. He was a white man with a belly that was going soft but muscled arms and shoulders that probably still did a hard day's manual labor around his properties. 'She's been on and on about it for a while. I'm trying to talk her out of it – it's the desert, for Pete's sake. And our son-in-law is an idiot. Why would I want to be around him all the time?'

'Has Henry Gallagher made you an offer?'

He leaned back in his desk chair, which shifted under his weight. 'Well now, that's the damnedest thing. He has. Out of the blue, really. It's making it a lot harder to say no to my wife, that's for sure.'

'Is he the only one who's approached you?'

He eyed her over the rim of his coffee mug. 'Yeah. It's not like I got a "For Sale" sign out front. Is he . . . is he in some kind of trouble or something? Is that why you're here asking questions?'

Sheila gave what she hoped was a nonchalantly dismissive wave. 'Oh, not at all. I'm just looking in to whether there are any . . . outsiders using intimidation on our local businesses. We've had some concerns reported to us, and we want to make sure that kind of thing doesn't happen.'

Say the word *outside* and locals immediately got their guard up. The funny thing was, Gallagher had fallen into that group just a short time ago. He'd only started buying up town businesses about four years earlier. It amazed her how quickly he'd come to be considered a local.

'Has anyone who's not from around here been to see you? Offered you access to any package deals? Like those ticket bundles that the tourism websites sell? Or to be part of a bus tour?'

He guffawed. The bus tours did not – repeat not – cater to the demographic interested in racing go-karts. Those folks wouldn't even be able to fold their rusty joints into the seats. As for the ticket package deals, there always seemed to be offers floating out there. He looked into it at one point several years ago.

'And it was a big load of horseshit, that's what. The terms were ridiculous. Had to let them see my financials and then keep track of the customers, whether they were package buyers or not. Starting my own mailing list is one thing, but I'm not going to force my customers onto somebody else's.'

Did anyone from a concierge travel firm ever approach him? Sheila kept her tone light and the wording vague. The answer was no. She got more specific. Still no. She used the name Gillam. Still nothing. He'd never heard the name. She thanked him and put down her barely sipped coffee. They both rose to their feet.

'You mind me asking how you even knew Gallagher made me an offer?' he said as he came around his desk to show her to the door.

She thought quickly, not wanting to put Dale on the hook. 'Just around. Nothing solid, you know. Local talk.'

He sighed. 'There's always plenty of that in this town. Half of it probably started by my wife.'

They stepped outside and Sheila shook his hand. 'You mind me asking if Gallagher's offer is a good one?'

He considered that. 'It's . . . fair. It's not great. Doesn't account for the capital expenditures I've done recently – new cars, resurfacing the tracks. But it's not lowball.' He shrugged. 'Which is the worst option, actually. If it was high, or low, it'd make the decision an easy "yes" or "no". Now it's . . .' He paused and looked out over the laughing children speeding past in go-karts. 'Now it's a tough one.'

TWENTY-ONE

A young man paying upfront in cash had checked into the Quickstopper RV Park and Motel. That matched the alert Sam put out five days ago.

'Kinda scruffy looking,' the motel manager said over the phone. 'But had enough cash to pay for a whole week. That's hard to turn down these days.'

'So you didn't ask for ID?'

'He said he lost his wallet. Was working on getting everything replaced.'

'You didn't press it?'

'Did I mention the cash?'

His tone implied that Sam was lucky he'd bothered to report it at all. Which was true, Sam thought as he pulled up to the place a half hour later. It didn't look like it could afford to turn away any customers, no matter how scruffy or ID-less. It was on the verge. A nudge in one direction and it could be a well-maintained little RV-park/motel combo. A nudge in the other, and it would become . . . problematic.

The manager, a big man with a beard to match, watched from the front office window as Sam parked and walked to Room 4. He rapped on the door, crisp and official. No response. He waved across the gravel parking lot at the manager. The guy shook his head. Sam groaned. He didn't have time for this. He gestured again, less a wave and more a stiff point. Big beard came out slowly, his Crocs crunching on the rock as he walked over.

'How long has he paid for?

'Two more nights. So yeah, I'm not letting you in until he overstays.'

Sam knew that. He'd need a warrant if he wanted in sooner than that. He knocked again. This time, he roused someone. Next door.

'Nobody's there.' The woman propped herself against the doorjamb of Room 3 and wiped the crust out of her eyes. 'So it'd be great if you stopped the damn pounding.'

It was three in the afternoon. Sam didn't even try to be sympathetic. 'Did you see him?'

She shrugged the shoulder not connected to the doorjamb. He pulled out his phone and opened his cache of photos. 'Is this the guy?'

Another shrug. 'Couldn't say. Maybe?'

He pivoted and stuck his phone in the bearded man's face. 'You got a good look. Is this him?'

The guy squinted. 'It could be.'

Sam took a step back so he could look at both of these crack observers at the same time. He wasn't showing them a blurry surveillance photo, for Christ's sake. It was a professional publicity shot. Every angle of Cooper's generically handsome face in perfect focus.

'I told you he was scruffy looking,' the manager said. 'Half-assed beard and hair down past his collar. Sunglasses.'

Sam lowered his phone, cursing at himself. The whole search for this jerk had been one step forward, two steps back. And nobody was helping. The Chief and Sheila were off God-knew-where and Ted had hit his hourly max for the pay period and so was off for two days. These two didn't know all that. And they didn't care. They just cared about how some young snot-nosed beanpole of a deputy was treating them. He forced a smile.

'I get what you're saying. It's true he would've changed from what's in this photo. He's been doing a bunch of hard living.' He turned to the woman. 'Do you know what time he left?'

She pushed messy hair out of her face. 'He was coming out when I got back from work. So about ten.'

'Does he have a car?'

They both shook their heads. 'Didn't seem to,' the manager said. 'I didn't see one, at least.'

That was good. Cooper hadn't had a car at the last two places he'd stayed. So this scruffy guy might indeed be him. Sam shoved his phone back in his pocket and stepped over to the window of Room 4. What little he could see through the drawn curtains was also a good sign. It looked like there was a backpack or bag of some kind on the bed. Which meant the occupant would be back. Hopefully. He backed away from the window and thanked the manager and the woman as he scanned the area. He needed to find a good place to wait.

There were too many damn entertainment choices in this town. Hours of canvassing after her stop at the go-kart track had resulted in nothing but blank stares or confused looks. Until the mini-golf place on the edge of the Strip.

'Yeah, we got approached.' The owner, a short, skinny, white guy with a crew cut, kept organizing child-sized putters as he talked. 'I declined. It was a month or two ago. Out of the blue. It was weird.'

Sheila laid her hand on the putters he was arranging across the counter. She wanted his full attention, because he certainly had hers. She asked about the conversation.

'Some lady called up and asked if I'd ever thought of selling.' He didn't remember her name. 'I was so surprised I just kind of stuttered around, and she kept on talking. Said I could get a good price.'

'Did she say *who* would give you a good price?' It could've been a Gallagher company employee putting out feelers. Just because it was a woman, didn't mean it was Gillam calling.

He shrugged. 'She would.'

He went back to lining the putters up by length while he remembered as much of the phone conversation as he could. Which was very little. She'd been very nice, but with more of a clipped, fast way of talking that meant she wasn't from around here. She'd said that she would pay him a fair price for the business and the land, but hadn't named a dollar figure. She said she could make it all go smoothly because she had one of those hotel front desk folks.

'I'm sorry – what?' Sheila's hand came down on the clubs again. 'I don't understand that part.'

'Neither did I, really. She said if I sold, everything would go smoothly because she had one of those folks who helps people at hotels. A what-do-you-call—'

'A concierge?'

'Yep. That's the word.'

Sheila peeled her fingers from around the putter she was now clutching. 'This has been very helpful. I really appreciate it.' She turned to leave and then stopped. 'How much did she offer you?'

'Nine hundred thousand. Which would be OK. Not fantastic for the amount of land I got, but not lowball neither.'

'And you said no?'

'Yep. A straight up no.' He laid down the last putter and leaned forward conspiratorially. 'But I heard scuttlebutt that the guy at Putt-Putt-and-More over on Shepherd of the Hills Expressway said yes. If you find out that's true, let me know, would you?'

Hank cursed himself. The stack of work files that should be here at the office with him were instead sitting on his dining room table. Where he left them early this morning as he rushed out the door to see Earl off on his trip. He bit back a sigh and called Duncan.

'Yeah, they're right here. I'd bring them to you, but Benny's taking a nap. Too full a day at preschool. Lots of sandbox time, apparently. The minivan will need a vacuuming.'

There was probably the equivalent of a beach in the backseat, he thought as he pictured his four-year-old son, excited and happy and very, very dirty.

'There are a couple of pages I need. Could you take some pictures and send them to me?'

'Sure. Hang on.' There was the scuffling of Dunc's house slippers and then the rustling of paper. 'Go ahead.'

He listed off a few things from the file he had on the soil report and asked Dunc to go to the next one.

'Charolais? That's good eating.'

'Huh?'

'Charolais beef. Makes great burgers.'

Hank set his pen down slowly. 'Explain.'

'It's a type of beef cattle. Like Angus. You didn't know that? Why you got a file on it, then?'

It wasn't the name of a person. He walked rapidly down the hall from his office to the conference room as he asked Duncan to photograph every page. Then he dug through the paperwork Sam and Ted had pulled from the wood filing cabinets. They had mentioned something. Details or names, maybe? He rifled through everything, and finally found it. In Ted's neat handwriting, a list of people culled from Gillam's records. Some had contact information, some only a few sparse details. Only one could conceivably be a big-time Kansas land owner. Twenty minutes and one wheedling conversation later, he was past the Steadfast Cattle Company office manager and talking with William Hamstead, owner of seven thousand acres of prime plains grassland, and as of four months ago, a six-bedroom mansion on Table Rock Lake. The sale matched the terms listed on the contract with no address in the 'Charolais' file.

'She's been killed? My God. That's horrible.'

Hamstead went fishing in the Ozarks every year and finally decided to buy a house instead of renting. 'Why yes, I guess it actually was her suggestion to do that,' he said when Hank asked. 'She ran the numbers for me and it made sense. She made the whole process smooth as glass.'

He was last in the area about a month ago. And he'd spent the weekend in Kansas helping birth multiple calves at all hours of the day and night. 'Is that your way of asking if I have an alibi, son?'

'I'm afraid so. We're doing it with all of her clients, though. Not just you.' He paused. 'Was the house you bought the only one she showed you?'

'No, there were three others, I think. This one had the best lake frontage and the biggest boat dock. Although the boat lift needed repair and the house's interior is a little dated.' He paused. 'Say, you wouldn't happen to know if she had ten grand laying around anywhere?'

Hank froze. 'Pardon me?'

'It was for new curtains. "Window treatments", my wife calls them. We couldn't get down there to get them installed, so Viv said she'd do it. We sent her a check, and the bank said it was cashed. For all I know, she spent it and the curtains are installed. But I thought I'd ask.'

Window treatments. Money for ordinary, mundane curtains. Which wouldn't need any further investigation. Hallelujah. 'We did find some money, sir. We'll need to confirm it's yours and go through some evidence procedures first, but then we will happily return it to you.'

He asked a few more questions and thanked the rancher. As he hung up, Dunc's photos popped up on his phone screen. He owed the old man a big thank you for his help. Maybe he'd even buy him a burger.

TWENTY-TWO

He was tired, and frustrated, and completely unsuccessful. He still hadn't tracked down the lousy deadbeat singer who – as far as he was concerned – had by far the best motive for killing Vivian Gillam. Who hated more deeply than family did? Nobody, that's who. And who needed his relief to show up more than he did? Nobody, Sam thought. He slid farther down in his seat and looked at the dashboard clock again. His colleague Bill Ramsdell was late. He looked out the windshield of his Bronco at the motel, squat and long across the narrow road far outside the Branson tourist district. The occupant of Room 4 hadn't returned.

It had to be Cooper who rented the room. He didn't have a car. He hadn't taken an Uber because that would've shown up on his credit cards, which Sam had been monitoring the whole time. He hadn't flown out of the little local airport. He hadn't taken a Greyhound out of the area. Sam had checked both and showed around that ridiculous publicity photo more times than he could count. Nothing.

And the guy certainly wasn't smart enough to have figured

out some incognito way to skip town. That was clear just by virtue of him being stupid enough to piss off Aunt Viv. And then there was— well, look who decided to show up. He rolled down his window.

'Hey, man. Sorry. Some asshole going eighty out on the Ozark Mountain Highroad. Had to pull him over.' Bill rolled his squad car to a stop facing the opposite direction, so that his driver-side window was right next to Sam's.

That was actually a pretty good reason. Sam relaxed a little bit. He filled Bill in, and then quickly backed the Bronco up and pointed it toward Brenna's. He was going to be late for dinner. It was her first-of-the-season barbecue. Thankfully, he was already in civilian clothes. Showing up in full uniform wouldn't exactly match the casual vibe she was probably going for. Speaking of which – he did need to figure out what to do with his gun. Couldn't leave it in the glove box. Couldn't leave it anywhere really. Not like Brenna and Felicia had a gun safe he could lock it in for the evening. He thought about that. He kept a couple sweatshirts and a pair of hiking boots over there. Would a gun safe be the next step? Too soon?

He hadn't arrived at an answer – to any of those questions – by the time he pulled into her driveway. He heard music from the backyard, so walked around the house instead of going inside. There were just a couple of people here so far. A woman she worked with at Donorae's, and a guy who had been her neighbor growing up. The lady next to him must be his girlfriend, judging by her hand in his back pocket. And Kyle. Great. He grabbed a beer and hoisted it at Brenna's older brother in mute greeting. He wasn't in the mood for the silent tests that Kyle and Corey liked to throw at him. He got it, really. If he had a little sister, he'd do the same thing. But they could've lightened up by now. He was suddenly glad the Glock was holstered in clear view on his hip.

He felt a hand on his back and turned with relief and that little lump in his throat he always got.

'Hi.' She reached up to kiss him. 'Come help me with the salad?'

They went into the kitchen just as Felicia sailed by with a plate of uncooked hamburgers in one hand and her camera tripod in the other. 'Americana. It's a new theme I'm trying out.' The screen door thwacked shut behind her and they were alone.

'You came straight from work?' She waved a tomato at his holster and then got out a cutting board. 'How was your day?'

'Busy,' he said. 'But uneventful.'

She looked at him out of the corner of her eye as she started to slice. He wondered what that meant.

'Are you still investigating that murder?'

He paused. 'Yeah. There hasn't been much happening on it. It's just . . .' He trailed off and shrugged. She gave him another sideways look. 'I don't feel like I'm making any headway, I guess.'

'Well, what are you trying to do? Find something? Or somebody? What leads do you have?'

He didn't want to get into it. He grabbed the bag of lettuce and offered to cut it open. She gave the tomato one last hard slice. 'Sure.'

Howard Barker apologized three times for calling on a Friday night. Hank bit back a sigh and assured him it was fine. He just wouldn't be home in time to help Duncan with dinner. Not such a bad thing.

'I'm happy to help, sir. What can I do for you?'

'Well, we'd really rather not pursue it any further. And we just can't seem to convince Lisa otherwise.'

He tried to continue, but Hank stopped him. 'I'm afraid I don't know what you're talking about, sir.'

'Oh goodness, I'd thought . . . well, anyhow. Lisa is determined to have there be consequences, you see. For the show folks. She keeps calling. Asking us to sign a statement about how we were treated. I thought she was doing all this because you wanted it.'

Interesting. Hank leaned back in his desk chair and thought for a moment. 'Did she say that directly?'

The elderly man paused. 'I suppose not. She was talking about laws and jail time and that kind of thing, but I guess she didn't mention you specifically, now that I think about it.'

That was fortunate for her, Hank thought, because someone invoking his name and authority would make him extremely unhappy. 'Did she say if she got that documentation from her own mother?'

She certainly did, Barker said. She'd said that having theirs as well would strengthen their case. She was still so furious about the whole thing. But she was young and energetic. And had always been a bit of a hothead, frankly. His wife loved her, but he'd always found her to be a bit much.

'Now that I know it's not information you're looking for, I feel better about telling her flat-out no,' he told Hank. 'We got out of the contract. That's all we wanted. Now we just want to be done with the whole thing.'

'Before I let you go, sir, can I ask you if she said anything about her second trip down here to Branson? The one just this last Sunday?'

'Well, now, let's see. She said she was making progress. But she didn't say specifically who she managed to meet with. Oh, and she did mention that traffic coming back was horrible. Said it took her hours longer than normal. She didn't get home until almost midnight.'

Hank thanked the old man and slowly hung up the phone. Traffic on that road wasn't very likely on a Sunday evening. If she'd lied about that and actually driven home unimpeded, then she would've still been in Branson within the timeframe Vivian Gillam was killed. He tapped his pen on the desk blotter. It was time for another chat with the tourist's daughter.

TWENTY-THREE

We're pulling into the parking lot now.
We're starting to get off the bus. This could take a while.

It was a little surprising, honestly, how quick Earl was with the texting. Or maybe Hank had just developed an ageist assumption after seeing Duncan hunt and peck his way around a smartphone screen.

About to go inside. Radio silence from here on out.

A crash came from the lobby. Hank jerked back and was halfway out of his chair when Sheila rounded the corner. 'Those goddamn blinds. The whole thing fell off the window.'

He sank back down and looked at the coffee now puddling on his desk.

'You should probably clean that up. Earl says it's about to start soon.'

He glared at her and stomped off to the alcove where they kept the break room supplies, as there was no actual break room in the tiny substation off Shepherd of the Hills Expressway. They were conducting the operation from here in Branson to be closer to the theater on the slim chance Earl needed help. Which was highly unlikely. His instructions were to do nothing but sit and watch the show. After he dialed Hank and slipped the phone into his breast pocket.

When Hank walked back into the office, Sheila had settled into the seat on the other side of the desk. She had a Thermos full of what smelled like herbal tea and a fresh notepad, and looked like there was no place else she'd rather be on a Saturday morning. He shot her a dirty look as he mopped up his spilled drink.

'You planning on writing down everything that's said?'

She raised an eyebrow in the way that signaled amusement, not annoyance. 'The things I think are pertinent.'

'What about things I think are pertinent?'

'Get your own notepad.'

'I'll rely on the recording, thanks.'

Missouri law allowed them to surreptitiously record for investigative purposes. Even though *Down Home Darlin'* said 'no electronic recording permitted'. Hank took a good deal of pleasure in violating Toothsome's edict as they waited through the shuffling sounds and pleasantries of people settling in. Then the music started to swell. Couple of guitars, a fiddle. Definitely a banjo. Hank started his stopwatch. How long before the entertainers took a break and the sales pitch began? Hank started fidgeting ten minutes in. He frowned at Sheila, who was calmly jotting down what looked like a grocery list. He got up and wandered around the room until the performers switched over to some kind of comedy skit. That did it.

'Holler when it's over,' he said on his way out the door. He'd rather wrestle rusty thirty-year-old blinds back onto a window than listen to that.

Sam had no idea how long it took for the ringtone to penetrate his sleep. He slapped around the cardboard box that served as a nightstand and heard his phone thud on the floor. It was Saturday, for Chrissake. He grumbled some stronger words as he buried his face in the pillow. It kept ringing. He groped around blindly and finally found it just as his brain kicked into gear. The only person who would be calling this early on a weekend was the one who'd relieved Bill Ramsdell on surveillance and who he'd told to contact him at the first sight of a certain Christian music star.

'Molly?'

'He's back. He's here. It's gotta be him. He was carrying a guitar.'

'Don't let him leave. I'm on my way.'

'Don't let him leave? How am I supposed to keep him—'

Sam hung up and grabbed a pair of pants. Sixty seconds later he was in the Bronco and headed toward the Quickstopper. He tried to call Hank on the way. It went straight to voicemail. He swore and tossed the phone onto the seat. That was just great. He whizzed past a thirty-five miles-per-hour speed limit sign doing sixty and took the turn on what felt like two wheels. Hank's non-answer at least reinforced his decision last night to have Molly report any news to him instead of a higher-up. Both the Chief and Sheila were so invested in the timeshare show angle to this case, neither of them were aware of anything else. Except office politics. They definitely seemed to be paying attention to those. He didn't blame them, though. If they weren't, they'd likely get a metaphorical shiv in the back from some of those jail guys.

He slowed down to a crawl and quietly pulled in behind Molly's little Honda Civic. He got out and went around to Molly's passenger side. She grinned and unlocked the door.

'Nice hair.'

He felt the crown of his head and groaned. He wasn't used to having to comb it. He'd shaved it a while back and finally decided to let it grow again. He raked his hands through it until he got a nod from Molly. He gestured toward the motel.

'When did he get back?'

She looked at her watch. Forty-two minutes ago. Sam nodded. He liked her precision. She really was turning into a good patrol deputy.

'He had a guitar and a book-bag type thing. And he wasn't too steady on his feet, either.'

That wasn't surprising. He eyed her in her sweater and jeans. 'You got your badge and gun?'

'Of course.'

'Then come on. Let's go say hi.'

Hank fixed the blinds with time to spare. The entertainment didn't stop until almost an hour into the show. During which Earl's tablemates still hadn't received the coffee and juice they ordered when they first sat down. Hank returned to his desk just as the dulcet tones of Travis Beckham started rolling out of the phone.

'Ladies and gentleman, have we got a treat for you. So far you've heard some genuine Ozark music and now we'd like to present you with some genuine Ozark property. We want to give you the chance to spend more time in this lovely town. How many of y'all have families? Kids? Grandkids?'

There were murmurings and Hank could visualize a sea of wrinkled hands raising up in response.

'And how many of you would like to spend more time with them?'

The murmurs got louder. A woman sitting close to Earl mumbled something about a grandson in Michigan. Earl started whispering back. 'Isn't it terrible not to see them? I got ten, myself. I'd love to have someplace for us all to get together.'

Sheila looked puzzled. 'Doesn't he only have three grandkids? He's just got the one daughter.'

Hank had no idea how big the guy's family was. But he loved that Earl was enjoying his undercover assignment.

'. . . can make on an affordable timeline.' Toothsome was talking more quickly now, injecting more excitement into his voice. 'And we'll talk more about that. But first I want to take you on a little tour. A virtual walk-through. If everyone will watch the screen . . .'

'Oh, how fun. Turning the lights down,' Earl whispered. Hank sighed and hoped that the old man's tablemates weren't going to mind a running narration of every little thing.

'You will be the first owners of this luxury resort's units. You'll get in on the ground floor. Unless you like a higher view, then we'll get you an upstairs unit.' Toothsome paused for laughter, which he got from the audience right on cue. Sheila rolled her eyes.

'You haven't met this Beckham guy,' Hank told her. 'In person, he'd have you laughing, too. He's got that charming, you-forget-he's-a-salesman thing.'

The 'tour' turned out to be artist renderings and gauzy nature pictures. There were no photos of actual buildings, according to Earl's neutral commentary. His neighbor Dina, the one with the Michigan grandson, was decidedly less charitable.

'When's it supposed to be done? Why would you buy if you can't see it? Are they gonna have a pool?'

Over the next thirty minutes, Toothsome went into the different-sized condo units, the detached cottages for larger families, the community space for crafts and exercise classes, and the spectacular views.

'That's just a drawing,' Earl whispered, 'but it might be Lake Taneycomo. From a nice point on the south shore, maybe.' He made it sound like he was guessing, but they knew he wasn't. The Crumblits had lived in Branson for generations. If anyone knew the views from the county's endlessly snaking waterways, it was him.

Toothsome sounded like he was winding his way through the audience tables. His voice would get louder and then less distinct as he wandered around asking folks about their families. How far away did the grandkids live? How often did they get to see them? How sad were they to not have a place for everyone to gather?

'I cannot believe people are volunteering this much information to a room full of strangers,' Sheila muttered, as yet another woman listed off her grandchildren's names.

'That's why,' Hank said. Appreciative applause rained through the phone speaker and Toothsome laughed with practiced delight.

'An even dozen grandkids! I think that deserves a little memento for each one.' Bits of metal clinked onto a tabletop quite close to where Earl was sitting. 'Official Time Well Spent grandkid coins. And this.' Papers rustled. 'You just read that and think on it, and I'm going to go over to this gentleman over here. He looks like a proud patriarch. Let's find out.'

He sounded closer. Hank stiffened.

'Well, yes. My name's Earl, and I got ten grandbabies. 'Course, the oldest ones are teenagers now. I would like to see more of them soon, before they're all grown up.'

Murmurs of agreement. Hank shook his head as Earl went on and on. He finally finished to a round of clapping and more tinkling metal sounds. Sheila had been trying to write it all down. She gave up and dropped her pen on the desk. 'He's never going to remember all this stuff he's making up. Didn't you tell him that the first rule of spycraft is "keep it simple"?'

Hank shrugged. 'Where's the fun in that? It's not like he'll get tested on it.'

'You never know,' she said, adding the ages of Earl's last two 'grandbabies' to her notes.

Toothsome's voice faded as he moved on to other tables. The elderly voices started to sound tired. Earl and his seatmate began whispering about breakfast. Someone farther away launched into a more pointed complaint. 'I paid for breakfast. I at least want some damn coffee.'

'Oh, we've got food, we've got more entertainment, we've got it all. But first, I gotta have a yes. I gotta have somebody commit to family togetherness. Do you say yes to that?'

There was a smattering of agreement. Some enthusiastic, some not.

'And who's going to say yes to showing your grandkids how much they're loved?'

Hank groaned. This was excruciating. It went on and on. Call and response. Faster and faster, louder and louder. Whipping them up.

'Do you say yes to Time Well Spent?' Toothsome finally shouted. 'Who's going to be my first here today? Who's going to sign for your family's future?'

A lady not far away from Earl called out. The crowd erupted.

Sheila threw up her hands and stomped out of the room. Hank felt like doing the same thing. Instead, he leaned back in the rickety office chair and thought. Much of this was textbook timeshare sales – dangling the promise of family togetherness and the option of leaving loved ones a 'valuable' inheritance. But Toothsome wasn't following the usual pattern of getting a potential customer alone and hammering at them in isolation. He was using the group. Making it do the work for him. Peer pressure. And he was good at it. He was an auctioneer and a preacher. 'Going once, going twice' and 'Can I get an amen' at the same time.

The first two knocks were met with silence. The third produced a few thuds and some mumbling. Sam rapped one more time, then tried the knob. It twisted easily in his hand. Molly fell into cover position and he pushed the door open. He was between the TV and the bed, swaying like seaweed in a gentle current. Sam could tell he was trying to stand straight, an impossible task considering the amount of pot he must have smoked to be smelling as bad as he was. Molly stifled a sneeze.

'You guys are cops, aren't you?'

Sam pointed to the badge on his belt and nodded. 'Are you Cameron Cooper?'

He wiped his nose with the back of his hand. Slowly. Then he nodded. The movement, going the opposite of his seaweed sway, made his eyes go wide with dizziness. He jerked his head and shuffled his feet at the same time, trying to make it stop. Neither worked, and he pitched face first onto the bed.

'Well,' said Molly. 'That's anti-climactic.'

TWENTY-FOUR

Three more couples signed contracts before Sheila came back into the office.

'The first one's got to be a plant.'

'What?' she said.

'That first lady. Who signed a contract.' Hank jabbed a finger at his phone. 'She's working for 'em.'

A fourth old man joined the club. That made five total, and balloons dropped from the ceiling.

'Oh, how exciting,' Earl said.

'What if I was allergic to latex?' Dina muttered.

The next person to join the fun by contractually obligating themselves to a ten thousand dollar payment (plus fees) would get an additional week free during the first year. That had two ladies raising their hands at the same time. The munificent Travis Beckham gave them both the deal. More cheering. As it died down, they heard a whisper.

'Folks're starting to get woozy. One lady's got her head down on the table.'

Hank carefully noted the time. It'd been more than an hour since the show started, and another ninety minutes before that when the glacially-paced group had started gathering in the hotel lobby in order to catch the bus. Earl started to say something else, but the twang of banjos cut him off. Upbeat and staccato. Everyone started clapping along.

'I'm going to lose my mind,' Sheila said.

Only two short songs, and then Toothsome was back at it. That pattern went on and on, with Beckham convincing a few people each time. It continued to have the rhythms of certain church services to Hank – music, praise, come forward to be blessed. He estimated half the audience had bought a time-share when they finally started to bring out the food. And they were the ones getting served first.

'That sure looks good,' Earl told Dina. 'I wish they'd bring plates over here. Looks like those folks who signed are gettin' first dibs.'

But Earl had followed Hank's instructions and not signed a damn thing. Neither had the lady he'd been paired with. 'I did pay for this show, you know,' she muttered to Earl. Then she repeated it much more loudly. The background noise dropped off. Sheila nodded approvingly.

'I said,' Dina re-repeated loudly, 'that I paid for this show, which means I paid for breakfast. And I'd like it, same as everybody else.'

Hank wondered how often this happened to Toothsome, who was making soothing sounds as he drew closer.

'Ma'am, we surely will get to you. I apologize. We're a bit short-staffed with our waitresses today. They are bringing food around as quickly as they can. While we're waiting, can I set this in front of you?'

There was the sound of shuffling papers and the click of a pen. Hank rolled his eyes. 'At what point is he going to accept that he's made all the sales he can today? And that he needs to feed *all* the old people in the room?'

A good deal of rustling came through the phone. It sounded like Earl was trying to get out of the way. Dina's voice was not quite as close now.

'No pool, so no thank you,' she said. 'Now, I take my coffee black and I want my pancake syrup on the side.'

There was a smattering of applause, probably from other non-signers. Beckham started to say what sounded like a swear word, then stopped. Seconds later, they heard clinking cutlery and pouring liquid quite close to Earl's cell microphone.

'I'm a little bit in love with her,' Sheila said.

Hank grinned. He'd given Earl strict instructions not to draw undue attention to himself, since he needed to be a tour member in good standing for tomorrow's show. But to have someone else make waves like this was fantastic. It showed them how Toothsome reacted under pressure. *Not very well.*

If only the single squad car on duty was available. But no. It was on a call all the way across the county. So instead, Cameron Cooper was sound asleep in Sam's backseat, and his smell was sinking into the Bronco's upholstery. Probably permanently. Sam sighed and rolled down the windows. At least the wind noise drowned out the snoring.

Molly arrived first and had the sally port door open for him. He pulled inside and found the new deputy standing with her. The girl one who seemed tough as nails.

'Amber said she'd give us a hand getting him inside,' Molly said as Sam got out and took a grateful breath of clean air.

It took all three of them to extricate his limp ass from the Bronco. He and Amber looped his arms over their shoulders and dragged him into the booking area. Molly hauled over a chair and they dropped him onto it. Sam held him up as Amber adjusted the camera height and snapped what had to be a hall-of-fame worthy mugshot.

'And what exactly are we charging him with?' she asked.

Molly held up an evidence bag containing the bare remnants of a joint they'd found in his jeans pocket. Such things were still illegal in this state. Sam grinned.

'Possession of marijuana. And property damage. And misdemeanor theft.' Might as well include those fancy hotel towels. 'And hopefully there'll be more to come.'

He was dying to get this guy in the interview room and start grilling him. But he knew he couldn't. Even if Cameron had been wide awake, Sam knew he needed to wait for Hank or Sheila. Having Molly report to him was one thing, but interrogating a murder suspect without a superior officer would be way over the line.

He adjusted his hold on Cameron as Amber muscled his hands into position and took his fingerprints. She finished and straightened with a critical expression.

'I've had stumbling drunks, but no stoners. So this has been good. Slightly different behavior. Interesting to compare.'

Sam wouldn't have thought of it as an intellectual exercise, but then he was getting the feeling that Amber didn't think the way most people did. He watched her pull gently on her new inmate's eyelid for a curious look at his pupil. Then she hauled him to his feet. Sam grabbed an arm and they maneuvered him down the hall and into the cell block. Where Bubba Berkins stared at them from the control room. He raised an enormous fat arm and hit the intercom.

'Put him in number twelve.'

Sam knew that cell was way at the end of the row.

'Number three is empty,' Amber said.

'I said twelve, Butch Boggs.'

Sam was so surprised he stopped dead in his tracks. Cooper stretched between them and let out a groan. 'What did he just say?'

Amber looked at him calmly. 'My last name is Boggs.'

'Well, yeah, I gathered that. I was talking about the other part.'

She shrugged and moved toward cell number three. Seconds later, three hundred pounds of Bubba came raging out of the control room. Sam had no idea he could move that fast.

'I gave you an order, Butch.'

Again? Sam almost dropped his hold on Cooper. 'That's not . . . I don't . . . you need to not be saying that,' he stuttered.

Bubba moved closer. 'This ain't your space, Karnes. You left us a long time ago. You don't get to give orders.'

He pointed down toward cell twelve. Sam felt himself flushing. He couldn't just stand here and let him talk to a rookie that way. To anyone that way. Before he could think of what to say, Amber spoke.

'This man is a medical risk. He is clearly incapacitated and likely has substance abuse issues. Per regulations, he should be housed in a place that is easily monitored and accessible by jail staff. Cell three fits those requirements. Cell twelve doesn't.'

She sounded like she was explaining circle-time rules to a preschooler. Sam bit his lip to stop the guffaw that threatened to come out. He turned back to Bubba, whose jowls were shaking. The look in his eyes made Sam want to crawl in a hole, but Amber seemed unfazed. She continued toward cell three like nothing had happened, Cameron Cooper stumbling along beside her.

They were both dying to talk to Earl once he got back to the privacy of his hotel room. He didn't disappoint.

'You shoulda seen the look on that guy's face when Dina told him off. Whoowee. Like she'd slapped him. I was glad I was sitting right there, to be honest.'

'What do you mean?' Sheila said into the speakerphone. She was getting very tired of this method of communication. It made her long for the cold clandestine meetings in the park.

'Well, it seems silly now that I'm trying to put it into words – but it was like his reaction woulda been worse if the rest of the table hadn't been men. Which is ridiculous, because clearly ol' Dina can take care of herself. But he started toward her and then looked at all of us and backed off. Then we got fed.'

Sheila looked across the desk at Hank, whose expression had

just gotten very dark. 'How many people, do you think, weren't feeling well?'

'A lot of folks, by the end. A few needed help out of their seats, including one gentleman at my table. But nobody swooned or anything.'

Those who had signed contracts got to leave the showroom first. Earl and Dina were two of the last ones out, but Earl said that Beckham's expression was nothing but pleasant as he walked them to the door, telling them both to take care of their grandchildren.

'Oh, and did you like what I said about my family? I figured the more grandkids I made up, the better mark I'd be.'

The man cracked Sheila up. She chuckled and started to dig through her notes.

'You did good, Earl,' Hank said as she searched for one particular sheet. 'You stayed on point the whole time.'

'Ah ha.' She cleared her throat. 'Do you happen to remember the details for all those fake grandkids?'

Silence.

'I'm not testing you,' she said. 'I wrote it all down. I'll send you a picture of it so you can read over it in the morning and say the same thing tomorrow if they ask you.'

Earl let out a sigh of relief. They went over a few more things and then let the man go so he could call his wife.

'There'll be no living with him after this,' Sheila said. 'If he was a spy before, he's a true undercover operative now.'

She realized what she'd said just as Hank looked up in confusion. He didn't know about her secret briefings with Earl. She hadn't told him because then she'd be admitting exactly how bad things were getting with the jail staff. And then Hank would – true to form – take some kind of action. And she didn't want that. Yet.

'I just meant that he's enjoying himself so much, he's probably one of those men who has a shelf full of spy novels.' She gave a little shrug and flipped the pages of her notes. Time for a redirect. 'You said the one who runs tomorrow's show doesn't have a record?'

'Right,' Hank said. 'But he is the one who argued with Gillam the day she died. And he clearly has a temper, just based on the times I've talked to him. I wish we had a better accounting of his movements that day.'

'Let me guess – home alone?'

'Yep.'

'What about Beckham?'

'Same thing.'

She sighed. 'And we still haven't found her damn nephew.'

'So there we go.' Hank finished off his coffee. 'Three solid suspects, and nothing to move us further toward any one in particular.'

It wasn't a good place to be, a whole week into the investigation. She'd wanted to haul both showrunners in for interviews already. But she knew Hank wanted to observe the shows in as unaltered a way as possible in order to learn more about what properties Gillam was buying, and to net better evidence in the elder abuse case. She could only imagine how hard Maggie was pressing him on that. Sheila just prayed that decision wouldn't come back and bite them in the ass.

TWENTY-FIVE

Hank's legs were longer than Sheila's, so he beat her down the hallway to the break room by a good bit. He waited for her before he started talking. 'Has he said anything?'

Sam shook his head. 'Heck, no. He was still snoring away the last time I checked.'

Hank nodded. That would teach him to forget to switch off the 'do not disturb' on his phone. He still hadn't done it when they finished debriefing Earl, and the Pup couldn't get through to anyone until Sheila finally turned hers off and saw the seven missed calls.

'It sounds like the two of you did good,' he said, turning to Molly March, who was sitting at a table clutching a mug of coffee and trying to keep her eyes open. She straightened in her seat and turned pink.

'Thank you, sir. It was . . . well, it was nice to get him. I didn't think I was going to have any luck when the whole night went by. But then he just came wandering out of the woods.' She turned to Sheila. 'I did clock out, ma'am. I only had to do a little past my scheduled shift, driving him back here to the jail.' She paused and fiddled with her mug. 'But I was wondering . . . could I stay and watch the interview? I know I'm not on duty . . . well, I mean . . .'

Sheila held up a hand. Hank could tell by the seldom-seen slight tilt of her head that she was delighted. 'I think that's an excellent idea,' she said. 'Both of you did a great job.'

She gestured toward the observation room. Deputy March's eyes lit up and she hustled down the hallway, coffee mug abandoned on the table. Hank watched her disappear and turned back to see Sam slowly putting his own mug away. He trudged out into the corridor with his shoulders slumped. Hank looked at Sheila and jabbed a thumb at Sam's retreating form. It took her a second.

'Oh. Ooops.' She called the Pup back. 'I didn't mean that you should be observing, too. You need to be in the room with us. You're the one who knows this guy.'

Sam's slump evaporated. He hurried off to see if Cooper was awake and Hank filled Sheila's coffee cup.

'Don't look smug at me.' She sighed. 'I didn't realize I'd lumped him and Molly together.' She thanked him and headed down the hallway, muttering something Hank swore sounded like '. . . the last one I can afford to alienate.' He winced. If Sheila was treading that carefully, the staffing problems had officially switched over from bad to worse.

'It's part of the creative process. I separate myself from the world. And the music comes to me.'

Well, that was one of the bigger loads of bullshit Sam had ever heard. A laugh escaped before he could stop it. The Chief gave him a go-ahead nod.

'That's why you ran out on a hotel bill? And took the battery out of your cell phone? And lied about your ID being stolen?' Sam said. He leaned back in his chair and stared at Cooper, who was slouched in a hard plastic chair across the table from him and Hank. His ankle restraint kept rattling against its floor anchor as he tugged at it. The noise was annoying, but at least he'd aired out a little bit and didn't smell like a marijuana dispensary.

'I'm in between projects right now. Cash flow is a little tight.'

'No, cash flow is tight because your Aunt Viv cut you off,' Hank said. 'Why do you think she did that?'

Cooper didn't respond. Hank nodded again. Sam opened the folder he'd placed on the table. He hoped no one could see he was nervous. To ask questions in the field was one thing, but this was an official interrogation. And the first one he'd ever been allowed to lead. He cleared his throat.

'You caused a thousand dollars in damage to the Kamarra Hotel. Vivian settled that bill for you. Then you caused a two-thousand-dollar mess at the Whistler Hollow Cabin Resort. But by then, she'd told you there was no sponsor to pay your bills. And you said this.' Sam read the email verbatim. '"You better find me someone new. I'm not leaving town and I'm not paying. Get off your ass and find me a gig or find me a sponsor. Or I'll be showing up at your door and you don't want that." That was Friday. And by Monday, she was dead.'

He stared at Cooper, carefully keeping his face blank.

'I didn't even know that until Wednesday.'

'Where were you staying on Wednesday?' Hank asked.

Cooper rattled his chain. 'I slept in the woods. After I left that Whistle Cabin place. Until I really needed a shower. So I got the room at RV park.'

'Why didn't you use your credit card?'

A shrug. 'The guy was willing to take cash.'

Sam turned to the next page in his folder. Which topic should he go to next? He thought the Chief might say something, but he just sat there looking comfortably relaxed. Although his eyes never left Cooper's face. Sam tried for the same level of focus, resisting the urge to glance at the two-way mirror. Before they started, Sheila said something about too many cooks in the kitchen and went to the observation room with Molly. If she were doing the questioning, she'd probably switch directions suddenly.

'Tell me about Natalie Lambert.'

Cooper jerked a little in his seat. Startled. 'What?'

'Your baby mama.' It was completely disrespectful to Natalie, but he needed to be forceful. 'The woman you had a relationship with, and a child with. Brody. He's a cute kid. Deserves a dad.'

'How . . . how do you know about her?'

Sam braced for the guy to deny paternity. Instead he started to sniffle. 'I was trying. That's why I came down to this shithole town in the first place. To be near the kid.'

It hadn't been a shithole when he was enjoying luxury accommodations and high-end room service, Sam thought. He felt himself frowning and forced the blank look back onto his face.

'It's so much pressure,' Cooper continued. 'I couldn't cope. I might've gone a little off the deep end.'

'Nope,' Sam said. 'I asked around. You were like this before. Drinking. Trashing dressing rooms. I think you came down to Branson because you couldn't tour anymore. No one wanted to appear with you.'

He felt Hank shift in his seat and out of the corner of his eye saw his boss fight back a smile. He hadn't had a chance to tell his superiors that he'd contacted other Christian musicians. Ones who had shared a stage with Cooper – or God forbid, a dressing room – returned his phone calls almost immediately. *He was a jerk to the stage hands.* And also *the guy was a total slob.* The most interesting: *Great performer, but also lost, you know? Like he thought he was owed something and wasn't getting it.*

'That's not true,' Cooper said.

'Yes, it is. It's great that you're acknowledging your son and all, but you're also down here because no one wanted you on tour anymore. Your mom asked Aunt Vivian to help you out. She did – big time. And what did you do? You kept acting like a jerk.' He paused. The next part was important. 'That put her in a difficult spot. You argued with her.' He held up the email he'd just quoted. 'Where were you Sunday night?'

'What? No. No way. I did not kill Aunt Viv. No.' He tried to push back, but the chair was bolted to the floor. He started to get choked up. 'I was just mad. Like you get with family. I didn't want her dead.'

He wrapped his arms around his torso and stared at the table. Sam repeated his question.

'I was at the cabin place. I had a party.'

'No, you didn't. You pretended to. But no one else was there. It was just you, making a lot of mess.'

Cooper started protesting. Sam cut him off. 'There were no other fingerprints. Just yours and the housekeeping staff.'

'They were about to evict me. So I figured I'd go out in a blaze of glory.'

'And leave your Aunt Viv on the hook for it?' Hank said.

Cooper shrugged and looked at the table. Sam slid a sheet of paper across the laminate surface.

'She wasn't on the hook for it,' Sam said. 'You were. She structured the agreement so if the sponsor fell through – and God Is Music, Inc. did dump you, that's for sure – you'd be responsible for all costs. Aunt Viv was no dummy.'

Cooper went pale. 'Really?'

Sam turned to the next page in his folder. 'How're you going to pay it?' That earned him another suppressed smile from the Chief. Cooper waved his hand like he was swatting away a fly. 'Fuck if I know.'

They went around and around on that subject for a few minutes, then Sam turned back to his folder. As he was finding the next document he wanted, Hank spoke.

'Why Christian music?'

'Huh?'

'Why . . . what's the genre called? Contemporary Christian? You could've just done regular pop music. Why do the other? You're not exactly somebody who walks the walk.'

Sam looked up. He never would have thought to ask that question. He wondered how it related to the case. Cooper gave the Chief a look of loathing. Sam didn't dare move. It felt like they sat there for ages before Cooper spoke.

'My first hit – which wasn't even that big of one – got interpreted as being about God. It wasn't, but . . . all the sudden I was locked in. The regular labels weren't interested. But the Christian ones were all over me. So hell yeah, of course I signed with one. Money's money.'

'And you have no problem not living the ideals that your music talks about?' Hank said.

'No. Why should I? People don't have to. Singers, actors,

politicians. You don't have to be your stage persona. It's just a brand, man.'

Based on his sponsors' reactions, they definitely did not feel that way, Sam thought. He waited, but Hank just sat there, holding Cooper's gaze until the younger man finally looked away. Sam shot a look at Hank and when he got no response, decided that meant he could continue.

'So you got no alibi for Sunday night. What about Sunday during the day? What were you doing?'

'I didn't kill my aunt.' It was almost a shout. 'There's plenty of other people that were pissed at her, too.'

'What do you mean?'

Cooper fidgeted for a minute, then dropped his head into his hands. 'Ah flug ger her Sunday . . . dumb house ogre . . . meet her.'

He and Hank looked at each other. Hank mouthed, 'Doing great, keep going.'

Sam turned back to his suspect. 'Say again?'

Cooper raised his head. 'I followed her. On Sunday afternoon. From her house over to a theater.'

What the hell? And how the hell? The guy didn't have a car.

'I borrowed Natalie's,' he said when Sam pointed that out.

'Did you ask her first?'

He shrugged. The Chief had had enough. He leaned forward again and spoke in a slow, even voice that made what he said even scarier.

'You realize why you're here, don't you, Cameron? We think you killed Vivian. So if you want to play coy with us about taking somebody's car, well that's just going to piss us off. Which isn't going to help when it comes to the bigger issue, is it?'

If Cooper had turned pale before, he went full-on Casper now. 'I called and told her I needed to borrow it. I had to go see my aunt.'

Now Sam was the angry one. Natalie lied to him. She'd said she hadn't seen Cooper in almost two months. He forced himself back to the present and asked what time Cooper had arrived at his aunt's house.

'I didn't. Well, I did. It was about two o'clock, I think? But she was pulling out. So I followed her.' He stopped. Sam made a *go on* gesture. 'I wasn't going to sit there and wait for her to come back. I didn't know how long she'd be gone. So I followed her and she ended up at some theater.'

He didn't remember what street it was on and he hadn't paid any attention to the sign on the building. He'd never even gotten out of Natalie's shitty little Chevy. He just parked near a hedge at the edge of the lot.

'Was it a big building?'

'Compared to what? Downtown Chicago? No. Compared to theater stuff here? Eh, medium-smallish.'

'What color was it?'

'Musta been boring, because I don't remember.'

'How long was she there?'

'She never went inside.'

Sam could feel Hank tensing beside him, but he didn't know why. Probably because he wanted to throttle this guy, too. 'So what did she do?' Sam said through gritted teeth.

'Some guy was just coming out the front doors. She got out of her car and they started arguing. Talky arguing at first, but then it went to yelling. Full on, right in the parking lot. I couldn't hear the beginning, but once they started getting louder, I could make some of it out. She went on and on about how the man wasn't spending his time well, and he was super pissed about food and audience health or whatever. He really got up in her face.'

'What did the man look like?' Hank asked slowly.

'Oh, that's easy. Big, buff, white dude with a shaved head.'

TWENTY-SIX

So Stone Cold's argument with Gillam had a witness. Hank sat back and considered that. The theater manager's version – a 'disagreement' – was clearly not completely truthful. It was a full-on yelling match, with the additional tidbit that he'd physically intimidated the much smaller Gillam.

'Were you there for the whole argument?' he asked Cooper.

'Yeah. It didn't last very long. She backed away from him and then got in her car and drove off.'

'What did the guy do?' Sam asked.

Cooper smirked. 'He stomped around for a minute or two. Waving his hands in the air and talking to himself. Still super fired up, you could tell. Then he got in his car and drove off.'

'Did you follow your aunt back home?' Hank said.

'No way, man. I was done. I had to get the car back.' He saw Hank's skeptical look and started to fidget. Finally: 'Look, not pissing off Natalie's mom about the car was more important than telling off Aunt Viv. She is one scary bitch.'

'Which "she" do you mean?'

'Natalie's mom.' The *duh* in his voice was obvious. 'Have you met her?'

To his left, Hank saw Sam give the slightest of nods.

'A lot of people say the same thing about your aunt,' Hank said.

Cooper waved that away. 'Nah. She's a tight ass, sure. But she's not scary.'

Hank made note of his use of the present tense. He leaned forward again, this time slouched a little, his hands clasped loosely in front of him. Encouraging.

'She's always there, you know? Her and my mom were pretty much it for me growing up. Then when my uncle died, she said she had to get out of Chicago. Start new somewhere else.' He stopped.

'Was that when you started "going off the rails? Acting out? Fucking up?" – heading down the road you're on now?'

'I don't need to be psychoanalyzed, man.' But his expression said Hank had gotten it right.

'So once you were down here, near her again, why didn't you shape up? Stop the drinking and the pot? And the general being a jerk?'

'Obviously you've never tried it. It's kinda fun.' Again, the *duh* came through loud and clear.

Hank sighed and flattened his hands on the cool table laminate, then asked if Cooper went directly back to Natalie's house. He nodded. Sam noted the time he claimed to have returned the car.

'Who else can prove this?' Hank said. 'Natalie lied for you

before. We have no reason to believe her now. And no reason to believe you, either.'

'I told you – I didn't kill Aunt Viv. What about the bald guy?'

'He has an alibi.' It was a complete lie. And it did exactly what Hank intended, stopping that line of protest outright. Cooper blanched and then started to fidget against his ankle chain again.

'Well, what about the lady in the minivan?' He was almost frantic now. Grasping desperately for alternatives. Hank didn't even bother responding. 'I'm serious. What about her? She saw the whole thing.'

Saw what? Hank swore to himself. He wanted to be done with this self-centered man-child. Wanted to get up and leave and go have a nice long chat with Stone Cold. Instead he gave Sam a nod.

'What whole thing? The murder?' Sam said.

Cooper shook his head. 'The argument. I wasn't the only one in the parking lot watching.'

This homicide had completely screwed the staff scheduling. Sheila frowned at her whiteboard. She'd need to make adjustments all the way into next week in order to keep to the no-overtime policy. If only they were given a decent-sized budget. Then none of this would be necessary. And she wouldn't need to be looking over her shoulder all the time.

She tinkered with the duty assignments a little and then sat down at her desk just as there was a hoot from the inner office. Hank burst out and ran to the printer. Seconds later, he was shoving car registrations in her face.

'Cooper said he saw a blue minivan.'

'You have a blue minivan.'

'I also have an alibi.' He waggled the papers at her. 'This blue minivan is registered to Lisa Fettic-Posky. Whose elderly mother took an ambulance ride to the ER after collapsing during a *Breakfast Buckaroos* show. Whose neighbors told me she was in Branson on Sunday.'

Sheila stopped swatting the papers away and instead plucked them from his hand. 'Really? So the nephew might actually be telling the truth?'

When the interrogation started, she'd regretted her decision not to participate. By the end, she was glad she hadn't been in the room. That little brat made her want to tear her hair out.

'I'm not willing to go that far yet,' Hank said. He walked back over to the printer and pulled out a driver's license photo. A middle-aged white woman a few pounds overweight, with shoulder-length brown hair parted sharply on the left. Her eyes bored into the camera. Sheila squinted at the name. 'Looks like Lisa is a forceful personality.'

'Based on the phone conversations I had with her – yes, she is. She offered to take up the cause of her mom's neighbors as well. A husband and wife the mom's age who went on the same tour.' He pulled another photo off the printer, which was starting to creak in a concerning way. 'This is the husband. Drives a Chevy Malibu not a minivan, but I think we need to put him in a photo line-up, too.'

This white man had to be in his eighties. Iron gray hair, broad nose, glasses. Pleasant expression, even in the license photo. She handed it back to Hank. 'And you trust the vandalizing, possibly-a-murderer pothead musician is giving us a straight answer?'

Hank thought about that. 'I think I do. Doesn't mean he's innocent, but I think if he sees the right guy in a six-pack, he'll identify him. 'Course, that doesn't mean he won't point to the wrong guy if the right guy isn't there. Because I do think he'll do anything to point suspicion somewhere else.'

'I agree with you on that,' she said.

'I'd like to pull a few more photos,' Hank said. 'Other people who've had someone harmed by these shows. But . . .'

She laughed at him as he trailed off. 'But your wife won't violate the law and give you any names, will she?'

'No.' He packed a whole lot of exasperation into that one word. 'So we need to lean on the court to hurry up and approve that search warrant request we submitted for their audiences – because you know those people are now on a mailing list. And the bus tour company's payment records. We asked for those, too, right?'

Sheila nodded. She could file piggy-back warrant requests with the new information from Cooper, showing how their case had strengthened. While that route was a pain in the ass, it'd be a whole lot easier than trying to pry information out of Maggie. She glanced at the clock.

'Go home. I'll get it ready and that way we won't have to deal with it tomorrow and can file it first thing Monday morning.'

'I'm not going to dump a crap job like that in your lap,' he said.

She waved him off. 'Go home to your family.'

'You have a family.'

'Yes, and he's got poker tonight. At my house. So I'm quite fine right here where it's nice and quiet. Now, shoo.'

That worked. And it wasn't even a complete lie. Tyrone did have his regular Saturday night poker game, but it was Rodney Hutchinson's turn to host. No matter. Hank's kids needed him more than she needed an early quitting time. She got to work and finished in a surprisingly short time. It was barely nine p.m. when she locked up and walked out to the parking lot. She tossed her tote bag onto the passenger seat of her Forerunner and climbed in. As she backed out of the space, a clunk came from the back. She frowned and then chuckled as she remembered she still had Earl's bird seed. She needed to remember to give it to him this week. She also needed him back on duty at the jail. He was her eyes and ears and without his reports, she had no idea what those bastards were up to.

She turned out of the parking lot and pointed the SUV toward Branson and home. The drive along winding, unlit Highway 160 always required more attention in the dark. She put on some Neville Brothers and hummed along as she passed scattered houses among stands of trees and rolling pastures. She just got to 'A Change Is Gonna Come' on *Yellow Moon* when the pair of headlights that had been behind her for several miles started to get closer. Fast. She hadn't thought anything of it at first – it was a two-lane country road, after all; it wasn't like there were many passing opportunities – but now they were practically up her backside.

Then the world lit up. A thousand watts flooded her vision. She swore and hit the gas. Her pursuer kept pace. It had to be a pickup truck, a huge one, with KC lights on a roll bar. The beams were too high off the ground to be anything else. She gripped the wheel and hugged 160's curves at ten over the posted forty-five miles an hour. But the truck only got closer. She reached a straightaway and pressed the accelerator to the floor, but her poor eight-year-old Forerunner couldn't give her more than another ten miles per hour before she had to slow again for the next curve.

The truck started to pull alongside, but they hit another curve and he dropped back to hug her bumper again. She thought about slamming on the brakes, but that wouldn't end well for either one of them. Him, she didn't so much care about, but her own self – well, she'd like to make it home in one piece. He crept forward and nudged her, his grill hitting somewhere halfway up her back hatch. She swore.

The skinny two-lane was about to straighten out again. If only she were in a squad car. Even the oldest one in the department had more kick than her poor SUV. She gripped the wheel and took the last bend as fast as she dared. It felt like the two left wheels were coming off the road. Not something those sensible Toyota engineers had designed for. She prayed the center of gravity was low enough to keep her from rolling.

The curve ended and she floored it. Starting the straightaway at a higher speed this time allowed her to quickly coax a few more miles per hour out of her engine. She started to pull away. Then the diesel asshole showed her how silly she was. The roar of his engine was almost overwhelming as he came alongside, but at least the blinding light was now on the road ahead instead of frying her field of vision from behind.

She risked a glance to her left. Definitely a jacked-up American pickup, possibly black. He swerved closer. He was going to run her off the road. Into the trees. She did some quick calculations. Distance. Time. Safety. She eased off the gas and was moving to hit the brakes when he jerked right. She had no choice but to do the same. The only thing that saved her was her foot already on the way to the brake pedal. She pressed down and managed to hit the unpaved shoulder at forty miles an hour instead of almost seventy. Dirt sprayed everywhere. She couldn't see the oncoming trees. Her seatbelt locked and she struggled to keep her hands on the wheel. By the time her shuddering car came to a stop on the rocky shoulder in between two trees, the truck was long gone. She pressed her hands to her face, then removed her gun from its holster and put it in the center console. Just in case they came back.

She adjusted her seatbelt and forced her car into a three-point turn on the narrow road. It took her two tries before she was headed back the direction she came, with only Aaron Neville keeping her company in the dark.

TWENTY-SEVEN

To be honest, Sam had hoped to find Cheeks at the semi-boyfriend's backyard trailer. But no. She was at mom's house on this sunny Sunday morning.

'Yeah. I know you told me never to come back. But I need to talk to your daughter. And I need you to step outside here on the porch.'

'Fuck you.'

Alrighty then. 'On the porch, ma'am.' There was no point in adding 'please' since she was probably only eighteen inches away from a behind-the-door shotgun and two seconds away from using it. Politeness wasn't going to improve that any.

They stood there and stared at each other. Inside the house, a baby started to cry. Sam smiled. Her move. She crossed her arms and let the kid wail.

Sam started to worry. He had a plan for this, and it was late. He was thinking he'd be forced to threaten her with arrest when Bill Ramsdell finally showed up. He rolled by in a cruiser, circled the cul-de-sac and parked facing the main road. He got out and planted his stocky six-foot-one self in a wide stance that gave him ready access to his handgun. 'Hiya, Karnes.'

'Ramsdell, hey. Ms Lambert here was just about to step out onto the porch with me.'

'That sounds like a good idea,' Bill said, his hand moving closer to his holster.

Natalie's mom stepped away from the door she was half-hidden behind and came onto the porch. Sam invited her to step down into the yard. She did with language Sam hoped she didn't use around her grandson. Once she was safely standing next to the damn Chevy hatchback, he returned to the front door and called for Natalie.

The crying had morphed into a kind of tired hiccupping. It got louder and then Natalie came out of the hallway into the front room. Brody was nestled against her, red and tear-streaked and miserable. Natalie didn't look much better.

'He has an ear infection. We were up all night.'

Sam felt sorry for her. Then he felt ticked off because he felt that way. 'You lied to me.'

She tightened her grip on the kid and took a step back. 'You said you wouldn't contact me with my mom around.' It came out as a cross between a whisper and a hiss.

'And you said you were telling me the truth.' He glared at her. 'But you did see Cameron last weekend. You even lent him your car. Which turns out to be pretty damn critical to our investigation.'

She dropped her gaze and then looked around the little front room, with its changing table in the corner and a stack of diapers on top of the TV stand. She was wearing the same T-shirt she had on the last time he saw her. The baby food stain was in a new spot, though.

'Look,' he sighed. 'You and I need to have a nice sit-down conversation. Here is not a good place. What would you like to do with Brody? Bring him with you? Or leave him with your mom?'

Her gaze flickered over at her mother, who was leaning against the car with her arms crossed and her expression thunderous. Sam reconsidered his offer of a choice.

'Let's go ahead and bring him,' he said, making the call that it wasn't a good idea to leave a baby with someone who was clearly not in a caregiving mood. 'You can follow us to the station.' Sam quickly waved her down the porch steps, cutting her off as she tried to say Brody would be fine with Grandma. 'That way he can ride in his car seat and stay nice and secure.'

But the mom wasn't moving. Once again, Ramsdell came to the rescue. He moseyed forward like he was a gunslinger in the Old West. 'Ma'am.' He gestured to the other side of the driveway with the hand that wasn't resting on his Glock. Megan Lambert gave him the same shotgun blast look and walked over to the scratchy weed patch that doubled as a lawn.

Ramsdell kept an eye on her as Brody and an incredible amount of baby junk got loaded into the tiny hatchback. Natalie climbed in the driver's seat and Sam bent down to talk to her through the open window. 'I'm going to go first, then you're going to follow me, and my partner is going to follow you.'

He really couldn't see her as the type to make a break for it, he thought as he pulled away from the house, but he hadn't seen her as the type to flat-out lie to his face, either. Plus, now he'd made her nervous, which would hopefully help once he got her in the interview room. Nervous people tended to talk a lot. They also tended to agree to things more easily. Like the search of a vehicle, which – thanks to him seizing on the safety needs of a cute one-year-old – was now off Megan Lambert's property and on its way to the perfect place for processing evidence.

The air smelled as dusty and stale as it had yesterday. Hank sighed and ignored the crooked window blinds as he walked through the shoebox lobby. He was a little surprised Sheila wasn't here yet. At least he knew Earl wasn't late. The old guy's texts had lit up his phone the whole ride over.

Ready for another great day! And I'm all fueled up. Cooked two Hot Pockets in the room microwave.

Waiting in line to get on the bus. Looks like everybody from yesterday is still here.

Fifteen minutes later:

Still waiting in line. Geez, these old folks.
Finally on. Somebody's trying to get a Waylon Jennings singalong going. Nobody's biting.
Got my fake relatives all memorized from Mrs Turley's picture. Thank you ma'am.
We're finally here. Seemed like we hit every red light in town. They're unloading the wheelchairs now. Time to go dark.

Still the secret agent. Sheila had called that one right. He set up the speaker phone and listened as Earl tried to find a seat for the *Breakfast Buckaroos*. Hank could picture the theater with the round tables for eight and the stage on the wall in the center. Earl tried to sit in the back – the better to see the whole theater – but got overridden by what sounded like a teenage girl who'd taken his ticket.

'This way, sir.' Her voice came through the speakerphone clearly. 'There's lots of room right up close to the action.'

'Oh, thank you but I'd rather sit—'

He was shushed and guided down to the front. There was muffled hubbub as people settled in, including his cranky seatmate from yesterday, who was a little distance away and already demanding coffee. Good for her. Earl called out a hello and then set about making new friends. Hank was listening to him compliment a woman on her bedazzled wheelchair when the substation door rattled open.

Sheila marched into the room, set down her Thermos and sank into her chair. She pulled out her notepad and sat back to listen. It was all perfectly normal. But not. First off, she was late. That wasn't unheard of, but it typically came with a loving gripe about Tyrone or some story about a 'damn fool' stalled in the slow lane. Now she just sat silently. Her usually glowing brown skin had an almost gray tinge. The skin around her eyes was drawn tight and the soft lines at the corners of her mouth had deepened.

She cocked an eyebrow at him and he quickly averted his eyes. What the hell was going on? Was Tyrone OK? He worried all the way through the opening number, which sounded remarkably like yesterday's closing act. He wanted to say something, but the emcee started up as soon as the music faded away. And he was close. The voice came through Earl's phone as clearly as if he were standing in the substation office.

'Wasn't that fabulous, folks? Such a fun start to what's going to be a great morning here for all of you Buckaroos.'

Sheila snorted and Hank groaned at the same time. 'He's talking to them like they're preschoolers watching a 1950s cowboy TV show,' she said. 'I don't think I can take hours of this. Wait, why are you laughing?'

'The incongruity . . .' He trailed off into another laugh. 'You haven't seen this guy. Name's Axel Orsi. He looks like a professional wrestler. All bulked up with a shiny bald head. Not who you'd picture talking that way to a bunch of senior citizens.'

Unlike Toothsome Travis Beckham yesterday, Orsi's voice didn't fade in and out while moving around the room. Stone Cold seemed to stay right near Earl's table. Hank began to suspect what the plan was.

'Say, can I ask you something?' Earl whispered five minutes later, as Stone Cold went on about the natural beauty of the Branson area. 'Did you buy a timeshare yesterday? At the first show?'

'No. I didn't. What use is a bunch of outdoor stuff for me?' the owner of the bedazzled wheelchair said mournfully. 'And I don't got kids. So there you are.'

'I do got kids. And grandkids,' Earl whispered. 'But I didn't buy one either. Come to think of it, I don't know that anybody at this table bought yesterday. Or those tables over there where my friend Dina's sitting.'

That was what Hank thought. They'd herded all the holdouts together so Stone Cold could concentrate his firepower. Bravo to Earl for confirming it.

'Now we're going to talk about how you can enjoy this lovely area on a regular basis.' Stone Cold was definitely not as smooth as Toothsome had been. He sounded more like he was reading from a script. 'Have some of you already committed to Time Well Spent? To spending time with the grandkids? To investing in your family's future? Give yourselves a round of applause if you've done it.'

He worked them into a pretty loud cheering section and then turned them on the others. 'Don't you think they should join you? Don't you think these folks up front deserve the same wonderful things in their future that you have in yours?'

Hoots and hollers rained down on the recalcitrants. No wonder they'd put the poor people up front. Easier to aim at. The atmosphere was less like Saturday's churchy call-and-response sales pitch and more like a monster truck rally, with a fired-up crowd egging on the contenders. It went on for a good ten minutes, at the end of which two more couples had signed contracts. Hank wondered how long the others could resist.

Then suddenly, the band was back. Upbeat, up-tempo music that didn't calm anybody down. After the third cycle of this, several people left had caved in and agreed to buy. They joined the others in goading the ones who were left. The wheelchair lady was in tears. Then there was a different kind of cheer and they heard the rattle of dishes and silverware as the band dialed down its volume.

'Looks like the waiters are starting in the back first,' Earl said. 'I'm sure we'll get ours soon.'

They couldn't make out wheelchair lady's response through the sniffles. Then Stone Cold started in again. Then more music.

'I don't think they ever got served,' Sheila said. 'They left the hotel more than three hours ago.'

'I'm giving it five more minutes, then I'm going over there and shutting the whole thing down in the name of public health. Or basic humanity.' He glowered at the sounds coming out of his phone and imagined what Maggie would be saying right now.

'There, there,' they heard Earl whisper. Then he waited for Stone Cold to pause for breath and raised his voice. 'My friend here needs some food. She's not feeling well.'

'She isn't the only one.' That sounded like cranky Dina. There was a small chorus of agreement from those around Earl, while the clinking flatware and satisfied murmurs of oblivious diners continued in the background.

'My, he's getting awful close to Dina.' Earl's whisper this time was less conspiratorial aside and more surprised worry. There was the sound of something hitting a table and then Stone Cold inviting her to sign a contract – in the same tone a person would use to invite someone to go swimming in concrete shoes. The bedazzled seatmate gasped and muttered something about her heart pills.

'You don't look so good,' Earl said. There was loud rustling and the sound of a zipper.

'. . . a little blue bottle in the side pocket . . .'

'If you'd only join us, ma'am, you'll see what a sound investment it is.'

'I'm through with this,' Dina said. 'I'm going to wait on the bus.'

'. . . can't have you leave without the group. There are—'

'Try and stop me, you pumped-up buffoon. I'm going to—'

A loud cry and clattering crash came through the phone. Then silence. By the time the yelling started, Hank and Sheila were already out the door and on their way.

TWENTY-EIGHT

'If you move, I'm putting you in handcuffs.'

Stone Cold started to protest, but was drowned out by the crowd milling around like a bunch of panicked chickens. Sheila was having to physically move people aside – very few of them were listening to her instructions – so that paramedics could get through with the gurney. They finally made it to the lady with the glittery wheelchair, who refused to let go of Earl's hand.

'Go ahead and ride in the ambulance with her,' Hank told him. 'See if she's able to tell you her next of kin.'

The poor guy looked horrified, then took hold of himself and nodded. He stayed alongside as the paramedics pushed the gurney through the squawking crowd toward the door. Hank turned to the adjacent table, where Larry Alcoate was kneeling in front of a woman who had to be Dina.

'You might have broken your hip, ma'am.'

'Just 'cause I'm old, you automatically think that?'

'No,' Larry said. 'I think that because you're laying on the floor with a tablecloth tangled around your legs. And since you haven't stood up yet, I'm guessing that you can't. Am I correct?'

'That's only 'cause of the damn tablecloth. Not 'cause of my hips. Just help me up.'

'I'm going to put you on a gurney and take you to the hospital.' Larry moved away just in time to avoid a swipe from a gnarled hand. He stopped next to Hank, who had stayed well out of arm's reach. 'You gotta clear these people out of here,' he yelled over the commotion.

'We're trying. Nobody's listening. I've got backup coming to help. I'll get you a path through – oh, Jesus, sir, watch out.' Hank lunged but was too far away to catch the old man who didn't see the step up to the next level of tables. He tottered and then went down like a rotten redwood. People scattered in all directions. Larry swore and leapt after Hank. They turned him over and all Larry needed was one look at the guy's broken nose before he reached for his radio. 'We're going to need more units. Hell, send them all.'

Hank helped move the man away from the crush of people as best he could. He rose to his feet to see Sheila calmly pointing a woman toward the exit. The woman flapped her hands and turned in the opposite direction. Sheila took a breath and scanned the entire room. Then she started to move, weaving quickly between tables and panicked seniors until she reached what she wanted. She shoved on the fire exit and the door swung open to an ear-splitting wail. And the flock of crazed chickens turned into a line of docile lambs. Everyone calmly headed for an exit.

Larry looked around in amazement. 'Well, if that isn't some kind of Pavlovian response, I don't know what is.'

Hank looked at Sheila across the room, holding the fire exit open, and gave her an approving nod. He got an eye roll in response. He got another one outside as they began to separate everyone into lines – one of healthy people ready to board the bus, and another of pending emergencies who needed either oxygen, blood sugar testing, or just a good hand-holding.

One of the Branson PD officers who'd responded to the call for help was able to turn off the fire alarm, and the whole area fell mercifully quiet. Hank spun on his heel and went back inside.

Stone Cold was sitting slumped on the edge of the stage, elbows on his knees and head bowed. His black dress slacks and blazer went a long way toward making his bulked physique look businesslike, but were now rumpled and stained. He looked up as Hank approached through the overturned chairs and ruined food.

'I don't even . . . this . . . what . . .' He spread his arms and then let them fall back on his knees.

'Yeah, there really are no words,' Hank said. 'Except maybe misleading advertising. And elder abuse. Oh, and there at the end, false imprisonment.'

Stone Cold eyed him in puzzlement and then understanding.

'You were watching? Or listening? How . . .? Oh, whatever.' He rubbed at his temples. 'This never happened before and . . . I was just following the procedure.'

'A procedure that said don't feed the people who haven't signed a contract?'

Stone Cold shook his bald head. 'They were going to get food. Just last. That's why they're all sat together. You get at least a few more contracts signed that way.'

'And the lady who wanted to leave?'

'Who does that? You're on a tour. I just asked her to stay with the group.'

Hank scoffed and waved his hand to encompass Orsi's muscled figure. 'You didn't ask. You intimidated. That's the same thing as using force.' It wasn't, technically, but Hank wasn't going to split hairs at the moment. 'You hulked over an old lady and made her trip and fall. You're going to face charges.'

'I never touched her. She's the one who assaulted me.' He pointed to a scuff mark on his black slacks.

Hank glared at him. 'Oh, I'm sorry. Do you need medical attention?'

Orsi cast his eyes heavenward and then back at Hank. 'That's not my point. I'm just saying that things exploded out of hand and none of this was supposed to happen. I was doing exactly what I was supposed to.'

'Yeah, I'm curious about that. You were doing what Time Well Spent wanted. What Vivian Gillam wanted. But she's dead.'

Orsi stared at him. 'I still have a contract.'

'Who's going to enforce it?'

'I have no idea, actually. I haven't been contacted by anybody yet. I'm starting to think she was the only one at the company.'

Hank didn't respond. He just stood there, wanting to see whether the guy would fill the silence. He didn't.

'Tell me again what you and Vivian argued about last Sunday.'

'Wait – is that why you're spying on the show? Because she showed up and yelled at me?'

'And then ended up dead. Don't forget that part. Plus, I have a witness who says you were doing plenty of yelling yourself.'

What little color there was in Stone Cold's face drained out. 'A witness?'

'Yeah. One who says you hulked over Vivian just like you did the old lady today. Seems to be a pattern with you.'

Orsi started to stand, then seemed to realize that would only support Hank's statement. He balled his fists instead. 'I want a lawyer.'

'Fine. You can call one from the station.'

The tour bus was only half full. Sheila stood next to the driver and did a head count, then moved aside as Bill Ramsdell climbed aboard with three large grocery bags full of orange juice and energy bars. Hank had pulled him off whatever he'd been doing to make an emergency stop at Country Mart. She estimated the cost and hoped the PD would be willing to pay for it. The show was in their city, after all. She saw Hank wave from the sidewalk and hopped off the bus.

'When Ramsdell's done,' he said, 'I need him to take Orsi to the station and book him.'

Even with a million things going on, the man still found time to overreach. They didn't have anything solid to hold him on, and Hank knew it. She bit her lip and kept quiet. 'You can have Bill when he's done passing out snacks. Then I'm going to ride back to the hotel and get witness statements.'

Hank rubbed his unshaved jaw. 'I can do that. You don't like to wait – you could head right now to the hosp—'

'Nice try. You're going to do it. You gotta face your wife sometime. Might as well get it over with.'

'That's easy for you to say.' He stomped off toward his minivan.

Sheila was now doubly glad she'd made him drive over from the substation. Not only could he get himself to the hospital without having to wait for a ride, but he also hadn't had the opportunity to notice the paint scrapes and busted side mirror on her Forerunner. She wasn't ready to explain that.

She climbed back aboard the huge tour bus and they set sail for the hotel. People were still pretty shook up, but the food was making things better. She turned to the driver, a nice-looking brother named Nolan, according to the tag on his polo shirt.

'Yes, ma'am. Been doing this about three years now. It ain't bad.'

It had changed recently. A couple of the shows got longer and the old folks more unsteady. And a bit schizo, if he was being honest. Some came out happy as clams and talking about the grandkids. And other ones were either crying or looking terrified. The main culprits were this show and the one the day before. Darlin' something.

'I told the tall white fella most of this. He was asking about the ambulance trips.' His eyes widened. 'My Lord, were there folks needing rides to the hospital? 'Cause of all those ambulances today? Did I strand some poor wives?'

'No, no,' Sheila said. 'It's fine. Us and the Branson police made sure all the relatives were transported. Anyway, you got in trouble for taking somebody before, didn't you?'

He shrugged. 'Yeah. They told me to keep my ass in the seat and my wheels parked. But today . . . that was beyond crazy. I'd happily broke the rules.' He looked over and winked. 'Plus, with your fine law enforcement self on my side, what could they do to me?'

She hid a smile and waved him off as she moved toward the back to start taking names and contact information. She continued as they unloaded at the hotel. Inside they were met by a flummoxed manager in a polyester vest talking to a real estate agent in a pressed pantsuit.

'Ms Silver?'

'Deputy Turley! How nice to see you. What brings you here on a Sunday afternoon?' She peered around Sheila. 'Oh, my. Are these folks all right?'

But Sheila was already turning toward the manager, asking for staff help to get people up to their rooms. She explained what happened earlier, using the more polite 'pandemonium' instead of the more accurate 'shitshow'. The man tugged on his tie and ran for the front desk phone. Sheila was following when an elderly couple nervously approached. The woman elbowed her husband in the side. He cleared his throat.

'Ma'am? We were one of the people who bought yesterday. A timeshare, you know. And well, after today, we're not so sure.'

People on their way to the elevators stopped to listen. A murmuring started from all around, which was slightly disconcerting considering how disheveled and manic looking half these old folks were. They all started toward Sheila like she had some sort of gravitational pull. She took a step back. 'There might be a time frame where you can get out of the contract,' she said slowly. 'I don't know offhand. It would be a civil matter, which I'm not as familiar with as the criminal side of things. I'd be happy to ask our county prosecutor if there's any kind of law.'

The wife patted her arm in thanks and stepped away just as Reggie Silver came sliding across the lobby tile, moving so fast she almost couldn't stop.

'Oh, there absolutely is. A grace period. Where you can back out of a timeshare contract.' She plucked a notepad out of her enormous tote bag. A glance at Sheila seemed to ask if this had anything to do with their earlier interview, but she didn't voice the question. Instead, she gently shooed the couple over to the tables by the breakfast bar. A dozen people followed. 'We do need to act fast. You only get five days to cancel.' Reggie started handing out sheets of notepaper. 'Your name, your address, your room number here at this hotel, and how much you bought the timeshare for.'

This was more – and crucial – information than Sheila had thought to ask for. She gave herself a silent scolding and stepped forward. 'And which show you bought at, please – was it today or yesterday? And if you've got the paperwork, please.'

'George – your copier work?' Reggie hollered at the manager.

'Yeah.'

'Well, get ready. We're going to give it a workout. We got some contracts to break.'

A weak yet grateful cheer went up from the crowd. Sheila dragged over chairs from throughout the lobby to handle the numbers wedged into a space designed to hold only a few breakfasters. Then she started to ferry over the contracts so George could Xerox them. As they waited for a stack to run through, she leaned against the counter. 'Why is Reggie here in the first place?'

'Oh, she comes by every other Sunday or so. To restock her business cards, give us some flowers for the table if we're fully booked. Draws more attention to her display.' George gestured toward the elevator and what Sheila guessed was prime captive-audience display space.

Love Branson? Retire here permanently! The area's #1 real estate agent can find you a home!

The almost tasteful, definitely in-your-face sign showed Reggie standing in front of a lovely brick colonial. A silver dish held business cards and a silver vase held fresh peonies. Sheila looked back toward the breakfast bar. Was Reggie hoping some of these folks would buy a house once they unloaded the timeshare? She didn't realize she said it out loud until George responded.

'Probably not. She's just good people. Happy to help others out.'

Sheila fought to keep a skeptical look off her face. Sure, the woman was helping fragile old people but she was also undoing the work of a former rival. One of those reasons was putting a gleeful smile on her face, and Sheila would bet it wasn't the altruistic one.

TWENTY-NINE

Every bed in the ER was full. The woman with the hip problem was in X-ray and the man with the broken nose was going to need a specialized surgical consult. Which she couldn't get him, because this was Branson Valley General and they didn't have those kinds of resources just sitting around drinking coffee and waiting on the two-percent chance they might be needed in an emergency.

She did at least have an endocrinologist on the way. That was one thing Branson had plenty of use for – a diabetes specialist. He'd be able to help her stabilize blood sugar levels. Which she knew were low, because she knew these poor people had been denied food. Because it had happened before. She was going to kill Hank.

'Dr McCleary? Can you take a look at this EKG?'

Maggie handled that and then a twisted ankle and a nasty anterior forearm laceration. She finished the stitches in time to see Larry Alcoate wheeling an ambulance gurney toward the exit. She caught up with him outside.

'What the hell? Did a herd of stampeding buffalo somehow get loose in the theater? Because, my God.'

Larry rubbed his eyes. 'I can't even describe it. They lost their damn minds. It was like a gimpy train wreck. Everybody falling off the tracks at the same time.'

'And nobody had been fed?'

'Naw, lots of people had, from the look of it. But not the tables up front. There were no dishes on them. That was where the heart attack was. And the broken hip. How's she doing, by the way? Feisty old broad.'

'No kidding. She's in X-ray right now. Keeps yelling about her missing cane.'

Another rig pulled up with two more flustered seniors. Maggie sighed. She had a nurse out sick and a medical assistant on maternity leave. That left her with only one of each and they were both already busting their asses. She pulled her blood pressure cuff out of her pocket. Larry waved her off.

'I'll stay. I can certainly check vitals for you in the waiting room.' He gave her a sly grin. 'Since I've already done the hard work for you and triaged the important cases.'

She laughed. 'Yeah, that's you. Alcoate Emergency Department Management Services. You should—'

She stopped as her minivan pulled into the circular drive. It parked in the spot reserved for law enforcement as she snuck a look at the updates on her phone. Larry saw who was driving and mumbled something about needing to be somewhere else. He and the gurney disappeared as Hank walked toward her. From the look on his face, he wished he could go with them.

She knew this wasn't his fault, but Jesus – he was supposed to put a stop to it, not make it worse. 'What the hell, honey?'

He stopped in front of her, looking calm and even-tempered. She knew better. The set of his shoulders and the almost imperceptible crease on the left side of his mouth meant the opposite.

'I'm sorry. I've been trying. We were monitoring the whole thing. He started getting intimidating and then . . . within minutes, there was the heart attack and the other lady fell.'

'"He" who? Who's intimidating old people?' She tried to keep her tone light, but was pretty sure it still implied 'and why have you not stopped it?'.

'The show emcee. He's the intimidator. And possibly a

murderer.' He shook his head. 'This whole thing . . . the guy on the first day – also a suspect – is the schmoozer. The one today is the enforcer. Brings out some intimidation for the people who didn't buy timeshares the first day. Brilliant, actually, when you look at the whole process. She really was good at what she did.'

'What the hell are you talking about?' He did this with his cases – tossed out incoherent comments as he thought things through. It would drive her crazy, except she knew she did the same thing to him with her work. Not nearly as often, though. 'I'll care about this later. Right now, I have fifteen people who shouldn't be here.'

'I need to get witness statements.'

She wanted to kick him and hug him at the same time. Instead she told him he could talk to people after Larry checked their vitals. 'And I need to go calm down a lady who just found out she broke her pelvis in two places.'

Her husband snapped his fingers and asked her to wait a second. He jogged back to the minivan and returned with an intricately carved wooden cane.

'Maybe this will help.'

It would, damn him. She took it and then laid a hand on his cheek. He turned his head and kissed her palm. 'Go heal the world, doc.'

'I'd settle for one small corner of Missouri.'

'Me, too.' She watched him try to smile and saw that shadow, the one he always tried to hide from her, there at the edge of his eyes as she walked away.

Thank God it was Sunday. Not because of the Lord's Day necessarily, but because Tyrone had it off. He'd be able to drive her back to her car, still sitting in the substation parking lot. She texted him and then went outside the building to wait. She sat on a brick planter and took a few deep breaths, clearing out the tang of stale coffee and Ben Gay that had settled in her lungs. An hour in a hotel lobby packed with nervously sweating old people would do that. She did have to admit, though, that things were ending a lot better than they started. People were clutching papers detailing their right to cancel under Missouri law and exchanging contact information with newfound comrades-in-arms. She sensed the beginning of a 'Buckaroo Bedlam Survivors' support group.

'Oh, goodness. You're still here?'

She turned from the warm spring sun and looked back into the shade of the building's overhang. Reggie Silver stood there in all her pantsuited glory. Sheila gave silent thanks that she didn't have to wear that kind of uniform to work. No throwing that in the wash when you got home.

'Are you . . .?' Reggie trailed off as she stepped closer. She had her car keys in her hand and her tote bag over her shoulder. If it had been big before, it was now full-to-bursting with papers and who knew what else from her successful obliteration of the tour's timeshare sales. Sheila wasn't impressed with the woman's naked delight in the situation, but she had to admit she was glad the two shows would end up empty for the weekend.

'Do you, um . . .' Reggie looked around the parking lot and back at Sheila. 'Do you need a ride somewhere?'

'That's nice of you, but no thanks. Someone is on the way.'

'Oh, did you ride here on the bus with everyone?'

Sheila nodded.

'They were telling me a lot of people were taken to the hospital.'

Sheila thought of Hank dealing with that – and his wife. 'Yes. There were several injuries when everyone panicked there at the end.'

Reggie clasped her hands together, keys jangling between her fingers. 'I am just staggered at how far Vivian Gillam was willing to go to make a buck. Trying to oust the competition is one thing, but having emcees intimidate old people is . . . well, it's nuts.'

Sheila thought back to their earlier conversation at the Silver Real Estate office. 'By competition, you're referring to Henry Gallagher?'

Reggie shrugged. 'I guess so. She was definitely moving into what was new territory for her. And there's only so much room in this town.' She pushed her key fob and a nearby Toyota Avalon blipped its lights. She took a step and then paused. 'Any word on that soil report? What property it's for?'

'Not yet. We're still looking into it.' She forced a smile that turned genuine as she saw her husband drive into the lot. She picked up the manila folder holding her own copies of the time-share paperwork, now warm from sitting on the planter bricks, and rose to her feet.

'Thanks again for your help in there. You put a lot of folks at ease.'

'Oh, it was my pleasure. Those timeshares are a scourge down here.' She gave a wave and trotted off to her car as Tyrone pulled up. Sheila slid into the passenger seat.

'Hi, babe,' he said. 'Does this mean you get to come home now?'

She just looked at him.

'Yeah. I didn't think so.'

Natalie wasn't paying attention. She stood there as the baby crawled around on the conference table – she had decreed the floor too dirty – and spent more time keeping him from falling off than answering Sam's questions. He realized he was tugging ferociously at his ear and forced himself to take a deep breath.

'Could you maybe hold him in your lap? Just for a minute or two?'

She ignored him.

'OK. Fine. But unless you explain why you lied to me, you're going down the hall to the jail, and somebody else can watch him crawl around.' False reporting was actually a low-class misdemeanor, and would be even harder to prove in this instance, since she wasn't reporting a fictitious crime, just lying about a favor. He'd feel like a jerk for threatening her, but he was still upset about it. 'Which are you going to choose?'

She grabbed her son and harrumphed down into a chair. Brody responded by yanking her hair. Bravo, kid.

'I didn't want Cameron in jail.' She gently picked the baby's fingers out of her hair and gave him a chew toy. 'Well, I didn't want his father in jail. I didn't want Brody to have a father in jail. It sucks. My dad was in when I was a kid. And I got friends like that, too. People look down on you and you gotta go visit them and it just . . . I didn't want that for my kid. And I figured if you thought he didn't have a way to go to see his aunt, then he wouldn't be a suspect.'

Sam sighed. 'Do you think Cameron killed his aunt?'

She stared down at the baby. A tear fell on the poor kid's head. 'When I lied to you – no. I didn't think he'd done it. Now with him being, like, on the run or whatever for so long . . . I don't know.' She wouldn't meet Sam's gaze. 'So I'm sorry. I hope it didn't fuck up your investigation.'

Well, she hadn't done it any favors, that was for sure. The baby started to fuss and as Sam waited for Natalie to dig a container of Cheerios out of her bag, a text popped up on his phone. Alice hadn't found anything in the Chevy hatchback. He tugged at his ear.

'Why'd you let Cameron use your car in the first place? Weren't you angry at him?'

'Yeah. But I was hoping if he had the chance to talk to his aunt and smooth everything over, then she'd start up the money again and we'd have a better chance of getting some child support.'

Sam looked at her, sitting there in the same damn T-shirt – washed so often it almost wasn't even cotton anymore – and found it hard to fault that goal.

'Did Vivian know about you? About Brody?'

She shrugged. 'I don't know. Maybe? But if she did, then that means when she cut him off, she basically supported him *not* supporting Brody. She was supposedly so forceful, why wouldn't she force him to go make money so he could pay child support?' She took the now empty bowl of cereal and gently bounced her son on her knee. 'So I like to think she didn't know. 'Cause it's hard to believe she was the bitch Cameron ended up saying she was. Nobody's that horrible all the time, you know?'

Sam knew. People were complicated. Which generally speaking could make life interesting, but specifically, it sure as hell made his job hard.

THIRTY

Tyrone thankfully hadn't noticed the busted side mirror before she left Monday morning. The Forerunner was now at the auto shop down the street from the office. She'd been promised it back by this evening. If she could keep him none the wiser, it would make home life a lot easier.

'Where's your car?'

Her work life, on the other hand . . . She sighed and looked up at Hank, looming over her desk like a hawk with vision too sharp for his own good. 'At the shop. It's overdue for a tune up.'

He gave her a look that was skeptical, suspicious and worried all at once. She decided that ignoring him was the best course of action. It lasted two seconds.

'Orsi – the *Buckaroos* showrunner – lawyered up last night and I had to release him,' Hank said. 'I think—'

'You. There you are.' The shout came from the hallway. A little white man with bristling hair and rodent eyes scurried through the doorway. Sheila and Hank groaned at the same time.

'You incompetent, dangerous, unqualified . . .' Edrick Fizzel sputtered to a stop, having apparently exhausted his repertoire of adjectives.

'Hello, commissioner,' Hank said calmly. 'What can I do for you this fine spring morning?'

Skinny white arms started flapping. 'You caused a riot. The emergency room is full of injured tourists. Injured at a show. Our life blood – tourist shows. And you caused a riot at one of them. People trampled. Total chaos. All your fault.'

Hank leaned against Sheila's desk and made a show of nonchalantly crossing his arms.

'I would say it was more of a melee than a riot,' he said.

Sheila snickered. Fizzel flushed a shade of deep maroon that she'd only ever seen on a color wheel.

'You . . . you will be held to answer for this. I'm calling a special commission meeting for tomorrow. And you're ordered to be there to explain your actions. And how far this department has fallen under your disgraceful leadership.'

Sheila braced herself. On the What-Not-to-Do-When-Dealing-With-Hank checklist, Fizzel had just ticked several boxes. She saw Hank's shoulders stiffen.

'And . . . and that wrongful termination lawsuit your deputies filed. We'll absolutely be discussing that. I almost forgot about it. You'd think that was the most reprehensible thing you'd done. But no, now there's also the Buckaroo bloodbath.'

Hank straightened. 'More of a fracas, really.' He gestured toward the door, which Sheila considered too nice an invitation to leave. He should have used a boot to the ass.

'You can't make me leave. I funded this building.'

'And I run it.' He moved one step closer to the little man. 'So unless you need assistance as one of my constituents, you need to leave so we can get back to work.'

Fizzel backed up with Hank following, his hand still raised in faux niceness. Once the commissioner crossed the threshold, spluttering nonsensically, Hank swung the door shut in his face. He didn't turn back around. She kept an eye on his stiff spine while she did a quick Google search. He finally took a deep breath and came back to her desk.

'It's up on the county website. Special meeting tomorrow at ten a.m. Agenda items are the discussion of sheriff's department litigation and feedback regarding weekend criminal incident and increase in the homicide rate.'

'Feedback?' he snorted. 'I'm not their subordinate. I'm just as much a duly elected official as they are.'

It went on from there – a lot of griping, some swearing, a few observations about Fizzel that used the words 'porcupine' and 'moron' multiple times – and then a curt 'thanks for listening'. He stomped into his inner office and closed the door. Sheila reached over and closed the second window of her web browser. No need for him to find out about that just yet. If at all.

'There are a few things you neglected to tell me the last time we spoke, Ms Fettic.'

'Oh?'

Hank was doing whatever work he could that didn't involve leaving his office. And this phone call had been a priority since Cameron Cooper told them about a blue minivan.

'Where were you last Sunday? Not yesterday, but eight days ago.' The day Gillam was killed.

'Out and about, I suppose.' She tried to disguise the question in her tone – *how much does he know?* – but it came through anyway. She was new at this.

'Out and about in Lee's Summit? Or somewhere else?'

Silence.

'I . . . I was in Branson,' she said finally.

'Why?'

She wanted to speak to the showrunners in person – to tell them she was filing a lawsuit, demand to know how they could be so greedy and heartless. But the trip turned out to be a waste of time. She wasn't able to talk to either of them. She gave up and came back home, hitting slightly heavy traffic and stopping for dinner on the way. That left the time window open – she could have killed Gillam and still made it home by midnight.

'You say you didn't speak with the show managers, but did you see either of them at all?' Hank said, bringing the conversation back to Branson.

'Oh, is that what you've been getting at? Yes, I saw the Buckaroo man. At least, I saw a man in the Buckaroo parking lot, arguing with a woman about the show. They were yelling at each other pretty loudly. Then they each got in their cars and drove off really fast, so I didn't get a chance to talk to the man.'

She said she didn't find out until a few days ago that the lady was the same local businesswoman who had been murdered. After all, she hadn't known the lady's name when she saw her in the parking lot.

'I'm sorry I didn't call you about the argument once I realized that,' she said. 'But I guess the Buckaroo man admitted to arguing with her, since you know about it. You know what, though.' She paused. 'You should be looking for that scruffy man, sheriff. Driving a dented hatchback. He was over in a corner of the parking lot the whole time they were arguing. And he looked pretty damn upset when they both left.'

Hank didn't mention that the scruffy man was in custody. 'The argument you heard – did that change your opinion about anything?'

'It'll be great ammunition for the lawsuit, that's for sure. That bald guy was furious about having to call so many ambulances. He was basically admitting that withholding food was a deliberate tactic.'

It wasn't her opinion of Stone Cold that Hank was interested in. He waited.

'Um . . . and I suppose,' she said, finally filling the silence, 'that it let me know there was another person involved in the whole thing? I certainly hadn't realized that before.'

'How did that make you feel?'

'Make me feel?' The derision in her tone about melted the phone line. 'What kind of a question is that? It made me feel like I should add her to the lawsuit, that's what.'

'Did you follow her?'

'What? Wait – are you asking . . . do you think? You've got to be kidding. I didn't kill her. I can't believe you would think that. That's outrageous.'

Hank leaned back in his chair. This lady wasn't doing herself any favors. He told her someone would be up to interview her later in the week. He wanted to go up there and do it right now, but he had to deal with the commission meeting first.

'You'll need to go through my lawyer,' Fettic said. 'I'm not saying anything else. I try to help you, and you make me a suspect. What's this world coming to?'

She slammed down the phone. Hank replaced his own handset and turned to his computer. The commission meeting could wait. His new priority was a search warrant request for Lisa Fettic-Posky's blue minivan.

THIRTY-ONE

Music Show Melee, Lawsuit Costs Provoke Hostilities at Special Meeting

By Jadhur Banerjee

Branson Daily Herald staff writer

Forsyth – Long-simmering tensions exploded into the open Tuesday as county commissioners blasted Sheriff Hank Worth's management practices and handling of this weekend's mass casualty theater incident, and he accused them of holding his budget – and the safety of local residents – hostage.

'Any personnel decisions that I've made were checked with the county's attorney,' Worth said at the specially called county commission meeting. 'Those deputies were fired for not reporting for duty. They didn't call in sick. They didn't have vacation approval. They just didn't show. So they were dismissed.' At that Worth paused. 'So I dismissed them. It was my decision, and I had every right under employment law to do it.'

Terminated deputies, including former sheriff candidate Gerald Tucker and deputies Randy Wilcox and Chris Dinson, filed suit last week against the county as well as Worth and Chief Deputy Sheila Turley.

'Those men had 50-plus decades of local law enforcement experience. Not like your newbie ass,' said Commissioner Edrick Fizzel, using the jabbing finger-point from the dais that he's well known for in local circles. 'Now we have to pay legal bills caused by your negligence.'

Worth, standing at the podium just feet away, didn't back down. 'I consulted the Association of Counties attorney service that this county uses for all its departments. I was told that I had authority under the employment agreements to dismiss those deputies. Only then did I move ahead with it. You can see all of that communication in the packets I've provided.' The lawsuit should be easy to defend, Worth added.

Pending litigation is usually discussed in closed session, but the commissioners chose to address it this time during a public meeting. They declined to say why.

'What if we don't defend it? You should pay for it out of your existing budget,' said Commissioner William Farnell.

The suggestion seemed to stun Worth. 'You've cut us to the bone already. We need new squad cars. We need a communications upgrade. It's to the point where you're not funding basic public safety. And now you're saying you won't pay for attorney costs under a county government system where you're clearly responsible for it?'

'Any anger you have should be directed at the former employees wasting your and the court system's time,' Worth added.

There should be a way to compromise on cost apportionment, said Lynwood O'Donnell, the commissioner known for his dislike of controversy and confrontation. Both his commission colleagues and the sheriff ignored him.

'You want to talk about public safety? Fine,' Fizzel said. 'What about the riot on Sunday? Where dozens of tourists were injured on your watch. That's what you call keeping the public safe?'

Fizzel was referring to Sunday's melee at the *Breakfast Buckaroos* show, where 15 people were injured after panic broke out in the middle of a performance. Worth pointed out the error of Fizzel's injury count and said the incident is still under investigation.

'The reaction of the crowd in that theater was the direct result of the show and its treatment of the audience,' Worth said. 'We responded immediately, de-escalated the situation, and provided aid. We did our jobs, and we did them well.'

The tourism industry provides much of both tax revenue and employment in the area, all three commissioners said, adding that protecting visitors should be the sheriff department's highest priority. Worth began to point out that the Buckaroo incident occurred within city police department jurisdiction, but stopped midway through his comment and instead asked how he was supposed to ensure tourist safety when his budget is repeatedly slashed.

'You'll get money when you earn it,' Fizzel said.

The long-serving commissioner is a frequent critic of the sheriff and has blamed him for the increasing county homicide rate, which has jumped markedly since Worth took office. The most recent murder happened just one week ago. Branson city resident Vivian N. Gillam was found dead in a field along Fall Creek Road. To date, no one has been arrested in connection with the killing. Worth declined after the meeting to discuss that investigation.

During the session, which lasted more than three hours, Worth repeatedly defended his deputies, including Turley. She became chief deputy after his election last year.

'Don't you think you'd be better able to respond to threats like the Buckaroo disaster if you hadn't fired good men like Gerald Tucker?' Farnell said.

At that, Worth picked up his stack of papers from the

podium and took a seat in the audience. He did not return to speak again during the meeting, but also did not leave.

Tucker lost last year's election to Worth, who had been appointed months before to fill the vacancy left when long-time sheriff Darrell Gibbons won a seat in the state legislature. Tucker was backed by two of the three commissioners, as well as prominent businessman Henry Gallagher. Gibbons, however, endorsed Worth in a move many viewed as being key to Worth's victory and illustrated the rapidly shifting allegiances that have always made Branson County a tricky place to survive politically. He had no comment on the board meeting Tuesday.

'That is a matter between those fine men,' Gibbons said from his office in Jefferson City. 'I'm sure they'll work it all out.'

'That reporter kid got his story up online awful quick. The smoke hasn't even stopped coming out of your ears yet.'

Hank pinched the bridge of his nose for what felt like the twentieth time in the last hour. Maybe this time it would help the headache. And the blood pressure. And the clenched jaw. He opened his eyes and looked at Sheila. She'd settled into the chair across from his desk. A steaming cup of tea sat in front of him.

'I know it's not coffee. Drink it anyway. It's calming.'

He glared at her. 'Is it two parts bourbon? Because that's about the only brown liquid that's going to calm me right now.'

'So how bad was it?'

'You're the one who read the news article. You tell me.'

She just sat there. He could try to outlast her but he wouldn't be able to, so he might as well save them both some time.

'I would rather have been dragged naked over sharp gravel.' He poked at the mug. 'No. That'd just be painful. Today was more than that.' He dunked the teabag as Fizzel's condescension replayed in his head. 'I would rather be forced to reinstall Windows on my computer. It would be less frustrating than that meeting.'

He had walked out of the commission chambers without getting a clear answer on whether the bozos would fund the county's defense against the lawsuit. Which was a victory, really. It meant they knew they had to. If they could have voted to refuse, they sure as hell would have. But man, was it going to cost him. Literally, in terms of his department's budget. And figuratively, in terms of God knew what else. His political standing, probably. His sanity, definitely.

'It would've been nice to have the county association lawyer there,' he said after some more manhandling of the teabag. 'Even to dial in on the phone. But I couldn't get a hold of him.'

Sheila snorted. 'Figures. Why would they be available to talk to their clients?' she paused. 'You think he'll give us advice about us getting sued personally?'

'I hope so. I hope he'll say he can handle that, too.' He watched her raise a very skeptical eyebrow and silently agreed with her. 'Or at least maybe he can point us in the right direction.'

He kept at the tea until Sheila finally grew tired of his fidgeting and snatched away the mug.

'Waste of a perfectly good cup of—' She stopped as her cell phone buzzed. She glanced at it and rose to her feet. 'Speaking of lawyers, you should see if Axel Orsi's will let him sit down for an interview.'

Now it was Hank who snorted. 'Not likely.' But Sheila was already out the door. He sighed and pinched the bridge of his nose again. It still didn't help.

She met Dale outside Henry Gallagher's fancy headquarters. It was almost the end of the workday and he was hoping the businessman would come out to his car soon. 'Better to chat with him in the parking lot than have to identify ourselves to a secretary. Don't look at me that way,' he said as she arched an eyebrow at him. 'This man brings in a lot of city tax dollars and I want to keep this quiet until we find out if he's involved.'

At least that dovetailed with her own reason for keeping it quiet – so Hank wouldn't find out. She nodded. It was only ten minutes before he walked out, juggling a laptop bag and several rolls of blueprints. Dale stepped forward and introduced himself. He turned toward Sheila.

'We've met,' they said at the same time. She forced a neutral look onto her face. He didn't bother.

'What do you want?'

'We're investigating a rash of high-end car thefts,' Dale said. 'There was a lot of activity the last two weekends. We were just wondering where you were those Saturday and Sunday nights – only to figure out where the thieves' might have chosen to avoid. You obviously haven't had any cars stolen, so that might mean the places you were, well, that they're better secured. Which would be helpful to businesses and homes that have been victimized. We're asking several other prominent residents the same question.'

That was one of the most ridiculous things Sheila had ever heard. What was Dale thinking? But the 'high-end' and 'prominent' strokes to Gallagher's ego worked. He gave a regal nod of agreement and listed off his activities as he put the blueprints in the back seat of his Range Rover. Dale took studious notes. She watched him carefully. There was no pause or flinch when he got to the Sunday that Gillam died.

'I was home. Which is a bit north, off Highway 65. But fairly isolated and fully fenced and gated.'

'Sounds like a nice way to spend a Sunday evening. Any guests?'

Now he started to look at them suspiciously. Dale scrambled. 'On that night or any of the other ones you spent at home? Just trying to figure out if it's possible your place is a known gathering spot for—'

'Ah. For high-end cars? I see. No guests that night. Only the previous Saturday. I must say, detective, this is a little odd.'

'Well, we're just trying to use every piece of information we can,' Sheila said. 'So we appreciate your time.' She wanted to grab Dale's arm and drag him away. Instead she had to wait for him to shake the pompous man's hand and chit-chat about his volunteer work with the local animal shelter. Was he going to donate money for another building to go with the first one he funded? Did he see an increase in demand with the springtime kitten season? She stifled a groan and started to inch toward her squad car, and he finally got the hint.

'You are a piece of work,' she said once Gallagher pulled out of the parking lot. 'How that actually succeeded . . .'

'I didn't think it would, to be honest. But we got what we needed.'

'At home with no guests. And we know he lives alone. So he has no alibi.'

Dale folded his arms across his wide chest and gave her a stern frown. 'Now we need to tell Hank. Well, *you* need to tell Hank.'

She thought about the county commission meeting. 'Now is . . . not the best time . . .'

She wasn't the type of person who put things off. Or avoided difficult tasks. Or come to think of it, the type of person who worried about driving home alone late at night. This last week had turned her into a person who did all three. And it was starting to piss her off. She sighed and trudged off to her car, leaving a befuddled Dale standing alone in the parking lot.

THIRTY-TWO

No one in Gillam's neighborhood had seen a clean-cut Christian music star. Right after the murder, deputies showed around the nicely lit publicity photo and came up empty. But now they had a scruffy, unwashed guitarist instead, so Sam was going door-to-door with Cooper's current look in hand. He'd showed the mugshot throughout the neighborhood with no luck until he got to a house near the residential street's intersection with Fall Creek Road.

'Oh yeah, I remember him.' The homeowner flicked on his porch light to beat back the approaching twilight and took the photo. 'He was in an old beater car. That's what made me notice in the first place. Don't see many of those in this neighborhood.'

The guy, stocky and with a graying goatee, had been working in his front yard when the hatchback drove by. It was probably a half hour later when it drove back out.

'Are you sure? It was that long?' Sam asked. Cooper had said his aunt was leaving when he arrived and that was why he followed her. That scenario wouldn't have taken thirty minutes. He thought about how to phrase his next question. Never lead a witness, the Chief always said. 'Did you see anything else around that time?'

'Well, the Vivian lady left.'

Sam frowned. The dude hadn't said anything during the first canvass about seeing Vivian Gillam in the afternoon. Just that he hadn't seen her that evening, when she'd gone to the yoga studio.

'The other cop who came didn't ask about the afternoon. Just that evening. So I didn't think it was important. Sorry. She left in between when the scruffy guy came and went.'

'Did it look like he was following her?'

'Maybe? He could've been a few minutes behind her. He certainly wasn't right on her bumper or anything.' The dude turned and looked down the quiet street, pointing to where it curved to the left and then continued farther into the neighborhood. 'If he sat there, he could see which way she turned when she got here at the intersection with Fall Creek. I never looked that way, so I'm not saying he did. I'm just thinking, you can only go right or left, then there's really not much for a ways. If he saw which way she went, it'd be easy to catch up with her before she got onto a more crowded street.'

That was a good point. And if it was true, it would be even more evidence that Cooper was lying in wait – not innocently tagging along after accidentally arriving as she left the house. Sam thanked the guy and started walking back into the neighborhood. He'd left the squad car in one of the cul-de-sacs around the corner. He got the length of three houses when he heard yelling. He turned to see the goateed neighbor jogging toward him.

'Somebody just sent out a message on the Nextdoor app saying that a guy named Nils wants to talk to you. He remembered something.' He read off the address, which Sam ended up not needing. The gaggle of people outside the house was direction enough. They all fell silent as he approached. A shortish, pudgy guy with trendy glasses was nudged forward.

'We, um, were all chatting about the police being here again.' He hitched up his glasses and cleared his throat sheepishly. 'And I said something about Leslie's visitor on Sunday, and that meant Leslie had an alibi, ha-ha.'

Sam looked at the group. A slender woman raised her hand a

little. 'That's me. I asked Nils what the heck he was talking about. I didn't have any visitors on Sunday. Or Monday even.'

'So I said, "well, what was that car parked on the street outside your house late that night?" And that's when we started asking around and all of us realized – everybody thought it was somebody else's visitor and so no one had mentioned it to you.'

The back of Sam's neck started to tingle. They weren't talking about Cooper and his borrowed beater. This would've been a car that fit in with the neighborhood. He carefully took down a description, gave everyone on the sidewalk his card in case they thought of anything else, and practically ran back to his car.

Earl, the Energizer bunny of almost-retirees, had gone back to work today and already had information to report. It was almost dark by the time Sheila made it to the rock outcropping in the park.

'Something happened with Bubba and the new girl. Sorry – new woman. Deputy Boggs. Some kind of physical altercation.'

Dear God. A dozen horrible scenarios flashed through her head, all of them ending with a traumatized Amber Boggs.

'I didn't see any of it, cuz of course I was at my desk in the lobby. But oh my, I wish I had. Although I suppose it was gift enough to see Bubba walking around with a black eye.'

Sheila stared at him. Bubba came out the worse for it? 'Was Boggs hurt?'

'Oh, heck no. I don't think a freight train could hurt that girl. Woman. Female. Person. She ain't moving for nobody.' She'd been walking down the cell block corridor with Bubba coming toward her from the opposite direction. As they passed, he slammed into her with his shoulder. With his three-hundred-pound frame. The lad in cell four said she smacked into the bars on his cell door pretty hard. She didn't say a word, just kept walking. She did her cell check and was coming back when Bubba waddled down the corridor again. This time, every inmate was paying attention.

'And Lord, she was ready for him. Sidestepped him like a dancer. He'd been leaning in her direction so hard, he kept going through the open space she left behind. Quick as anything, she was on the other side of him. And bam. Dug her own shoulder in. With that and his momentum . . .' Earl had to rein in his delighted grin before he could get any more words out. 'He hit those bars with the side of his face. Big ol' red mark down his cheek and the start of one hell of a shiner.'

Sheila's smile started to match Earl's. 'And you're sure on all this?'

'Oh, yeah. I saw Bubba and decided to use my break time to walk to the nice little bench out by the sally port. Quickest way there is through the cell block.'

Which Earl technically wasn't supposed to enter.

'Didn't figure you'd mind,' he continued.

She most certainly did not. She was so proud of Boggs she wanted to hug the kid. Probably wiser to just compliment her, though. She asked Earl a few more questions and gave him instructions for the next couple of days.

'It's all starting to come to a head, isn't it?' he said quietly as she stepped toward the path that would take her back to where she'd left her Forerunner at the edge of the park. She considered his question and nodded.

'Yeah. It is. Especially after today. If I can get him formally disciplined for this, and add it to what's already in his file, I might be a lot closer to being able to fire him.' She scoffed at herself. 'Then he'll be able to join Tucker's lawsuit. But at least he won't be stirring up shit at work every day.'

She said good night and watched as Earl trundled off toward the parking lot. She wasn't sure if Boggs's actions would ultimately help or hurt her and Hank. Even if it wound up hurting in the end, though, Bubba's black eye sure felt good right now.

The conversation with the county association lawyer was running through his head on a loop, so it took Hank longer than it should have to realize someone was following him. He radioed dispatch, but no one had called in a request for assistance. He looked in the rear-view mirror again. The twilight coupled with the headlight glare made it hard to see who was behind the wheel. He didn't feel like leading the person straight to his front door, so instead of continuing home, he turned onto a side street near Gretna Road and pulled over. The car did the same, stopping a few lengths behind him. Hank gave Dean at dispatch his exact location and as much of a description as he could before checking his Glock and getting out of the squad car. He stood beside his driver's door and waited.

Suddenly the headlights flipped off and Hank had a clear view. He reached in for the radio and updated Dean, then started toward the sedan and the cueball head visible even in the dark.

'Mr Orsi.'

The *Buckaroos* showrunner had the engine off and his hands on the dash in full view. He was doing everything but waving a white flag. Hank wasn't buying it.

'What exactly can I do for you this evening?' He tried to keep his tone even.

Stone Cold's sizable hands flexed into fists and just as quickly flattened back out. 'I . . . I . . . how are the old folks? I haven't been able to find out. The hospital wouldn't tell me anything.'

That certainly wasn't what Hank was expecting. 'Two of them are still in the hospital. The man with the broken nose and the lady with the cane.'

'Did she end up breaking her hip?'

'No. Pelvis.'

Stone Cold swore, putting together a combination of words Hank had never heard in that particular order. He ran a hand over his bald head. 'I'm so sorry.'

'If you're that concerned about other people, why would you do it in the first place? Starving and pressuring them – it had to have been clear to you from the get-go that what Gillam wanted was pretty shitty.'

Stone Cold tensed. 'It was just a sales tactic. A nudge.'

Hank eyed him. The guy was deliberately talking to him without his lawyer, and Hank would be an idiot not to take advantage of it. 'That sounds like something your attorney would say. I want to know what you really thought when you signed with Gillam, and then what happened during that argument on Sunday.'

Stone Cold shifted in the driver's seat and scoffed. 'I thought I was saving my damn show. We're shoestring, man. Bare bones. I thought it would be easy money down here, but it only is if you get in with somebody. A tour company, or a timeshare. Otherwise you're selling tickets at the door, and that shit only works if you got brand recognition like the Chinese Acrobats or Shoji Tabuchi.'

When Gillam made him the offer, it seemed like it would solve everything. Steady crowds, and all he had to do was spin a sales pitch and change the timing on the food. Easy. He had no idea there would be blood sugar problems.

'I don't believe you,' Hank said flatly. 'That was the whole damn point. Get them shaky and confused and then pressure them to sign contracts.'

'No. She never said that. She just gave me the sequence, what order everything had to go in. I didn't think anything of it. Until the second dude collapsed. The first time – OK. Whatever. Twice? Then two more? And then you show up?'

He sounded confounded by it. Was he that naïve? 'What did you do before you started this show?' Hank asked.

He'd worked construction. Laying bricks and decorative rocks that meant bending and lifting and kneeling all day. He was good at it, but his body just couldn't do it anymore. He sold his construction book of business and used that money to buy the show. It was already up and running, and he thought he'd just step in, no problem. But the purchase didn't come with any tour partnerships and he didn't figure out how crucial that was until he was already committed. And then Vivian Gillam walked in.

'Like I said, it was a good deal. Until everything started happening.'

'And how did that make you feel?'

Orsi angled his head to get a better look at Hank standing outside his car. 'What are you, a therapist?'

'Fine,' Hank said. 'We can do it a different way. You were angry. You were so angry that you had a yelling match with Vivian in your parking lot on the day she died. And then you went to her house later on, and you beat her to death.'

'Whoa. Hell, no.' Now he was puffing up, stiffening in his seat, his shoulders filling all the available space. Hank put his hand on his holster. Orsi saw it and took a breath. 'I didn't kill her,' he finally said. 'I don't know where she lives, and I didn't kill her.'

'What did you say to her during the argument?'

Stone Cold told him. Lots of 'your fault not mine' and 'not going to hold back the food anymore'.

'And what did she say?'

'It was all about what you asked me, what I told you.'

'You didn't tell me anything.'

'I know. I told *her* that. And she said that if I violate the nondisclosure, then the wrath of the Almighty Business God would come down on me. That I'd be screwing myself royally, and her, too.'

That made it sound like Gillam was answering to someone. 'The "wrath of the Almighty Business God" is exactly what she said?'

'Yep.'

'Any idea who she was referring to?'

'Nope. But it worried her. 'Cause it was also a panicky kind of yelling, not just a pissed-off yelling, you know what I mean?' He paused. 'Like she thought things were slipping out of her control. She was definitely rattled.'

'What happened after she said all that?'

'She got in her car and left. Yelled at me to keep doing everything like I had been, until I heard back from her. Then she drove away. And that's all I got, man. I don't know anything else.'

'Why did you decide to talk to me without your lawyer?'

'I figured it was the only way to find out how the old folks were doing. Plus, the lawyer's a douchebag. I need to find a new one. What I'm going to pay him with, I don't know.' The last part was muttered under his breath as he started his car. Hank watched him drive away and wondered how much of what Orsi said was true. Either all of it or none of it. And his gut feeling, which usually helped in situations like this, couldn't tell which.

THIRTY-THREE

It was almost dark and the temperature was cooling quickly. Not the crackling cold of a few months ago, but the crisp snap of an early-spring evening. Sheila filled her lungs with the potpourri of tree blossoms and took the fork in the path toward her SUV.

She wondered what Tyrone was cooking for dinner. And she wondered how she'd even be able to pay attention to his day after everything Earl just told her. What was she going to do about it?

She kept on, walking and thinking. She could take a page from Boggs's book.

Use their momentum against them.

She needed to get witness statements before any of those inmates got released and disappeared to who-knew-where. Would the word of a cell row full of no-accounts be enough to counteract what were sure to be Bubba's lies? Maybe. She needed to warn the county HR department, because he'd probably want disability leave. And he'd probably sue. Ha. He'd have to get in line. Her thoughts flitted from there to her own lawsuit and whether—

The next thing she knew the gravel path was coming to meet her. Hard and fast. She went sprawling, barely getting her hands out in front of her. She slid forward on her palms and her chin as her lungs exploded in a blunt-force exhale. Her left foot was the only part of her that hadn't moved. She heaved herself onto her left side and got her right hand on her service weapon before taking the time to look back at her boot. It had stayed hooked over the spaghetti-thin steel cable stretched across the trail.

She scanned the trees on either side of her. Nothing. She yanked her boot off the cable and sat up, then slowly rose to her feet, her hand never leaving her Glock. She was still several hundred yards from her vehicle. She stood still and listened. Nothing but night-time insects. They weren't what was giving her the feeling she was being watched, though. She patted at her hair and calmly set off toward the Forerunner. At least she hoped she looked calm. She kept off the path because Lord Jesus, if she was on it and looking down for another ankle-height wire, the next one could be placed level with her voice box.

She was about halfway to the car when she saw a flash of white off to her right. Pasty farmboy white. She spun and lunged toward it. *You gonna run now that I'm on my feet? You goin' back home to your mama? You ain't even gonna be safe there. I'll get you. There. Anywhere.*

She didn't know if she was talking or thinking. But she was definitely running. Branches lashed at her face and she kept skidding on the mildewed mat of leaves left over from the winter of freeze and thaw. She was tracking by sound now since the white was no longer standing still. She followed crashing footsteps and wheezy breathing and was almost there. Almost to him. She thought she saw the road flash by on her left but she wasn't sure. She heard him slip and pushed faster at the advantage.

And then . . . nothing. The tree limb found her middle. She doubled over and her chest exploded with pain. The tree limb swung back, winding up again as she pitched forward into the dirt. It got her again before she was fully down. The next blow came on her side, then her back. Then . . . nothing.

What the fuck are you doing? Are you insane?

She tried to focus but the buzzing was too loud. She couldn't tell what was there and what wasn't. If she could just stop breathing, then the stabbing pain in her side would go away. Good. She'd try that.

We gotta go. Now.

No. She didn't want to. She sank deeper into the buzzing.

It was so dark. She lay perfectly still until her body was able to tell her that she was oriented face down. In what tasted like a pile of moldy leaves. She listened and heard only buzzing. She couldn't tell if it was coming from inside or out. No human sounds. She rolled onto her side and spat out a leaf. The pain seared her middle and flamed around to her back and then came up to her arm and then somehow down again and joined up back where it started. Where it kept bursting into fireballs of agony.

She did another quarter roll. Now on her back, she could see stars through the trees. So her eyes were still working at least. Small favors. She tried to sit up, which turned out to be a very bad idea. She curled up in a ball for a while until the worst of the pulsar pain retreated and she was left with only yellow sun-temperature pain. She kept her eyes on the stars as she felt in her shirt pocket for her phone. The screen was broken. She managed to get the emergency call button to work, but when it picked up she couldn't talk.

'What is your emergency? Are you alright? Where are you? Sir? Ma'am?'

She finally coughed out the name of the road where her car was parked. 'Forerunner. Blue. Ambulance.'

'I need you to stay on the line with me.'

She put the phone back in her pocket, which nicely muffled the incessant questioning. She had to make it to her car. They'd never find her out in the middle of the goddamn woods. She took one last look at the stars and rolled onto her stomach again, then forced herself onto her hands and knees. The pain made her gag. Could she just crawl? No. She had no idea where she was in relation to the road. She dragged herself over to a tree and used it to leverage her sorry ass to a standing position.

That it had come to this . . .

They'd been careful. Her and Earl. But careful about being seen. About being overheard. Those were the worries. Physical safety? Not a worry. She laughed as she spat a glob of blood onto the ground. That made the world tilt. She clutched the tree until it stopped. Then she forced herself to look around. She had to find the road. A section of trees to her left were thinner than everywhere else. Maybe. The shadows were less dense, anyway. She'd head that way.

Three steps away from the tree and she was eating leaves again. She lay gasping on her stomach as the pulsar reignited.

She wasn't going to let them do this. She was just trying to do her job in this fucking town. She swiped at the wetness dripping down her cheeks. Ain't nobody going to see her cry, not even the trees. She got her elbows under her and then made it to her hands and knees. And crawled.

THIRTY-FOUR

What was this place coming to? A woman found beaten on the side of the road? Jesus. Maggie looked at the vitals that the ambulance crew had called in and started prepping. First a CT scan and then possibly the OR. She gloved up and went to meet the rig.

Larry Alcoate was the first one out, looking ashen and shaky.

The diagnostic part of her brain took note – maybe the start of a virus. Then the gurney slid out of the back and she saw a hand the color of mahogany. She felt her knees weaken. She pushed the other medic out of the way and looked down into Sheila's oxygen-masked face.

'Yeah. We found her out by Caudill Way. Laying in the dirt. The city cops are on the way out there now.'

She barely heard him. She was already pulling the stretcher toward the entrance. This was her greatest nightmare. Injured police showing up at her ER. Her fears mostly centered on one person. It wasn't him, but it was the closest thing to family there could be. She grabbed Sheila's hand and yelled back at Larry.

'Call Hank.'

He ran lights and sirens the whole way and arrived shaking so badly he could barely get out of the squad car. He leaned against the door for a minute and scanned the roadway for Raker. The guy had to be out here. Larry told him they'd called city police the minute they realized what – and who – they'd found. 'It's bad, man. Honestly, I wouldn't bother with the hospital first. I think she's going to end up in surgery. You're not going to be able to see her.'

He'd left Duncan and the kids staring open-mouthed as he bolted from the dinner table, a fork still in his hand. Now he realized it was sticking out of his shirt pocket. He tossed it in the car and started toward the flashing lights. Three Branson Police cars lined the road and their evidence folks were unloading floodlights from a van. He spotted Raker's squat silhouette.

'We think we've found the spot where she was attacked.' He turned toward Hank. 'What the fuck is going on? What was she even doing out here?'

'I have no idea. This wouldn't be a park she'd use to go jogging or anything. It's nowhere near her house.'

Raker looked back at the woods. 'She doesn't go out to jog. Uses a treadmill at home. Can't get harassed that way.'

Hank hadn't known that. He felt even more sick.

'Come with me,' Raker ordered and started into the trees. Hank obeyed. They got to a section about four hundred yards in where there clearly had been a struggle. A lean, middle-aged officer pointed farther in.

'There was running first. Probably from the path. Which is what she had to be on. Walking to or from her car. Then the running through the trees.' He thought for a minute. 'Likely walking *to* her car, from the look of the tracks. But—'

A shout cut through the air. Everyone went running, cutting away from the tracks and crime scene tape. Another officer stood on the path, dusting dirt off his knees. 'Goddamn wire. Right there. Tripped right over it.'

Hank swore.

Raker exploded.

'I want this whole park sealed off. I want a grid search. I want to know if this was random or if Turley was targeted specifically. I want answers. Now.'

His men scattered and went to work. He paced for a minute, then spun and glared at Hank. 'You and I both know this wasn't random. You don't string wire across a barely used park path on the off-chance you can trip someone and take their wallet. You do it because you already know who's going to come walking along. Who would be following her, Worth?'

Hank stared down at the wire. This was no longer internecine department drama. This was assault. With, dear God, great bodily injury. And that meant . . .

'I'll say it again.' Raker stabbed a finger at Hank. 'Who followed her? What do you have her doing? What danger have you put her in?'

'You know we fired Tucker. And those others. Now they've sued us. They want their jobs – and their overtime – back.'

'And you made her the point person?'

'She's in charge of staffing.' He stopped. That sounded like what it was. Shifting the blame. Weaseling out of it. He started again. 'All of this is me. My decision to crack down on the overtime. My way to balance our budget. I made that very clear.'

'Oh, so you thought if they retaliated, they'd surely just come after you? That Tucker, of all people, would follow some kind of decorum?' Raker glared some more. 'You're an idiot.'

One half of his brain was glad Sheila had such a devoted friend. The other half prayed Raker would stop talking. Every word was a knife to the gut. That he deserved. He looked down at the torn-up trail. 'It should've been me.' The words were barely a whisper.

'Yeah, well, it was never going to be you.' Raker turned away. 'Because you're a six-foot-two white guy. And she's not.'

Travis Beckham. Honda Accord.

Axel Orsi. Nissan Altima.

Lisa Fettic-Posky, the ticked-off daughter of a timeshare victim. Blue minivan. But her husband owned a Audi A6 sedan.

Aaron Engelman, another victim relative. Brand-new Hyundai Sonata. Sam was pretty sure he wasn't the one who killed Vivian Gillam, but you always check.

None of the vehicles were a match, though. The color was a bit off, or the body style, or some other little point. But it had been dark when the neighbors saw it that night. They understandably might have gotten some details wrong. He was looking over everything again when his phone buzzed.

Dude that's messed up about your boss.

It was a hunting buddy who worked for Branson City PD.

??? IDK what you're talking about.
You didn't hear? She's in the hospital. Got beat up at some park. It's all over our comms.

His phone hit the table with a clunk. City's communication and dispatch were separate from theirs. He hadn't heard a thing. Nobody had told him a thing. He raced to Branson Valley General. He was just pulling into the parking lot when Hank called.

'There's no point going inside,' he said. 'She's still in surgery. Until she's out, we need to focus on why she was at that park in the first place.'

'I have no idea. Does Mr Turley know why?'

'No.' The Chief's voice sounded like it was coming from a deep well, hollow and lifeless.

'You don't really think it could be those guys, do you?'

'Tucker blew up a boat. Harassed anybody he could once I

assigned him to the jail. I've seen him drive by my house a few times since I fired him. I can definitely see him stringing wire across a path. To intimidate her, scare her, that kind of thing.'

'But they said she was beaten up. Not just tripped on a path.'

'Yeah. She was. And that's the thing. That goes way, way beyond.' Hank was sounding completely lost. Sam's worry increased exponentially.

'What does City PD need us to do?'

Hank let out a breath. 'Nothing. I've been ordered to do nothing. But why was she at that park? That's *our* question. Because it has to be related to something with us. The staffing. Or the Gillam case. Something about us.'

He was right. Sam thought a minute. When he'd talked to Sheila that afternoon, nothing had been out of the ordinary except for one muttered aside about somebody getting on her nerves. Well, that was normal, too, actually.

'Can you think of anything?' Hank asked.

'No,' Sam said, looking out his windshield at the entrance to the ER and the person who had just trudged through it. 'But you need to get here. Your wife is out of surgery.'

Hank hung up on him. Sam pocketed his phone and slowly got out of his car. He didn't want to ask. He was terrified of what she would tell him. He forced himself to walk toward the building. Dr McCleary didn't see him until he was under the portico.

'Oh, honey, don't cry.' She put her hand on his shoulder. 'It's . . . well, she's in recovery now. You can come into the waiting room, but I need you to get a hold of yourself, OK? Tyrone is here, with his sister. They . . .'

They didn't need Sheila's work colleague blubbering in their faces. He nodded and swiped at his nose. She gave his arm a kind squeeze and guided him through the doors, stopping to grab a tissue from a sanitizer station on the other side. By the time they got to the surgical waiting room, he had stopped sniffling and crammed the Kleenex in his pocket. And man, was he glad. He didn't need to be adding to the misery that huddled on the hard bench against the wall. He'd never seen Mr Turley without a smile on his face. The guy was always cheerful and ready with a joke or some friendly question about your life. Now he sat hunched over with his elbows on his knees and his hands laced in prayer. A woman with the same light brown skin and sharp cheekbones leaned against him. She looked up as they approached.

Sam didn't know what to say. He introduced himself. She was who he'd thought – Mr Turley's sister, Tessa. He sat down a respectful distance away and tried to force the image of a beaten Sheila out of his mind. Dr McCleary disappeared behind the surgical unit doors and the room fell silent. Until the Chief burst in. He'd probably run all the way from the parking lot. He caught his breath in one big gulp and stepped toward the Turleys.

'Tyrone. I'm . . . I'm so sorry.' He knelt down in front of Sheila's husband, who raised his head for the first time. Sam thanked God he wasn't the one on the other end of that stare. He saw the Chief stiffen but his voice stayed calm. 'I need to ask you a question. Everyone – city and county – is working on this. We will find who did this. Do you know why she was there? At that park? Was she meeting someone?'

Mr Turley lowered his head. Hank's shoulders slumped. Just a fraction, but enough to make Sam cringe for him. The silence was awful. Until the sister saved everything.

'You got to think, Ty. Did she say anything? She would've been late coming home, right? Did she tell you anything about that?'

Mr Turley unclasped his hands, flexed his fingers. Didn't raise his head. 'It was her normal late. About once a week, for the past two months maybe. She said it was intelligence gathering.'

That was too long a time period to be anything but the staffing problems. The overtime revolt. The bloodletting. Sam almost vomited at the term they'd thrown around so loosely. Which was now literally reality. Hank thanked Mr Turley and strode from the room. Sam followed.

'She has an informant. It's got to be somebody working in the jail,' he said as Hank started to pace in the hallway. 'Do you think it's one of the new recruits?'

'Maybe.' More pacing. 'Or somebody right under my nose.' He yanked his phone out of his pocket and dialed. 'Where are you right now? OK. Did you meet with Sheila tonight? At the

Lakeside Wilderness?' A pause. 'You gotta tell me, Earl. She's been attacked. We're at the hospital.'

There was an explosion of talk on the other end of the line that Sam couldn't fully make out. When it finally stopped, Hank ordered the old man to lock all his doors and sit tight until he received more instructions. He hung up and turned to Sam. There'd been an incident at the jail. Berkins had been made a fool of by a new deputy. The new *female* deputy.

Under different circumstances, Sam would've reveled in the story. Now it was just the tipping point that was sending them all over a cliff. He said as much.

'Yeah. I think you're exactly right,' Hank said. 'The last straw. For Berkins and the other jail guys, and by extension, for Tucker and the fired ones. But to go this far . . .' He pointed at Sam. 'So I need you over at the Crumblit house tonight. I'm not having him attacked, too.'

Sam nodded. It wasn't going to be the interesting part of the investigation, but he sure could see why it was necessary. Besides, it'd be best not to be anywhere near the Chief and Detective Raker and the wrath of God they were about to unleash.

THIRTY-FIVE

The woman looked down at the business card in her wallet. And then up at the TV high on the wall. And the lady's picture on the screen. Then outside, to the wall of dark beyond the fluorescent lights. So dark. Her eyes made the circuit again and then, hands shaking, she picked up the phone.

It was a shit gas station, down K Highway south of Kirbyville. Two pumps and a store that sold more liquor than soda. Hank pulled in behind a very angry Raker.

'I don't want you here.'

'Deal with it. I'm the one who brought you the lead in the first place.'

He did let the detective push past him at the door, the bell above it announcing them with a weak clack. The woman stood behind the counter, nervous as hell.

'Hello, ma'am,' Raker said. 'You're the one who contacted Deputy Karnes? About the TV news report?'

She nodded. 'He gave me his card when I came to pick up my boys. At the jail. They weren't under arrest. Just stupid. Stupid teenagers.'

Raker nodded encouragingly, which was impressive restraint. Hank could practically feel him vibrating with impatience. 'About the report on the attack . . .?'

The woman wrapped her long, angular arms around her thin middle. 'Before I saw that, two guys came in. Not regulars. All amped up – not on drugs, but like they just ran a race or something.

'They finally bought some beef jerky, a Mountain Dew for the older guy, a fifth of Jack for the younger one, and ten dollars worth of gas on pump two. But the older one was pissed. While they was browsing, he kept shoving at the young guy. Who wouldn't stop whining. He kept saying, "I thought she was going to catch up to you. All I did was stop her. All I did was stop her. It wasn't my fault." And then the older one says, "Scare her. Not kill her, dumbass."'

The woman looked at them with eyes so tired the rings underneath looked like bruises. 'That's when I pretended I had my headphones on and hadn't heard anything.'

Raker raised an eyebrow. 'But that's not when you called it in.'

'I wasn't going to. You keep your mouth shut out here, you know?' Her eyes flicked toward the window. His squad car was in plain view. She hugged herself a little tighter. 'But then I saw her on the TV. The chief deputy lady who was attacked. She was there at the jail, too. She let me explain everything about the neighbor kid and our situation.' She paused. 'She was nice. When she didn't have to be.'

Hank's heart broke even more. Raker didn't even flinch.

'Do you have surveillance cameras?'

She pointed at the far left corner. 'There's one outside, too, but it don't work. Keeps getting shot out.'

She led them into the back after locking the front glass doors.

She and Hank figured out how to cue up the creaky VCR while Raker paced and fidgeted and made an irritating nuisance of himself. Finally the right time frame started playing. The two men came in, just as amped up as she'd said. They could see their stature – the young one skinny and not very tall, the older one in his early fifties maybe and stocky – but their features where obscured by baseball caps pulled low. There was something about the young one, though. The cocky walk looked familiar.

The pair paid and left, disappearing from the camera's view just as they reached the vehicle parked by the pumps. 'Stop it,' both men said at the same time. The poor woman startled at their tone. Hank apologized and asked her to rewind it. This time they ignored the shoppers and focused on what was outside the window.

'You can barely see anything.' Raker swore. 'The license plate isn't even in the camera view at any point.'

Hank straightened. That didn't matter. Because he would recognize that tricked-out, jacked-up pickup with the chrome roll bar and KC lights anywhere. Even in grainy black-and-white.

Edrick Fizzel, Jr.

Hank whispered the name. He didn't need to. Not even a shout would wake her as she lay there drugged and tubed and motionless. He moved his chair closer. He thought about taking her hand. Then imagined the arched-eyebrow kibosh she would give him for such sentimentality. If she were conscious. He laced his fingers instead.

'We're looking for him now. Raker is . . .' Well, Raker was out for blood, that's what. And Hank intended to join him. 'He's leading the search. We've got Junior's truck on video. And I think the one with him could be Randy Wilcox. That guy and Tucker have been stirring up shit on local websites ever since we fired him.'

Fizzel Senior, he of the county commission, had backed Tucker in the sheriff's election last year. They were definitively aligned. It would be an easy thing for one of them to convince Junior to have a little fun by intimidating an adversary. Because Junior – Eddie to his friends, a waste of space to everyone else – had neither a sharp intellect nor a history of good choices.

He talked that through some more, still whispering, until Tyrone got back. His sister had finally hauled him off to the cafeteria and from the look of it, forced him to eat half a ham sandwich. He was holding the other half as he walked back in the room. He dropped it on the tray table and sank into his chair on the other side of Sheila's bed. Hank told him about Junior.

'Son of a commissioner, huh?'

'That's not going to matter. He's going to go to prison.' He stood to leave.

Tyrone scoffed. Tessa, by the door, gave him a grim smile.

'I'll keep you updated,' he said as he walked past.

'You do that.'

That monstrosity of a truck had to be somewhere. Probably hidden in someone's barn. Along with its owner. He had a feeling the fuck-up kid wouldn't wander far from his prized possession. He surveyed the flagstone rectangle where it normally parked and then turned again to the hyperventilating owner of the land itself.

'Commissioner Fizzel,' Raker said, 'tell me again the last time you talked to your son.'

Fizzel's arms flapped at the very nice two-story brick house to the right of where they were standing. 'I'm not saying anything until you're out of my house. I'll have your badge. You don't have a warrant, you don't have cause, you don't got any right.'

'I don't need a warrant.' Raker walked to the middle of the front lawn and watched his officers swarm the place. 'We're hunting a fugitive. Right now, that's all we're looking for. When the warrant gets here, *then* we'll be looking through everything else on your premises. And your phone records. So think real hard for a minute.' He turned from the house to the politician. 'When did you last talk to your son?'

He thought his city councilmen were bad. But damn. This guy. How Worth had managed to not strangle him was amazing. Right now he was hopping around like a frog on a hot sidewalk, complete with plaintive croaking.

'You can't . . . this isn't . . .'

'You're in tight with Gerald Tucker. Your son's been seen with his associates. Specifically one Randy Wilcox.' He pulled his phone out of his wrinkled slacks and stuck it so close it almost touched Fizzel's red nose. 'This man. Seen on video just after the attack on Chief Deputy Turley.' He swiped to the next still from the convenience store video without taking his eyes from Fizzel's face. 'And look – here's his companion.'

The red drained out and left an ashen pallor on Fizzel's face. Raker leaned in. 'You always know your own kid, don't you?'

THIRTY-SIX

She stared at the ceiling. It wasn't her ceiling. There was no crack in the plaster on the left side. She tried to turn her head, but nothing happened. Nothing moved, but nothing hurt, either. She expected it to, but she wasn't sure why. She sighed and let herself slip back where she'd come from.

The next time, she could look around a little. Machines and monitors and a swingy curtain. Huh. And a man sitting next to the bed, asleep with his head in his arms. Her husband. She tried to bat away the cotton in her brain and come up with his name. She nodded off instead.

The cotton was gone the third time she awoke. Now she was full of glass shards. They worked their way from her abdomen back toward her spine and then up through her shoulder blades. She focused on the monitor next to her and tried to breathe through it. Then her eyes began to hurt. The room was too bright. Who thought putting overhead lighting in here was a good idea? She forced her head to roll from the left to the right, away from the monitor and hopefully the excruciating ceiling glare.

'Oh. You're awake.'

She needed to blink several times before the blur sharpened into a semblance of a person. White, dark hair, otherwise nothing but a hazy outline. She gave up on the blinking and just listened. She was young, from the sound of it. Teenage-ish.

'They told me you weren't going to wake up anytime soon. That's why they stuck me in here, just 'til they have a room for me. I guess you had surgery, too, huh?'

That would explain the hospital. But she was pretty sure it didn't explain the pain. That happened before she got here. She just couldn't remember how. She tried to think, but Chatty Cathy wouldn't shut up.

'. . . and I knew I'd probably never get another chance – I mean painted buntings? Do you know how rare that bird is around here? – so I went quietly, and I was paying so much attention to my equipment that I didn't see the hole. And boom.'

Her blurry arm pointed at her blurry leg. Sheila didn't care.

'Broken in two places. Can you believe it? Just from falling in a hole and . . .'

She dragged her head back to center. Maybe not looking at her would say *not interested* in a way that her mouth currently couldn't. The glass shards started dancing through her middle again just as the curtain in front of the door slid aside. Even blurry, she knew who these two were. She told the tall one to go away. It came out 'gawain honk'.

'I'm not going anywhere.' He started to drag over a chair.

'Hold it.' The other one pushed him aside and started checking tubes that hung from poles and threaded their way somewhere Sheila couldn't see. Her arms, she supposed. Then Maggie leaned in and peered into her eyes, almost popping out an eyeball in the process. Sheila groaned.

'Sheila honey, you shouldn't be awake. It's too soon post-op. We're going to get you some more pain meds.'

She liked the sound of that. No more glass shards. No more yammering roommate.

'Maggie, I need to talk – wait, Felicia? What are you doing here?'

'Hi, sheriff. I broke my leg this morning. Two places. They had to put in pins.'

'How did you manage to do that?'

She fell in a hole, Sheila wanted to shout. But her voice still wouldn't work. She tried to swat at anyone within reach, but her arms weren't working either.

'At the job site. The landscapes are great this time of year, so I was out there getting more photos. For the promotional materials. I thought I'd avoided all the construction, but I didn't see the hole.'

'Construction where . . .?' Hank drew out the words. The kid said something about T Highway, which ran along the south side of Lake Taneycomo. Hank stiffened. Even through the pain, Sheila could sense him closing in on something. Which meant it was important. Which meant she should know it, too. She tried to think as Maggie shot something into her tubing. Why was T Highway important?

'And Felicia, who exactly do you work for?'

Her eyes started to close.

'It's a new timeshare condo business, but I mostly work out of the Gallagher Enterprises office. Which makes sense, 'cause I report directly to Mr Gallagher anyway.'

Her eyes snapped open. Gallagher. He was competing for business, wasn't he? With who? The cotton was back, deadening her brain from the inside out. 'Sopta drucks.' All three of them turned to stare at her. She glared at them and struggled to move. Finally, her right hand obeyed. She reached across her jagged middle and ripped the IV out of her arm.

Maggie yelled. Hank swore.

'Gallagher . . . competing. I . . . trying to look into it . . .' She had to stop and gasp like a late-stage emphysemic patient until she was able to suck enough air back into her lungs. 'He no alibi.'

She felt Maggie working on her arm and tried to push her away. Her body wouldn't cooperate.

'Alibi?' Hank sounded dumbfounded. 'He's involved in this? How? Competing? With who? You didn't tell me.'

She tried to think. The land on T Highway was what they thought Gillam was selling. Wasn't it? How could that connect . . .?

The cotton slammed into her with the force of a thousand pillows. She tried to fight it, but was no match for Maggie's new IV mega-dose. The last thing she saw as her eyelids slid blessedly shut was Hank. Even with blurry vision she could tell he was furious.

'Yeah, we think we've found him.'

Raker stood alongside a chain-link fence that ran around the property of a man named Mark Payne. It fit all the requirements. Isolated, big barn, hard to see from the road, owned by a known associate of Junior Fizzel. He hadn't planned on telling Worth. But the guy was relentless. Which, to be fair, was warranted in this particular situation.

'I don't want you here,' he said into the phone.

'You haven't even told me where you are yet,' Worth said.

'I know.'

Multiple people had pegged this Payne guy as a longtime friend of Eddie Fizzel. And that barn could easily hold the little asshole's big truck.

'So are you going in?'

'We're waiting for the warrant. And for SWAT. No telling how many guns they got up in there.' That was another reason he didn't want Worth around. If it was just the two of them, they'd easily talk each other into storming the place on their own. Alone, Raker could force himself to be sensible.

'So you've got a minute?' Hank said.

'What? No. I'm about to raid a suspect property. I don't "got a minute" to—'

'Dale. Stop. What do you know about Henry Gallagher? And Gillam?'

Raker stopped pacing the fence line. 'What, um, makes you ask about that?'

'Sheila was looking into him. As a suspect. Do you know anything about that?'

How had he found that out? And why the hell bother to bring it up now?

'You won't let me in on Fizzel, so I'll follow this instead . . .' Hank paused. 'I need you to tell me what you know.'

Raker sighed and resumed pacing. That's all they needed, Worth going off half-cocked at the town's preeminent businessman. He couldn't see any way to avoid it, though. He outlined what he knew. 'And when we talked to him, we didn't mention it was part of a homicide investigation. Why piss him off unless we're sure he's involved?'

'Sheila kept saying "compete". Did she mean compete with Vivian Gillam? How would he be competing with her if they're both involved with the development of the same property?'

Raker froze. 'Wait, the T Highway property? How is Gallagher involved with that?'

Hank told him.

'That would only make sense if they were working together.' He started to pace again, turning down the volume of the dispatch updates on his radio and trying to think. 'We need to talk to Gallagher.'

'No. *I* need to talk to Gallagher. *You* need to find Eddie.'

The call clicked off. Raker stared at his phone, actually glad Sheila was unconscious. She wouldn't have to see the mess her boss was about to make of everything.

Hank hadn't been in this building since he'd arrested a Gallagher Enterprises employee more than a year ago. The company headquarters was almost empty then. Now it hummed with activity, all of which stopped as he announced himself to the receptionist in the lobby.

'Yes, that's what I said. The sheriff. And I want to see Henry Gallagher. Right. Now.'

Whispers followed him up the stairs to Gallagher's office. The man's obvious annoyance would've made him smile if he wasn't so irritated himself.

'What do you want, Worth?'

'To talk about your property on T Highway.'

Gallagher tossed the folder he was holding onto his desk and spread his hands in a short-tempered *well?* gesture. 'I'm busy.'

Hank sauntered into the room and sank into one of the guest chairs. 'Why'd you hide that it was you who bought the land? Under a newly incorporated company with a random name?'

'Why do you care?'

'Because you, all of a sudden, are at the center of a murder investigation. Again.'

Gallagher's pale complexion reddened. Hank held up his hand. He shouldn't have brought up the killing on Gallagher's old showboat. He needed to stay focused on the current problem. 'I only want to talk about Vivian Gillam and the property you're building a resort on.'

Gallagher sat down and eyed him. 'She's why you're here, and then that's the question you ask me? Why I created a new company to purchase the land?' The *you complete moron* was unspoken but loud and clear. 'I hired her so no one would know I was involved. Pretty easy to understand.'

What you don't understand, you moron, Hank thought, is that I need you to say it. Out loud. For the record. He swallowed a snide retort. 'And why would that be important? Wouldn't you want people to know your latest grand venture?'

Gallagher leaned back in his leather desk chair and steepled his fingers. 'Eventually, yes. But not as it's taking shape. Not as I'm trying to acquire properties. And you're going to ask me why again, aren't you? Like some two-year-old. Why, why, why.'

Let him be condescending. Keep him talking. Anything to distract him from calling his lawyer.

'If people knew I was involved, the asking prices would skyrocket. I realized that after I approached the go-kart owner. Everything needed to be kept quiet. Nothing could have my name attached. Not even other people in my company knew.'

Properties. Plural.

'So you're also behind Gillam trying to buy the Hickory Sticks Motor Lodge?' Hank said. 'The Putt-Putt golf place?'

Gallagher just sat there. Fine.

'You were certainly keeping her busy, with all that and then selling your timeshares through the breakfast shows and . . .' He trailed off at the look creeping over Gallagher's face. Astonishment and disbelief overriding patrician haughtiness in real time. Hank waited.

'She was what?'

Hank stayed quiet.

'We aren't starting sales until construction is further along,' Gallagher said finally. 'Until we can show people a finished unit.'

'That's not true.'

'Excuse me?' The haughtiness was back.

'She made deals with local shows. They've been doing sales presentations for your property. With very strict requirements on withholding food and drink from vulnerable old people.'

'That is patently ridiculous and . . .' He slowly came forward in his seat. 'That incident I read about in the paper. You were quoted.'

'Yeah, because I was there. Responding to multiple sick and injured senior citizen tourists. Who had just purposefully been denied food – at a breakfast show – while being pounded with a sales pitch for your project.'

There was just a heartbeat worth of pause. 'I have no idea what you're talking about. I haven't authorized any show presentations.'

'So you're telling me that Gillam – that this consummate professional – went rogue?'

'I'm telling you I don't know what the hell she was doing.'

Hank leaned back in his chair. Time to take a left turn.

'That's easy to say now that she's dead. Nobody to contradict you.'

Gallagher glanced at his desk phone. Hank knew he didn't have much time before the bastard kicked him out and called his lawyer.

'You knew she was murdered. Why didn't you come forward, tell us that the two of you had a business relationship?'

'The killing seemed random. Horrible, awful, random violence.' He managed a sorrowful frown. 'My business wouldn't be relevant.'

Hank fought to keep his hands from curling into fists. 'You know that's bullshit. Everything is relevant in a homicide investigation. Staying quiet means you must have something to hide.'

'You and your conspiracy theories. You're worse than the idiots in tin-foil hats.'

Now his hands were fists. 'Where were you on Sunday the eighth? From noon until sunrise on Monday. Your exact movements.' Dale had said he didn't have an alibi, but Hank wanted Gallagher to answer the question with full knowledge that it was related to the murder. The businessman repeated what he said earlier, adding details about going for a walk and when he went to bed. Hank thanked him and then leaned back in his chair.

'Did you kill her?'

The man's face, already thin, hardened into gaunt stoniness. 'How dare you. Get out.'

Hank didn't move. 'Answer the question.'

'No.' Gallagher's arm snaked out and his fingers wrapped around the phone receiver in front of him. 'I'm calling my attorney.'

'Fine.' Hank shrugged. 'Tell him that the sheriff's department thinks you were angry with Ms Gillam over your business dealings. Tell him you refused to answer questions. Tell him you're a suspect.'

He rose to his feet and walked out. *Tell him I'm coming for you.*

THIRTY-SEVEN

Mr Crumblit and the missus had been safely driven to his police officer brother-in-law in St James. Who, along with his department-issued Glock, had an impressive collection of rifles and a few Dirty Harry revolvers. And an itch to use them, judging by the look on his face. 'Just let them try, son. Those piss-ant two-bits won't get anywhere near Sandy and Earl.'

Sam thanked him and returned to Branson – after stopping for a Red Bull and some Advil because, man, what he spent the night on at the Crumblits' might have looked like a blue plaid sofa, but it felt like Missouri limestone. He would have been better off in a sleeping bag on the front lawn. He was just finishing the drink when he pulled up at Brenna's. Someone had borrowed her car and she needed to go get it and some other details he hadn't paid attention to. He just wanted to get her where she needed to go and then head back to the hospital and Sheila. She hopped in the car and did a double take.

'You look horrible. What happened?'

He tried to speak, but nothing came out as the image of Sheila's beaten body crowded everything else out of his mind. 'You go first,' he finally managed. 'What's up with your car again?'

She'd driven Felicia's sister to the hospital last night. The sister had stayed there late, and so Brenna left her the car and took an Uber home. Now the rest of the family was coming, so the sister no longer needed to borrow Brenna's car to get herself back home. Sam blinked away the grit in his eyes. 'You drove her sister? Where?'

'I told you. The hospital. Felicia broke her leg. Bad. We went to see her, and my car's still in the parking lot. I thought her sister would need it to get back here, but their parents are coming, so she doesn't.'

'Well, that's convenient.'

'It is? Why?' She turned in her seat and stared at him full on with what felt like X-ray laser beams. 'You tell me what's wrong, Sam Karnes. Right now.'

He strangled the steering wheel for a minute. She refused to let up with the laser beams. 'I was just there,' he said. 'Sheila got hurt. She was in surgery. Now . . .' Now he didn't know. He hadn't gotten an update in hours.

'Oh, my God. That's horrible. I . . . I'm so sorry. I never would've asked you to come get me. God, why didn't you say something?'

'I didn't want . . .' He trailed off.

'Didn't want to what, worry me? You're an idiot. I'm not some fragile snowflake.' She certainly did look more like a fierce ice storm at the moment. He tried to apologize. She stopped him. 'We can talk about this later. Right now, Mrs Turley is the most important thing. And Felicia. Let's just get to the hospital.'

He kept watching the road, but could see out of the corner of his eye that she was forcing herself to calm down. She sent off a text to Felicia's sister and then stared out the window, tossing out random thoughts to fill the silence.

'Nice flowers in that yard.'

'They cut that tree down over there. That's a shame.'

'I haven't seen one of her signs in a long time. She used to be everywhere, didn't she? That's a new picture though—' As they sailed past, she stopped talking and twisted around in her seat. 'Stop. Stop the car. Go back.'

It was the tone of her voice more than anything that had Sam slamming on the brakes. Luckily, the residential street was deserted. He reversed the Bronco and they drew even with the sign, swinging gently from its pole. Brenna hopped out and snapped a photo with her phone.

All he could do was stare at her as she got back in the car. What was she doing?

'It could be her.' She stuck the phone in his face, her face lit with excitement. *Strike Gold With Silver.* 'The one I was talking to Mr Worth about. She used to come in to the shop. It could've been her arguing with the dead lady that day. Out on the sidewalk. Because she came in right after. I didn't remember until I saw her face.' She pointed at the picture. 'We need to tell Hank.'

Sam wished he could tell Sheila, too. She was the one who'd interviewed Reggie Silver. He'd seen it in the case reports. But there was nothing in the notes about Silver speaking with Gillam recently. Which means Silver hadn't mentioned it. Even though it seemed pertinent, considering the deadness of the other woman. He dug out his iPhone and told Siri to call the Chief, then took the next turn at full speed. There was a split second when he thought he should drop Brenna off somewhere first, keep her safe. But between her gleeful expression now and the smack-down three minutes ago, he decided to keep his mouth shut and hit the gas.

'Move move move.'

The Missouri State Highway Patrol SWAT team fanned out, the black tactical gear laughable against the bright spring greenery. Raker and the team leader cut through the gate five minutes after Judge Sedstone signed the search warrant. He didn't much care that he had no paper copy in hand as the Bearcat pulled up the dirt driveway. A photo of the document and his gun would do.

'You gonna be cool with this?' The leader eyed him. 'You're looking a little, uh, agitated.'

'I'm fine.'

'Ah, shit. You know her, don't you? The officer who was attacked?'

'We've met.' He walked away before the guy could ask more questions and took a close look at the house. It was ranch style, painted dirt red with an old shake roof dotted with plywood patches. Multiple exits. He signaled the men holding the battering ram to ready themselves, and began to pound on the door.

He held her hand. The monitors beeped and the IV dripped and he tried not to weep. Then he left Brenna at the hospital to track down Felicia, who apparently kept getting moved from room to room, and looked up the address for Silver Real Estate Services.

Brenna IDed the lady who might have met w vic at Donorae's.

No response from the Chief.

It was Reggie Silver the real estate lady. Should I head over there?

Nothing. Where the hell was he? Sam felt the fact that Silver might have lied about how recently she saw Gillam needed urgent addressing. He decided not to wait on Hank.

Heading there now. Will update u.

He walked in and showed his badge since he was still in his wrinkly civilian clothes from yesterday. 'Ma'am, I hear you met with Ms Gillam at Donorae's Gourmet Coffee pretty soon before she died. Can you tell me what that was about?'

He declined to have a seat and instead stayed near the doorway with his arms folded across his chest. The Red Bull was wearing off and he was in no mood for chit chat. Ms Silver smoothed her pantsuit and leaned against a shiny wood table in the center of the office. Probably the spot where people signed away their lives in exchange for a house.

'Ma'am?'

'I might have run into her there. I see lots of people, deputy. I know everybody in town practically.'

He decided to pretend Brenna's supposition was fact. 'No. You met Ms Gillam outside the shop and had an argument. What was it about?'

'Well, I take many meetings, young man.' She tapped her chin with a finger, sending a whole lot of bracelets jangling on her wrist. 'It might have been about local property values – lots of people ask me about that. Oh, or where I get my signs made. I did make a recommendation to someone recently. It might have been her.'

'You told Chief Deputy Turley that you hadn't had contact with Ms Gillam in years and didn't like her. Why would you be helping her out with advice?'

'Love thy neighbor, deputy.'

Sam's eyes widened before he could stop them. 'OK, then. If you love your neighbor, why didn't you mention before that you met with her? When people came to you trying to solve her murder? How is that love if you're withholding information?'

He knew the Chief would be more circumspect. And Sheila would be more composed. But he was what he was, and right now that was tired and frustrated and so, so angry. And all he got in response was a blink. And a jangle. And finally, denial.

'I just don't remember. I'm sorry.'

Sam pressed, but she stuck to that story. 'Fine,' he finally said. 'I'll be back. With a warrant – for your calendar and your business records, all that stuff. And I'll see what you were really talking to Ms Gillam about.'

He turned on his heel and walked out, making an effort not to stomp. He was crossing the parking lot to his Bronco when his phone rang.

'I just talked to Gallagher,' Hank said.

Sam stopped walking. 'What? Henry Gallagher? Why?'

'You didn't know he was involved? That Sheila was looking into him in connection with all this?'

'I honestly have no idea what you're talking about.'

'He's buying up properties to turn into timeshare developments. He hired Gillam to hide his involvement – said people would hike up prices if they knew he was the one interested. Recruiting the music shows wasn't supposed to happen until later. He says she was doing that part on her own. That he had nothing to do with the sales presentations.' It was clear the Chief thought that was bullshit. Hank's voice was so loud Sam had to hold the phone away from his ear.

'OK. Enough on that.' Hank took a breath. 'Are you at Silver's office?'

Sam told Hank what the woman said as he climbed in the Bronco. 'And, um, I might have threatened her with a search warrant.'

Hank gave a weak chuckle. 'Nothing wrong with that. Especially after she wasn't honest with Sheila.' He told Sam to start work on a warrant affidavit, although it was iffy whether a judge would grant it.

'I'd rather be hunting for Eddie Fizzel.' Sam didn't realize he'd said it out loud until Hank responded.

'Me, too. But if we've got to put our faith in anybody, Raker's a good one for it. He should be going into that associate's house soon.' He paused. 'We just got to hope Junior's there.'

Yeah.

THIRTY-EIGHT

The boom didn't come from the battering ram. The house shook and smoke started to billow from the back as the ram cracked through the front door with only the slightest of noise. Raker ran toward the hallway, glad he was wearing protective eye gear and a helmet. The commander was yelling orders as Raker headed deeper into the smoke, which smelled like . . . summer. He pushed the thought aside and advanced, a SWAT officer covering his rear. The first bedroom was clear of people. The second had a busted-out window and a charred hole in the carpet with the husk of a NitroOctane firecracker in it.

'Out the back. Out the back,' Raker shouted as he coughed his way back down the hallway. Two others cleared the rest of the house while he ran around it. The perimeter team was swarming like ants across the back field where the trees were rustling in the stiff spring wind. He leaned against the siding for a minute, trying to clear the Fourth of July from his lungs and eyeing the distance to the woods. The suspected accomplice could be a world-class sprinter for all he knew. But Junior – well known at every fast food joint in the Ozarks – sure as hell wasn't. Raker turned and headed for the only other thing nearby.

The nicest car in the parking lot rolled slowly toward the exit. It was a new Range Rover with Gallagher behind the wheel. Hank was right behind him. Nobody ever looked twice at a minivan. Especially one with back-end body damage that wasn't fully repaired, a fact that still had Maggie plenty irritated. Gallagher turned south and headed for the Highway 76 bridge over Lake Taneycomo. Hank dropped back a few car lengths. He had a pretty good idea where the guy was going.

He knew he was just killing time. Trying to avoid thinking about Sheila. Wanting to be on the raid with Raker. Gallagher was not going to lead him to some treasure trove full of incriminating emails that proved he knew what Gillam was doing with the timeshares. If there was proof, it would come from investigating where Gallagher was the day she died. He should try for a warrant to look at his Range Rover's GPS. And the GPS on all his other fancy cars. Rich people could be a real pain in the ass.

Hank eased off the gas and dropped farther back as a sedan whipped in front of him. They trundled over the bridge in the middle of a line of cars that rapidly thinned out as they got farther away from the lake. They took the curve at the cemetery and then veered left onto T Highway. What was his plan once they got there? Confront him again, only this time in a more picturesque setting? Demand to know why he was determined to dominate every aspect of the Branson tourism industry? Ask him why he wasn't building a pool?

His hands reflexively tightened on the wheel. It was not good to be this fixated on somebody. He knew that. Sheila clearly did, too. She'd kept that avenue of investigation from him. Out of the case notes and completely hidden. Which, if he was being honest with himself, had been the right decision. Proof of it was right here, with him obsessively tailing a suspect who wasn't at risk of absconding – instead of sitting at the bedside of one of his best friends.

He nudged the side door of the barn open a crack, any sound he made covered by the confusion outside. Dust hazed the air and it smelled like motor oil and mold. He couldn't see anything but a slice of tool bench and part of the big sliding door at the front of the building. He shifted slightly and pushed the door wider. And caught the glint of polished chrome on a very large front bumper.

Now for the bumper's owner. He waited while the SWAT officer who had cleared the rest of the house moved silently toward him and took up a position to cover him. Raker slithered through the thin door opening as well as his bulk allowed and got low. There were clear lines of fire from multiple spots, but no bullets came at him. He ducked behind a riding lawn mower and waited for the SWAT officer to join him. Then he was forced to waste time having a hand-signal argument with the guy over who would get to approach. Finally, he just stuck his hand in the younger man's face and started to move. It was his case and his friend in the hospital. The out-of-towner could damn well play backup.

He moved as quickly as he could until he was pressed to the side of the truck. Now – cab or bed? Where would Junior be hiding? He was near the back tire, so he decided to try the truck bed first. It had a canvas cover pulled taut across the top. He was reaching for one of the fasteners attached to a hook on the side edge when he saw another officer duck through the side door. Then another. He relaxed fractionally and tugged the fastener. It popped off, as did the next three in quick succession as Raker moved down the length of the bed. He ripped the canvas back and kept moving. His argument partner, rifle at the ready, was right behind him, springing onto the back bumper in order to look inside. Raker yanked at the last cover hook, right at the back of the cab, then reached up – Jesus this truck was big – and pulled on the passenger door handle. Once it was unlatched he kicked it open so he wouldn't step directly into the line of fire of whoever was in the cab. Then, both hands gripping his gun, he swung around and aimed directly at the driver's seat just as a diesel roar filled the barn.

'Get your hands up,' Raker shouted. Junior was crouched so low behind the wheel he couldn't see over the dash. He shifted into gear. Raker leaped onto the running board. Junior hit the gas.

Raker heaved himself into the cab as a SWAT officer in front of the truck threw himself out of the way. The Ford surged forward and crashed through the giant sliding wood doors at the front of the barn. Raker, almost laying lengthwise across the seats, grabbed onto the little shit's shirtsleeve as the passenger door swung shut onto his lower legs.

Junior was screaming like a hysterical thirteen-year-old girl and trying to shake him off, still hunched too low to see out the windshield. He was going to kill them both. Raker tightened his grip on the flannel shirt and yelled at him to stop. Junior stomped down and the truck surged forward even faster. Lord how he wanted to just shoot the bastard. He struggled to bring his right hand around as he slid back and forth along the seat, his legs still sticking out of the truck and getting slammed by the door with every bump.

'No, no, no. Not me. Don't even know her. Don't even know her.'

'Stop the truck.' The flannel tore and Raker was suddenly hanging onto his ride by nothing but a split seam. Still laying across the seat on his left side, he managed to bend his knees and get his legs fully inside the truck. He wedged himself between the seatback and the dash in almost a fetal position. That made him stable enough. He braced and pulled his right arm up. The gunshot boomed in the cab. And Junior finally stopped screaming.

THIRTY-NINE

The construction was further along than Hank thought it would be. Two-by-four skeletons all over and concrete-lined pits that would probably become basements. He was on the eastern edge of the property after parking farther up the highway and walking back. He'd kept going as Gallagher turned into the driveway, getting his white Rover dusty in the process. It was now parked near what looked like a half-built clubhouse, which had more ground floor walls than the other buildings, but only the beginnings of a second story. Construction equipment sat idle and the only figure visible was the tall businessman as he flitted through the building. Why was no one here working? Hank moved slightly toward the lake, changing the angle of his view through the vegetation that shielded him from Gallagher. There. Near a cluster of trees the construction had left alone – a web of yellow caution tape and a big orange 'Danger' sign. Where Felicia must have fallen. Snapping her leg and apparently shutting down the project, at least temporarily.

He was wondering how close he could get without technically trespassing when he heard the rumble of another car engine, muffled by the increasing wind. A sedan appeared, inching its way down the driveway. It was the same one that had sandwiched itself between the minivan and the Rover on the drive here. It parked behind the SUV and the driver got out. And shut the door slowly and silently. Interesting.

Hank moved closer. This was not a meeting. The visitor would have pulled in right behind Gallagher and joined him immediately if that were the case. He turned back toward the clubhouse, but Gallagher had disappeared. He inched along the property line, careful not to cross it. The visitor, face hidden by a sun hat, looked around at the skeletal condos and then, guessing correctly, headed for the more finished clubhouse. Hank snapped a photo of the car and its license plate and argued with himself about moving closer. Then came a clattering crash and a sharp yell and he was pushing through the bushes and sprinting toward the noise.

It hadn't been hard to figure out the raid location. Sam knew plenty of guys in the city PD, and it was all everybody over there was talking about. He knew he wasn't supposed to be involved. The sheriff's department was supposed to stay out of it. He pulled the Bronco over and sat there, fidgeting. He had to find something to do or he'd go crazy. What else was there? He could apply for a warrant for that real estate agent's records. But he'd never done one that complicated on his own before. He'd always had help. From Sheila. He leaned his forehead on the Bronco's steering wheel and fought back tears.

He forced his thoughts away from Sheila and back to the homicide investigation. He pulled his battered notebook out of the center console and went through it. Something felt incomplete. He flipped through again, thinking back on his conversation with Hank. Flip, flip. There it was. What had been a comprehensive list now was not. He whipped out his phone and called dispatch. Dean came through super quick. Two vehicle registrations. One of them matched.

He called Hank. There was no answer.

The clubhouse interior was a maze of framed walls, some already stuffed with insulation, some still open. He dodged through them, trying to find the two people who had to be inside somewhere. He passed construction debris and the sun hat, torn and dangling from a nail at chest height. A loud yelp came from above just as he rounded a corner and saw the stairs. He took them two at a time as a splintering crack cut the air. He emerged onto a high expanse that was nothing but plywood floor and a few lonely posts guarding the edges. Gallagher lay sprawled at the feet of a middle-aged woman wielding a two-by-four. A gash at his temple was starting to bleed and he wasn't moving. She lifted the wood like she was using an ax and brought it down across his shoulder as Hank shouted at her to stop. He pounded across the open space and lunged for her as she tried to swing again.

Hank grabbed her left arm and yanked her as hard as he could. She stumbled into him, still clutching the wood with her right hand. Now she used it like a tennis racket, swinging it with a forehand grip and catching him full force on his left side. He felt one of his ribs crack. Gallagher moaned and started to crawl away as the berserk woman wound up for another swing. He wrapped her in a bear hug, pinning her arms to her sides.

'Drop it.'

She didn't. All she could manage was a weak whack on his leg. He squeezed. She whacked him again and started to struggle. Gallagher was dripping blood as he tried to get to his feet, his arm dangling grotesquely at his side. 'Get to the stairs,' Hank shouted over the wind. Gallagher stared blankly and staggered sideways. The woman stomped on his foot and twisted back and forth. He squeezed as hard as he could and told her she was under arrest. She looked up at him, silver-white hair barely moving in the wind, and scoffed softly.

'This is over,' he said, his face inches from hers. 'You're going to stop, and we're going to go downstairs and get help for him.' Neither one of them glanced at Gallagher, now back on his knees. She stopped fighting and looked out toward the lake view dazzlingly framed by half-erected posts. And then she kneed him in the balls.

Hank doubled over and the world went white. She turned and bolted in the opposite direction. Toward the edge farthest from the stairs. Hank staggered after her as Gallagher shouted something unintelligible. He called out again as the woman started to jump. *Basement.* The cemented pits visible in the other buildings flashed through Hank's mind. He leapt and caught her arm as she went over the side. And then they were both staring down, not at a fifteen-foot drop onto freshly churned dirt, but a thirty-foot plunge onto concrete.

She screamed. Hank, flat on his stomach and full of plywood splinters, struggled to keep his grip on her arm. He yelled for her to raise her other hand. She tried but couldn't manage to grab onto him. He slid closer to the edge. He wasn't going to be able to haul her up unless he could get to his knees. And he couldn't do that while bearing all her weight.

Suddenly a leg swung down. One clad in expensive work slacks. Gallagher dangled it over the side, getting lower than Hank's arm could. He wrapped his one usable arm around a post and braced himself. The Berserker swung and used the momentum to reach up and grab his pant leg. Gallagher was jerked forward but managed to hold on. Having even that bit of weight off him gave Hank enough relief to get his knees under him. He inched backward, pulling and heaving and swearing until the Berserker was lying on the plywood next to him. She stared up at the sky, tears streaming down her face.

He forced his exhausted arm to reach to the back of his belt and unclip his handcuffs. He had never wanted to use them on a person more than he did on this woman. He cuffed her and turned to Gallagher, who had pulled his leg back up and slumped against the post. Blood was still dripping down his face. He tried to help the battered businessman down onto his back without jostling the injured arm. Then he crawled the few feet to the edge, leaned over, and vomited.

FORTY

He got there just in time for the explosion. The barn doors blew outward. Planking and hay bales and some unfortunate chickens all went rocketing into the air. Junior's pride and joy leapt through the hole in the building as SWAT guys swarmed out from the house and the back field, running toward the mess. Everyone on the street-side perimeter with Sam started scrambling for cover – and their guns – as the monster truck swung in their direction. Too astonished to move that quickly, he was the only one still looking at the barn instead of the truck as a SWAT officer ran out waving his arms and screaming a warning.

'Hold your fire,' Sam yelled at the same time a gunshot cracked. The truck slammed to a stop. The yelling officer raced toward it, getting there at the same time Sam did. Sam reached up and grabbed the driver's door handle. The officer gave him a nod and Sam yanked it open so the other man had a direct sight line into the cab.

'Hands, Fizzel. On top of your head. Now.'

The door was blocking Sam's view, but he could hear scared, whiny breathing over the grumble of the diesel engine. The officer ordered Junior to swing his legs out and away from the gas pedal. He must have obeyed because Sam saw the officer almost imperceptibly relax. His next words had an entirely different tone.

'You OK, Raker?'

What? Sam tried to peek around the door but was pushed out of the way by the onslaught of people now around the pickup. They reached up and hauled out Eddie Fizzel, babbling and whimpering. And crying. Sam wanted to punch him. Instead he backed away and rounded the front. The shiny grill was satisfyingly scratched and twisted. The passenger door wasn't even latched. He pulled it open to find Mr Raker curled up on his left side, head toward the driver and sizable rear end pointed at Sam. His legs were braced against the dashboard and his pants were torn. His right hand held his service weapon and there was a bullet stuck in the roof of the cab near the back window. He raised his head and sighed at the look on Sam's face.

'I'm gonna need some help getting out.'

Larry Alcoate found them. Gallagher out cold with a broken collarbone, head gash and likely concussion. Reggie Silver dirty, disheveled and sitting handcuffed to a wood post. Hank curled in a fetal position and covered in splinters.

'Dude. I got no words.'

'Good. Help me up.'

Once on his feet, Hank watched the paramedics load Gallagher on a gurney. Bill Ramsdell and Derek Orvan stepped to the side as they made their way down the stairs. He gestured at Silver and the deputies started to uncuff her while he checked his buzzing phone.

'Wait.' He reread the text from Sam.

Silver's car matches description of sedan seen in vic neighborhood on night of murder. Gray Toyota Avalon.

Two minutes later:

Gallagher doesn't own any sedans. Just SUVs and a sports car.

He walked across the plywood and stood looming over Silver. He had a better chance of getting her to talk here than at the station. 'Why did you kill her?'

She glared at him.

He knelt down and stared her right in the eye. 'We can prove you were in her neighborhood that night. We have witnesses who saw your car. And we have hair and fibers in her car. You might have wiped off your prints, but you didn't catch everything. DNA is so hard to get rid of. And now' – he spread his hands wide to take in the bloodied construction site – 'a judge for damn sure will let us take a sample from you to match.'

He paused and let that sink in. She didn't look away. He had to give her credit for that.

'So I'll ask you again. Why did you kill her?'

She shifted away from him, babying the arm he grabbed onto when she went over the edge. She looked out toward the view of the lake for a good long time. 'This is my town. My place. I was born and raised here. I've worked hard my whole life. For this place. We were finally getting back on our feet, after the Great Recession. Those hedge fund bastards who were buying up bankruptcies finally stopped, and we were getting proper homebuyers again. People who would stay, take care of the property.'

And then Vivian Gillam came to town. It took Reggie a while to catch on, that the damn woman was snatching up higher-end properties before they hit the market, on behalf of investors. Who then rented them out even shorter-term than the hedge fund people had – to celebrity musicians or fat cat fishermen. That was worse than renters, honestly. At least those folks used the grocery stores and schools and such.

It kept getting worse, until the only business Reggie could get were the shacks out in the rural parts of the county. A good honest business rivalry would've been fine. But Gillam operated in the shadows. It was impossible to compete.

'So I got to work shifting gears. I would go commercial. I started with that strip mall out on Branson Hills Parkway, by the RecPlex. Then an empty pad near the quarry south of Hollister. Things were starting to take off. And then there she was.'

Nosing around. All over the place. Warren at the Hickory Sticks said Gillam straight up offered eight hundred-and-fifty grand. Reggie asked if he'd like her to be his agent on the deal, and he put her off. So did all the others, people she thought were her friends. People she went to church with. People whose kids she bought Girl Scout cookies from. People whose Little League teams she sponsored.

Then a few weeks ago, she ran into Travis Beckham at the supermarket. She'd helped him find his little bungalow about four years ago. He told her he was excited about a new timeshare presentation for his show. He expected to make big money, on new property developments.

'I asked how he came upon this deal. And he said there was a businesswoman, branching out from her successful business in Chicago. She had brought it to him. Like it was an honor to be chosen.' Reggie shrugged, the handcuffs rattling against her bracelets. 'That would've been everything. Residential, commercial, tourist. Branson's not a big enough place. There's not room for two when one of you is willing to destroy everything.'

Behind him, Hank could sense that the angry stiffness of Ramsdell and Orvan was softening. Local solidarity maybe? They came to arrest a killer and instead found a defender of hometown values. They hadn't seen Vivian Gillam's beaten body, though. He had. And it made it easy to keep his focus. That and the fact that she hadn't actually admitted to killing Gillam yet.

'How did you move her body?'

Nothing. She shifted uncomfortably against the wood post and the handcuffs clinked again. Her wrenched arm had to be killing her.

'We're not going anywhere until you tell me.'

'That won't play well with a jury.'

'Neither will assaulting a law enforcement officer.' He looked toward the ambulance parked in the drive. 'Plus, we're just waiting for the ambulance to leave. Wouldn't want to get in their way, would we?'

Ramsdell snickered. Reggie startled at that and looked up at the men behind Hank, who were shedding their sympathetic softness. Hank felt their hostility start to return. So did she. The bracelets jangled nervously.

'She wouldn't meet with me. To talk about it. I tried for a whole week. So I went to her house. A Sunday night and she wasn't home.'

She parked down the street and waited a bit. When Gillam came 'round the corner, she hopped out of her car and hustled down the street. She walked into the garage right behind the car and suddenly the door was down. 'She hadn't seen me. Didn't see me until she got out of the car. Then she was so mean. Yelling and threatening and that voice was just echoing in the garage.' She shook her head, trying to clear the sound from her memory. 'And then she was on the ground. I had to drag her around the car and get her into the backseat. Then I drove her to the field. Dragged her off the road a ways so it would look like she'd been hit by a car. She was already in workout clothes. She could've been jogging. An accident . . . it was an accident . . .'

He leaned in. 'No, Reggie. It wasn't. No matter what you tell yourself.'

FORTY-ONE

'It's PD policy for someone involved in a shooting to be brought to the ER to get checked out.'

'You didn't actually shoot him. He's fine. He needs to be in a cell. In my jail.'

'Oh, no way.' Raker turned himself into an immovable wall. 'He's going up to Springfield. Even you are not that much of a hothead to think it's a good idea to put him in a place he's got sympathizers, that also happens to be controlled by a man he has just made a lifelong enemy of.'

Hank stood in the hallway along the back of the emergency department and glowered at his friend. Raker waved him off.

'I got guys watching him. Plus, I have it on good authority that the doctor examining him doesn't put up with shit from anybody.'

Hank scoffed. Then the doctor appeared.

'I'm not treating him,' Maggie said, taking Hank's wallet out of his back pocket and feeding one of his dollar bills into the Coke machine. 'No way. Conflict of interest. In about every way imaginable.'

Why was no one being cooperative, bending the rules? At least Sam had. He'd gone out to the scene of the raid despite orders otherwise. Which was how Hank knew that Edrick Fizzel, Jr wasn't hurt. Unfortunately.

'However,' she continued, popping the top of her Cherry Coke, 'that means I'm available to examine you two jokers.' She stepped back and took in Raker's torn pants and what looked to be the start of horrific bruising on his shins. And then Hank's scraped face and awkwardly held arm. 'Your shoulder?'

He nodded.

'That it?'

He winced and avoided looking at Raker. 'Just that and a rib. That's it.'

She eyed him with a look that said she knew he was lying but couldn't figure out how. He was saved from deflecting by a howl that exploded out from the triage area and echoed down the hallway. Maggie sprinted toward it. He and Raker, guessing who it was, took the distance at a stroll.

'By the way,' Hank said as they moseyed down the hallway, 'Cameron Cooper's mother bailed him out. She plans to ask the judge to allow him to go back to Joliet with her.'

Raker sighed. 'Whatever happened to tough love?'

'I know. I just hope she decides to extend her coddling, or at least some cash, to the grandchild she didn't know she had.'

'That,' Raker said as they entered the exam room, 'will be interesting to see.'

He was cut off by another shriek. Poor Junior getting a shot. 'Tetanus. He poked himself on wire when he climbed out some window,' the other ER doctor said. 'You'd think he was a five-year-old.'

Hank looked at the skinny little punk and felt his throat tighten. 'But he's not. He's a grown man who decided to ambush someone in the woods and almost kill her.' He took a step forward and Junior's eyes bugged out. He started squirming and waving his arms. The other doctor hesitated, unsure whether it should be him or one of the four cops in the room who needed to stop Junior's outburst. Hank took another step forward.

'Man, it wasn't me. It wasn't. I was just there for back up. You know? Helping out a friend.'

'Which friend, Eddie?'

'It was all his idea. Totally. Not mine. I wasn't the brains. I just . . . man, I'm just a friend. An innocent friend.'

'You were there, though, right?' Raker said.

'Well, yeah.'

'Who put the wire across the path?'

'Him. Totally him. Had me stand there to make sure it would hit right at the ankles.'

'Then what happened?' Raker asked, stepping on Hank's foot to keep him from moving any closer.

'Then we went back into the woods. Cuz it was gonna be fun to watch. She went flying ass over tits.'

Hank yanked his foot away from Raker's sizable boot and took another step. Junior's squirming turned to thrashing. Raker grabbed the back of Hank's belt. The little punk squeaked in terror and the words came out in a torrent.

'She went nuts, man. She got up and her gun was out and she started crashing through the trees looking for us. We were far ahead to start, but he ain't so fast and she was coming and it was like: what do I do? She's gonna catch us. We didn't have our guns. She had a gun. We didn't – I can't believe we forgot 'em but she had one and we didn't and she was gonna shoot if she caught us and so I doubled back 'round and—'

He stopped with his mouth half open and his brain finally half in gear. 'I think I want my dad. I ain't gonna say anything else.'

Hank stepped all the way to the bed, dragging Raker with him. He started to speak but Raker clamped a meaty hand on his uninjured shoulder.

'Which friend were you with, Eddie?' the detective said. 'You were just helping out. We believe you. We'll tell your dad that. Because why should you go to jail, and him not? So who's fault is it really?'

Junior inched away from Hank as far as he could. 'Randy Wilcox.'

Raker released Hank. But Sheila's boss wasn't done. He leaned down. 'And . . . who else helped plan it?'

'Nobody.'

Raker let go of Hank's shoulder. Junior flinched and scooted as far away as he could on the narrow bed.

'Who, Eddie?'

Junior looked at Raker and then around the room, finding no sympathy in any of the faces. He stared up at Hank, pressed his skinny lips together and shook his head.

'Who scares you more than me?' Hank said quietly. 'Who could possibly be worse than the friends of the officer you beat up?'

Silence. Which was confirmation enough. Only one person held that kind of sway in this social circle. Gerald Tucker.

Not for the first time, Hank wondered how Maggie could stand being trapped inside a hospital all day. He was already feeling claustrophobic and it hadn't been more than an hour. He sure as hell wasn't leaving, though, without taking advantage of someone's incapacitated state.

'I figured you'd show up while I was in here. I'm surprised it took you this long.'

Gallagher was sheet-white, with a bandage covering most of his forehead. His shoulder was immobilized and his arm in a cast.

'Yeah, well, I had something more pressing to attend to first.'

The businessman had to think harder about that than he normally would have. 'Oh, your deputy. The one who was attacked. How is she?'

Hank didn't know. He pushed the thought aside. 'We've arrested Commissioner Fizzel's son.' It wasn't the nicest thing to do to a guy stuck full of IVs and monitors, even if he was one of the corrupt politician's strongest supporters. The heart monitor went a little faster and Gallagher sighed.

'That kid is an idiot. Why on earth would he . . .' He trailed off, looking exhausted.

'Oh, he didn't come up with it on his own, that's for sure.'

A nurse bustled in to check the monitors. She frowned at Hank. Gallagher reassured her and she left in a huff.

'She broke more than your collarbone?'

'Yeah. The humerus. They're making me see an orthopedist before they'll let me go home. Also a neurologist. Apparently getting bashed in the head can cause some lingering side effects.' At least the guy's wry snootiness was still intact.

'Did she say anything before she attacked you?'

Gallagher scoffed. 'No. I only heard one footstep and was in the middle of turning when she clobbered me. Then she was yelling things, but I have no idea. I was trying to protect myself, not paying attention to . . .' He trailed off and raised a hand to his eyes. Hank rose and turned off the overhead lights, leaving only the sunlight filtering through the window blinds. 'Oh, that's much better. Thank you.' He dropped his hand. 'Do you know why she attacked me?'

'Vivian Gillam was ruining her livelihood. You were in league with Vivian Gillam. Ergo, you were ruining her livelihood.'

'Oh, God. She's the one who killed Vivian?'

Hank nodded as he sat back down at the foot of the bed. 'She was the area's top real estate agent. Gillam moved in, stole her residential business and then started to take away any possibilities on the commercial side – some outsider coming in and destroying everything.' He stared pointedly at Gallagher, who didn't even have the grace to look sheepish. Although it was hard to tell with the bandage.

'I'm not that concussed. I know what you're getting at. You're saying I've come in and destroyed everything, too.' He waved his good arm dismissively. 'This is where I point out that I've been here longer than you have.'

'Barely. And I'm not trying to buy up the whole damn town.'

'Oh, yeah. You're just over there minding your own business, making friends everywhere you go. Leaving everything just like it was. Changing nothing.'

They stared at each other through narrowed eyes. Hank didn't want to concede that the guy had a point. But if it got him something in return . . . He gave a semi-committal shrug. Gallagher relaxed a little.

'I need to know what you knew about the timeshare presentations.'

'Nothing. Until today, when you showed up at my office.'

Hank didn't believe him but had no way to prove it. If Gillam were alive, he probably could've flipped her. Cut a deal for a lighter penalty so she'd testify against Gallagher for elder abuse. Now she wasn't around to contradict his denials. By killing her, Reggie Silver accomplished nothing but ensure that the person probably at the root of it all got off scot-free. He rubbed at his temples.

'Will you keep trying to sell the timeshares?'

Gallagher considered that. 'I have to. I don't have a choice. Not with the horrible presentation tactics, don't worry. But I've sunk a lot of money into that site on T Highway. I have to be able to fill the units.'

That might be the first honest thing the man ever told him, Hank thought as he rose to his feet. He might as well try for more honesty with something he'd always wondered about. 'Why here? There are tourism opportunities everywhere. Shows and amusement parks and timeshares all over the place. Why not stay where you were in Des Moines? Why choose to come to some insular, eccentric town that's hours from a major airport?'

Gallagher smiled ruefully. 'Well, your money goes further

down here. I'm well-funded, but not billionaire-funded. I'm not going to be building downtown skyscrapers or Disney-sized theme parks. Down here I can actually accomplish things. Capitalize on the country's . . . philosophical split. Bring in people who maybe don't want to vacation in California anymore. Give them a nice Bible Belt place to go.' He lifted his one good shoulder in a shrug. 'And down here you can catch both ends of the market. The young families looking for wholesome entertainment, and then the senior citizens. Timeshares are perfect. Grandparents buying in for the grandkids. It's a pretty stable market. Everybody gets old.'

'Not in my line of work, they don't.'

FORTY-TWO

They stood outside the station, clumped together like a band of pigeons as they waited for Hank to come out of the building. Sam and Mr Raker were in the detective's car, parked close enough to hear everything but not close enough to be too noticeable. Plus, it was best to give the Chief a wide berth right now.

There had been what Sam's gramps would call a good, old fashioned knock-down, drag-out fight that morning. Hank protested for a good half-hour before giving in and agreeing to hold a press conference. Mr Raker told Hank it had to be done because the riot at the theater was such big news. Dr McCleary got on speaker phone and said the same thing, plus stuff about him needing to think about looking successful for the next election. That really stressed him out. Then Mr Raker pointed out that he could also use the opportunity to announce that the sheriff's department had arrested the latest killer – which would go a long way toward counteracting criticism about the rising murder rate. At which point Sam had to take Hank's desk stapler out of his hand before he threw it at the wall.

The whole thing had been entertaining, but also agonizing, he thought as he sipped his coffee and eyed the reporters jostling around the lectern. None of it would've even been necessary if Sheila was conscious. She'd have issued orders and that would have been the end of it. He felt his eyes water and pretended he was stifling a sneeze.

'Finally,' Mr Raker muttered. 'Here he comes.'

Hank walked out. He was in his uniform, a rare sight. So was Ed Utley, the city PD chief. That had been Hank's idea, inviting the guy to share the limelight since the PD had helped a lot with the theater riot fallout. To Sam, it just proved that Hank really wasn't as bad at the political stuff as he thought he was. He watched his boss arrange himself at the lectern and look at the microphones like they were poisonous snakes.

'Thank you for coming today.'

At least his voice sounded calm.

'First, I'd like to announce the results of an investigation that my department – in partnership with the Branson Police – has recently concluded.' He looked at his notes and then pushed them aside. 'The ruckus at the *Breakfast Buckaroos* music show on Sunday, and the injuries to innocent people, was no accident. It was the result of a deliberate campaign by several area theaters to withhold food and water so that their elderly audiences would be more vulnerable to high-pressure timeshare sales tactics. Basically, they were trying to starve people into submission.'

There was a murmur from the TV folks. The dude from the local paper was writing furiously in his notebook.

'We have evidence that this scheme was organized by a woman who worked in town as a property broker of sorts. She had deals with multiple theaters, all of whom then took advantage of unsuspecting tourists who thought they were getting a nice breakfast and a show. Instead – if they didn't sign up – they got an endless presentation, no food, dangerously low blood sugar, heart palpitations and in some cases, a trip to the emergency room.'

Questions started getting shouted. The pushy guy from Channel Three was loudest. 'Who is this person? Have you made an arrest? What on earth would the charges be?'

'Elder abuse. Financial exploitation.' Hank stared the guy down as his cameraman snickered. 'We haven't made an arrest, but that brings me to my second point here today. The person we believe recruited these showrunners is Vivian Gillam.'

The newspaper dude almost dropped his notebook. Everyone else looked confused.

'As I'm sure you remember,' Hank said in a tone that said he knew full well that they didn't, 'Ms Gillam is the woman found dead near her Branson home ten days ago. Our investigation into that murder led us to uncover the theater presentation scheme.'

'So she was killed because she was starving elderly audiences?' the *Branson Daily News* dude said in full-on skeptical mode.

'Not exactly,' Hank said. 'She was killed by a business rival, who is now under arrest. Someone who didn't like Ms Gillam coming into town and snapping up properties, taking away crucial sales. Trying to consolidate what's always been small and locally owned.'

The newspaper guy whipped out his phone and started texting like a madman.

'Name, please,' called out Pushy Channel Three.

Both Hank and Chief Utley seemed to brace themselves.

'Reggie Silver. Regina. Fifty-eight. Lifelong Branson resident.'

'You're kidding. She was my parents' real estate agent,' blurted the Channel Ten cameraman, who was a dude even younger than Sam.

'Well, she's now in custody and will be charged with murder.'

Sam and the detective looked at each other. Hank hadn't mentioned the charges for assaulting Mr Gallagher.

'If it was anybody else, I'd say Hank was trying to protect privacy,' Mr Raker said. 'But it's Gallagher. Did he get beat up bad enough that Hank's actually taking pity on him?'

'I don't know,' Sam said slowly. Maybe the Chief was just being kind, or maybe there was different reasoning at work. Something where he was thinking four steps ahead of everybody else. With Hank, that was always a possibility.

Chief Utley didn't mention the assault either as he started answering questions about theaters and the police department's proposed safety monitoring. Hank stepped well away and tried to blend in with the shrubbery. The newspaper dude followed. He asked a question and then the two of them haggled back and forth for a minute in quiet voices no one else could hear.

'I wonder if he found out we arrested Junior,' Mr Raker said. 'He's pretty dialed in around here.'

'Nice of him not to blab it to everybody else then,' Sam said.

'I believe that's called preserving a scoop, my boy. It's not . . . wait.'

The reporter was asking another question. Hank looked surprised. He shook his head, and then the reporter pointed to something on his phone that caused Hank's jaw to drop. He spun on his heel and disappeared into the building. The reporter put his phone away and moseyed across the parking lot to his car. As Sam watched the spring in the reporter's step get higher with each stride, his own spirits sank.

What now?

FORTY-THREE

'Did you really use the word "ruckus" on live TV?'

'That went out live? Damn.'

Hank pulled up the room's only chair and sat down next to her bed. She looked awful. Skin more gray than brown, tree branch scratches criss-crossing her face, tubes snaking out from her arms. And he didn't even want to think about the surgical incisions that had to be under her hospital gown.

'I didn't know you were awake. I would've told you first.'

'That's all right. I enjoyed you getting grilled by TV reporters.' Her voice was raspy and weak. 'Reggie Silver, huh? Was Gillam starting a property empire too much for her?'

'She wasn't starting her own, actually. She was helping Henry Gallagher expand his.'

Sheila's eyebrows shot up. 'What?'

Hank explained, ending with the construction site attack. 'He was actually in a room down the hall from here. Silver walloped him pretty good.'

'And yet he helped save her from falling.' She shot him a skewering look. 'Is he still your devil incarnate?'

He didn't bite. 'Thanks for letting me know you were investigating him, by the way.'

That got him half a smile in response. 'I would have. Eventually.'

If she hadn't gotten ambushed and assaulted. He leaned forward.

'We got him. Raker did, actually. And Sammy. It was Fizzel's kid. Edrick Junior. We got him and his big truck on video. Stopping at a convenience store afterward. Him and Randy Wilcox.'

He let that sink in. It didn't take long, even in her pain-medicated state. He got another half smile, this one weighted with resignation.

'They figured it out,' she said. 'They followed me and I didn't see. Or they followed Earl.'

They both knew it was more likely Earl.

'Yeah,' Hank said. 'We know he was your jail spy. He's safe with family out of town.'

'Good.' She gave him a look he couldn't read. 'It was the only way I could think of to keep an eye on what was going on in the jail. I had to keep some kind of handle on it, keep a watch over those new deputies. They're my responsibility.'

'Not just you. None of this is just you, Sheila. You shouldn't have been the one to pay the . . .' He trailed off. He swallowed hard, forcing the bile and rage back down. 'They're both in custody. Junior's already up in Springfield. Before he stopped talking and called his daddy, he said it was all Wilcox's idea to string the wire across the path. And Wilcox says he was just hanging out with Junior, didn't know about the wire, and was horrified when Junior started attacking you.'

He told her about the convenience store video and what Kathy Lancaster had overheard. 'So it does seem like the original plan was just the wire.'

Sheila stared at the ceiling. 'But then I chased them.'

'Of course you did.' He was indignant at her defeatist tone. 'I would have, too. That was bullshit. They deserved to be arrested for that alone. You were doing what any of us would've done.'

She seemed to be counting the ceiling tiles. Finally, in almost a whisper, she said, '. . . just so angry. I couldn't see. Couldn't think. So sick of it. Being followed. Being sued. Being undermined, threatened. I just wanted them down on the ground in handcuffs. I wanted my gun in their faces. And my knee on their throat.' She looked over at Hank. He nodded. He certainly didn't disagree with her for that. Her head rolled back until she was staring upward again. Her eyes started to water and he looked away.

'I didn't announce Junior's arrest at the press conference,' he said, eyes still averted, 'because Utley from City PD wants to do it separately, probably tomorrow. I said it was all his. I don't want within a mile of it.'

She gave a weak chortle. 'Look at you, playing the political game. Refocus Daddy Fizzel's ire on the city police instead of you.'

'And by that point, Wilcox will be up in the Springfield jail, too. It took a while to find him, so he was still getting processed this morning.'

'Wilcox doesn't do anything without Tucker's say-so,' she said after a minute. 'Tucker either knew about their plans, or he gave his general approval for some kind of action.' She went silent, pondering the ceiling. 'But he's so distanced, we can't get him.'

Hank leaned forward and slowly smiled. 'Not necessarily. There's one more thing I need to tell you. The kid from the newspaper cornered me after the press conference. He wanted to ask about the lawsuit dismissal.'

'Huh?'

'The lawsuit against us and the county was withdrawn this morning.'

When Jadhur told Hank an anonymous tipster had just alerted the paper to the dismissal, the relief that flooded through him was almost overwhelming. Not having to worry about his and Sheila's family assets or a furious county commission was like the weight of the world coming off his shoulders.

She perked up. 'Why would Tucker do that?'

'Well, I have a theory. It involves a patron, of sorts, who might have exerted some pressure on Tucker last night.'

'A patron who backed Tucker in the election when he ran against you?'

Hank nodded.

'A patron who you rescued from getting beaten and possibly killed at a construction site yesterday?'

Hank couldn't help smirking a little. 'I wasn't thinking about any ripple effects at the time, that's for sure. But I'll take it.'

'Are you sure that's what's going on? What if Tucker just has something else up his sleeve?'

'I stopped in at Gallagher's room before I came in here,' he said. 'He was just about to be released. I told him I didn't mention the attack on him when I spoke at the press conference. It would give him some time, but he should be prepared for media attention once people found out about it. He thanked me for the heads up. Then I asked if there was anything I should thank him for.'

That got a small smile out of Sheila. Thank God.

'You are a wily son of a bitch. What'd he say?'

'That his medication wore off last night, and he couldn't sleep. So he watched TV and made some phone calls to take his mind off the pain until the nurse came in to give him more. Then he said, "So there's nothing to thank me for. Seems to me, we're square." And he walked out of the room,' Hank said.

'Does this mean you're done with letting him be a thorn in your side?'

He made a show of considering that. 'Probably not.'

She rolled her eyes and then closed them. The dark circles underneath were worsening. He rose to his feet and looked at her small figure in the narrow bed. Maggie figured she would be here for at least another week, then rehab and probably long-term physical therapy. He had no idea how long she'd need to be off work, he just prayed she'd be fighting to come back as soon as possible. That would mean those bastards didn't win. That would mean she was OK. And she had to be OK. None of them would survive without her.

He stepped away and quietly slipped through the door, closing it softly behind him as he went.

ACKNOWLEDGMENTS

Writing this book was different from any other I've done. This one I wrote during the depths of the Covid-19 pandemic – and I am so lucky that as the challenges multiplied, so too did my support network. An amazing group of women kept me busy and laughing: Rae James, Holly West, Michele Drier, Chris Dreith, Penny Mason, Karen Phillips, Danna Wilberg, Virginia Kidd, Pat Canterbury, Anna Dever, Geri Nibbs, Peggy Dulle, Mary Ellen Shay, and Wendy Hornsby.

Once again, it was wonderful to work with Carl Smith and Kate Lyall Grant at Severn House, and to be the recipient of another beautiful, atmospheric cover from Piers Tilbury. I would never have found such a good home for the Hank Worth books without my agent, Jim McCarthy, who has been in my corner for every book. Also invaluable were my early readers, whose expertise and sharp eyes elevate every word. Paige Kneeland, Carol Adler, Mike Brown – thank you more than I can say.

I want to thank all the people who have championed the Hank books, including Janis Herbert, Tina Ferguson and everyone at Face in a Book independent bookstore, as well as Sam Schlafer and the wonderful people at the Lincoln Public Library and libraries everywhere. And a special thanks to Kimberly Evans Paul for bidding on a character name at the Sacramento Literacy Foundation auction. Her donation benefited a great organization, and her request to name the character after her father, retired sheriff's lieutenant Earl Evans, meant that I got to imbue special meaning into one of the book's key characters, Earl Evans Crumblit.

There are, as always, three people who make this all possible. Thank you, Joe, Carolyn, and Meredith. I love you.

And lastly, this book is dedicated to my mother- and father-in-law, who lovingly welcomed me to Branson many years ago, and have made me feel at home ever since. Thank you.